OLD GHOULS

A Greek Ghouls Mystery

ALEX A. KING

Copyright © 2023 by Alex A. King

All rights reserved.

No part of this book may be reproduced in any form or by any electronic or mechanical means, including information storage and retrieval systems, without written permission from the author, except for the use of brief quotations in a book review.

This book is absolutely not dedicated to the guy in my neighborhood who burns garbage on perfect spring days when my windows are open.

You, sir, are a malakas.

CHAPTER ONE

Some people go through their lives with a flock of personal heroes to keep them on a steady path and guide them through times of darkness. Their heroes are real people, who have done remarkable things, worthy of the pedestal.

The person clinging to my pedestal was Indiana Jones.

My low-key obsession with Indiana Jones began when I watched him swap a bag of sand for a golden idol and knew he was doomed to fail, and not just because I'd already read spoilers on the internet. There was no way a small sack of sand would weigh the same as a lump of gold that size, and Indy was screwed the moment he whipped out that burlap bag. What impressed me was that he found cool, interesting artifacts, and he did it with a smirk. I couldn't smirk because when I tried people automatically assumed it was gas, but even as a teenager I had a natural affinity for finding lost things, a lot like Professor Jones.

I'd like to say I went into the "finding stuff" business for reasons unrelated to Harrison Ford's famous fictional professor of archaeology, but I'd be lying. And for years I'd dreamed of scoring a client committed to sending me on my own Indy-worthy adventure.

Today I had that client, and this was my Indiana Jones moment. I had the hat. I had the backpack. I had an enormous dog by my side, alternating between licking his butthole and grinning at me.

What I didn't have yet was a neat row of ducks.

One duck refused to get in line, and that duck was my grandmother. My dead grandmother. She'd recently returned from a prolonged imprisonment inside a jar made of Himalayan salt, and now she was haunting my apartment and performing dozens of wardrobe changes daily because dead Yiayia had more outfits to choose from than living Yiayia. At this particular moment she was dressed like Evie in *The Mummy*, and she was refusing to do her job as my assistant. A job she'd requested.

"Please, Yiayia. Let me test it."

She dug her 1920s heels in harder. "As Greece's prime minister said to Mussolini: No!"

"It won't hurt."

"Do you know that for sure, eh? Did science tell you? Did you see it in a coffee cup? No. That is my answer."

My gaze cut to the oscillating fan. Seemed benign enough. The only way you'd hurt yourself with this thing was if you leaned over the fan while it was turned on and your hair got caught. But what did I know? I wasn't a ghost. Yiayia didn't have long hair but she was as dead as dead got, and her ghost wasn't in the mood for science. "We could start with the lowest setting."

"No."

"I thought you were adventurous."

"Only in bed, and on the kitchen counter, and sometimes on the back of a donkey."

Way TMI. Alive, Yiayia's filter had been flimsy, at best, but now it was nonexistent.

I picked the personal-sized fan off the coffee table. "What about this itty bitty baby-sized fan?"

She eyed it with suspicion. "Maybe that one."

Recently the island had experienced a wicked storm of the supernatural variety, and the winds had been strong enough to send all of Merope's ghost population into hiding. According to the dead, they were afraid of being blown out to sea. Ghosts have issues with salt water, and salt in general, so wafting over the sea wasn't their idea of fun. That's when my theory was born. I'd begun to wonder if I could keep ghosts at bay, if necessary, using fake wind. AKA: fans.

My name is Aliki Callas, and in all my thirty-one years, nobody has called me Aliki ... except judges and half the people on the Greek island of Merope that is my home these days. Everyone else calls me Allie. I was raised in the US and dragged to Greece, eye-rolling and whining, when I was in my tweens because my grandmother had—in her words—*mouni* cancer. Her cancer turned out to be curable with a dose of antibiotics and a commitment to cotton underwear, but the damage was already done. My parents had upturned our lives and we were Greeks now—my same parents, who pretty much lived on a cruise ship now.

Oh, and by the way: I see dead people.

Ergo, the fans.

I plucked the handheld fan off the table and blew on the blades like I was the last cowboy standing after a gunfight. "Ready?"

"No, but blow me anyway."

My grandmother was precisely the kind of person who would make a blowjob comment at a time like this.

I flicked the switch. The rubber blades slowly came to life

and began to spin with the world's smallest amount of enthusiasm. I aimed them at Yiayia and waited for a reaction.

Nothing happened.

"Watching that reminds me of the time a man gave me a spinning *poutsa* dance to the Greek version of *Careless Whisper*."

"Please never say those words again."

As the blades lazily turned, the same nothing kept repeating itself.

Yiayia stared at me with her eyebrows high and transparent, like the rest of her. I flicked the slider. The fan went back to sleep.

"I was really hoping that would work," I said, disappointed.

"Those things are *malakies*. They sell them to the *touristas* to make them feel as if they are doing something about the heat, and to encourage them to part with their money."

That sounded true. When summer rolled around, Merope's retailers added a rainbow of useless yet colorful items to their stock. Like bees and hummingbirds, tourists were naturally attracted to bright colors. Those blindingly orange espadrilles, so fun here in Greece, would be sore thumbs once unpacked in their new homes. Espadrilles aren't made for city streets. They're for trudging across sand, from umbrella to umbrella, to avoid the sun's daily hissy fit.

"Packing it anyway," I said as I shoved it into my backpack. The ferry was leaving in fifteen minutes and I needed to be on it if all my Indiana Jones fever dreams were to come true.

Yiayia vanished for a moment with a soft pink pop. When she reappeared she'd changed into a flapper dress and fluffy slippers. "This case is a bad idea. I have a feeling in my colon."

"Does the Afterlife have therapy? You should look into that."

"Only for permanent residents. Promise me you will be careful."

"I'll be careful."

"Do not do anything I would do."

Solid advice. In life, my grandma was a walking scandal. She did five outrageous things before breakfast every day to keep her skills sharp and her reputation in the mud.

"Seeing as how you're my assistant, you could come with me. All you have to do is hop inside the jar, like Jeannie."

Ghosts can't travel across bodies of salt water without hitching a ride in a secure container. Lucky me, I had one such receptacle sitting on the coffee table. An opaque pink jar, handcrafted from Himalayan salt. The same jar where my grandmother had been temporarily imprisoned before I popped the flat cork and unleashed her on my life.

Yiayia recoiled in horror. She plopped down on the couch and reached for the remote. Her fingers slid straight through. An oversized ginger cat appeared out of nowhere and got down to the feline business of making biscuits on her lap. My grandmother didn't have enough lap to contain Dead Cat, but he didn't seem to mind that he was spilling over her edges. He kept kneading while maintaining eye contact with me. A power move—power I was happy to let him have because he was my pickle bickle dead kitty-boo.

"O-o-okay, I'll take that to mean you're working from home today. I'll be fine. Cerberus will be on high alert, won't you?"

Cerberus bounced in a circle. Good thing Greece was bound by law to craft their dwellings and businesses to withstand earthquakes and giant dogs.

As far as I could tell, Cerberus was half Newfoundland, half bear, half mountain. The math didn't work, but that's because he was so much dog. He was staying with me temporarily until I could find him a new forever home. Just because I'd bought him his own fluffy bed and hitched a wagon for him on the back of my bicycle, didn't mean I was keeping him.

"Put the jar somewhere else," Yiayia said. "I cannot stand to look at that thing. It gives me PDSD."

Post Death Stress Disorder.

I shoved the pink jar into my bag because you just never knew when a salt jar might come in handy.

"Let's ride," I told the big dog.

Ten minutes later I was at the dock, waiting on the ferry to start boarding. At this time of year, ferry service was lackadaisical because they didn't have tourists to impress. Things got moving when the captain's mother showed up to yell at him for not doing his job quickly enough. Greek men are born afraid of their mothers, and they never stop.

Today was destined to be a day of ferry jumping, until I reached the small, nameless island my client had circled on a map. Finders Keepers, my very own business, is dedicated to—as the name suggests—finding things, information, and occasionally people. Most of the time people pony up cash for me to locate lost or coveted items. My inbox is always sprinkled with people who need assistance with gift-giving. Sometimes people or businesses pay me to dig up information. When I have to find people, things gets more complicated and pricey. But I've never failed. This trip to an unnamed island was my first real brush with genuine treasure hunting. My client had promised me that I wouldn't be able to resist doing this job for him, and he turned out to be right, damn him. As soon as he said "lost artifact" I was done for. I'd instantly pictured myself as a modern day Indiana Jones, slashing my way through a jungle to raid an old tomb. Of course I would never actually raid a tomb because that would be wrong, and Greece wasn't a country of jungles, so the hacking and slashing was out, too. According to my client, the island was home to an old temple, where a certain clay pottery doodad sat gathering dust, waiting to be cleaned, wrapped, and gifted to an undisclosed person.

I had questions—so many questions—but delusions of grandeur and my own movie franchise danced in my eyes.

Two hours later, the small boat I'd rented from an ancient but canny fisherman on Mykonos bumped up against the island.

"I will wait here, yes?" He pulled a Nintendo Switch Lite out of a waterproof pocket and waved it under my nose. Before I could answer, he was already lost in a game.

Cerberus leaped out ahead of me. He didn't care that the water was cold and wet. I did. Which was why I was wearing waders.

The nameless island was small and shaped like a blob. The terrain was covered with scrub and twisted trees that looked like a bad omen. For a flicker of a second, I thought about hopping back into the boat and zipping back to safety, where the places had names. The problem with unnamed things is that they can be anything.

"Why you want to come here, eh?" the fisherman called out. "There is nothing."

The fisherman was wrong, there was plenty of something on the island. Unfortunately, that something was ghosts. The beach was haunted out the wazoo with dead fishermen, casting their nets along the pebbled shore. Not recent deaths, either. They were dressed for a fishing party a few thousand years ago. I ignored them, didn't make eye contact. Just because I can see ghosts, doesn't mean I want to make conversation. Something happens after death, and once people are untethered from their bodies, they tend to lose self-awareness and their inner filters. And because these spirits had been here so long without crossing over, they were bound to be socially awkward. They'd want me to do things. Things I didn't want to do for free.

I wasn't here to solve unfinished business. I was here for the artifact and nothing else.

But just because I purposely ignored the ghosts, didn't mean they didn't give me the hairy eyeball. As Cerberus settled at my side, the ghosts set down their nets and lines and watched us march up the beach to the tree line.

Chatter moved through the fishermen like pinkeye in preschool.

"Is that a person?"

"I think it is supposed to be a woman."

"Why is she dressed that way? How will she ever get a husband dressed in a man's clothes?"

Pfft. Waders were for everyone who wanted to be in the water, but not *in* the water. My eye twitched as they followed me, excited, enthusiastic, and overly critical for beings that didn't have their own show on E!

My client had given me no instructions, no directions. He'd said I wouldn't be able to miss the temple, although countless Greek history aficionados and archaeologists had either never encountered this island or hadn't deemed it noteworthy. Probably the former. Every pebble from Ancient Greece was considered important enough for modern Greeks to slap a plaque on it. For some reason, nobody knew or cared about this place, except my client and now me.

That should have been another omen. The day was filled with them.

I trudged through the trees, gently moving branches aside and performing all kinds of gymnastics to scoot past some of the more vicious scrub. The ghosts wafted through the trees because they could.

"Where is she going?"

"Where do you think? There is nothing on this island except us and the temple."

"The temple! Ah-pah-pah! It is forbidden."

"I know it is forbidden. You know it is forbidden. But this woman who dresses like a man has no idea that it is forbidden."

"Or perhaps she does."

"That is even worse."

I faltered for a second and made it look like I was tripping on a tree root and not reacting to their conversation. A forbidden temple? This couldn't be any more Indiana Jones if it tried. And here I was without a whip.

"She is clumsy," one of the ghosts said. "She will never be able to take the treasure."

"We will see."

"And if she does?"

"We will see that, too."

"I am going back to my fish."

"Not me. I want to see where this goes. It could be eons before we ever see another person."

Not a word about why they hadn't passed on, choosing to fish for eternity. Fishing for an hour was my idea of hell. Doing it for thousands of years was cuckoo.

Cerberus woofed. Up ahead, the trees thinned out and a weathered, bleached pile of stone stepped into view, shadowed by leaves. Ancient. Sun-battered. The temple wasn't so much standing as it was kneeling at the foot of the trees with winter's thin light trying to pummel its back. The partially collapsed stones formed a crescent moon shape. A monument to some long gone god? Temple of Artemis?

The ground was littered with rocks and pottery shards, jutting up out of the ground, ready to puncture an unsuspecting foot. I was a pro. As an aunt, I was prepared for the hazards of LEGO. But still, all this broken crockery, how would I know which doodad I was looking for? My client said that I'd know it when I saw it. Which wasn't great as descriptors went.

Careful with my footsteps, I crept around the edge of the structure. Who had built it and when? Why didn't anyone know or care that it was here? Who were the fisherman? Why didn't the island have any other signs of human life? Or life signs at all, come to think of it. There were a few birdcalls in the air but nothing else. Shocking that some bored tycoon hadn't slapped an overpriced resort on the beach.

As I rounded the far side of the temple, another structure rose up from the back. A sort of antechamber without any actual larger chamber. So maybe this was just the chamber and not an antechamber at all. Columns in various degrees of integrity formed four walls. There was no real roof to speak of. Just bones that had been picked over by time and weather.

One dead man followed me. Watching. Waiting.

For what?

Besides him and his industrious pals who'd returned to fishing, there was nothing woo-woo here. No sensation of danger, no weird weather. Just old stuff and Cerberus, who was mostly peeing on the scenery.

"This is a miracle," the ghost said. "Gnec, where are you? Come see. Today is our lucky day. This child is about to find the vessel."

Child?

Child!

Aww, he thought I was young. Today must have been one of those good days where I looked like I was on the side of thirty where bladders were more robust and knees did their job without complaining. My instincts said to beam at him and thank him for mistaking my wind-chapped cheeks for the freshness of youth; good thing my common sense stepped in to prevent me from revealing my woo-woo skill. It dragged me back to the job at hand.

"Should we peek inside?" I asked the dog who definitely wasn't my dog. His tail flicked slowly from side to side. Uncommitted. If something was up, he wasn't getting a read on it.

"Okay, let's do it.'

Cerberus dived between the pillars like an agility champ. More circumspect, I angled between them, trying not to ruin a future archaeologist's hopes and dreams by crushing a pot.

There was something inside the chamber-antechamber. A pair of pedestals. One empty. One holding a clay pottery doodad. Not so much a vase or pot as it was an oval with a flat bottom. About the size and shape of a pineapple, but without the leafy bits on top.

I moved closer. It was covered with squiggles lined up in neat formation. A language I didn't recognize, and I knew a lot of them by sight.

The air rippled slightly. Two ghosts appeared. One of them was the spirit that had called me a child. His pal, presumably, was Gnec. The two long-dead men were dressed for a day in the neolithic agora, circa 4000 BC. Probably the market wasn't called an agora back in those days, but I wasn't sure what the neolithic folks called their marketplace. Gnec and the other one had kicked the bucket when they were middle aged—probably ancient for neolithic times. They wore chitons made of skins and had some kind of dead animals strapped to their feet. Weasels, I thought. Their toes had whiskers. Both men were carrying staffs which were basically sticks with skulls tethered to the top with leather strips. Small animals. Probably what was left of the weasels. Nice that they used the whole carcass instead of letting it go to waste.

"She is going to take it," the first one said to Gnec.

Gnec grunted. "You mean steal it."

"How can it be theft when it belongs to no one?"

"I still say she will steal it. It belongs to the island and those of us who put it there. Remember what happened to the last one who stole from the island, Tut? Do you remember, eh?"

"Nothing happened."

"That we know of," he said darkly.

Tut waved his objections away. "I still say it is a miracle. This is not exactly what we intended, but it will be for the best, you will see."

Questions poised on the tip of my tongue. Desperation bubbled up inside me. I wanted to know more about the island, the ghosts, this artifact I was supposed to bring back to my client.

You know what? This whole thing was starting to stink. That flat-bottomed pineapple pot with the strange writing had to be important, and not necessarily in a good way. Its location alone indicated that it was potentially significant to Greece's scholars. If I took it, I could wind up wearing a pair of my maybe-boyfriend's bracelets. That wasn't how I wanted to try out his handcuffs.

And yet I'd been paid to do what I do: find the cool artifact and bring it back to Merope.

Nobody gave Finders Keepers—and me—money to question why they needed a replacement for their mother-in-law's favorite tablecloth. They didn't need to. All I required was a detailed description and photo, and—bam—one identical tablecloth. This was no different. That pineapple with the archaic writing over there was a tablecloth made of clay.

"I wonder what will happen when I pick it up?"

I asked the question aloud, hoping the ghosts would provide me with the answer.

And sure enough, one of the dead men—Gnec—snorted. "We will see."

Tut, the other one, did a palms-up. "Nothing, that is what. You will have some pottery. Go ahead, pick it up. For science."

As ancient as the dead men were, I was surprised they knew about science. Given that they weren't making woo-woo sounds and muttering dire warnings, I decided to forge ahead.

"Time to do the job," I told Cerberus.

The massive dog hunched down and pooped. Another omen or the call of nature? He gave me the "have you got my back?" side eye as he did his business.

Once he was finished, I crossed myself Greek Orthodox-style, hoping religion would intervene on my behalf and save my bacon if necessary.

Yes, I picked up his poop. I was no monster.

With the baggie stowed away, I crept forward, scanning the grounds for traps.

The second pedestal was covered in dirt and other random bits of nature. Like the rest of the temple, the surrounding area was sprinkled with debris. It didn't look dangerous in here, and besides, the ghosts were sure nothing terrible would befall me if I grabbed the fancy pineapple. There was no place for a giant boulder to lie in wait for someone like me to pick up the thingy.

Heart hammering in my chest, I picked up the clay pot gently with my gloved hands and carefully wrapped it in a towel. Then I eased it into my backpack.

Mission accomplished.

I called out to Cerberus, who was watering a tree, and we set off for the boat.

Not going to lie, I kept glancing back to see if we were being followed by Nazis, Indian cult members, or Nazis—again. The only things behind us were the Gnec and Tut, who were speculating when they'd see more people.

The knots in my gut didn't loosen until I'd leaped into the boat.

The ghosts of the fishermen on the shore rose as one, their focus on something I couldn't see. The light show from the Afterlife was my guess. They ran, skipped, and jumped, hooting and hollering. Then they vanished.

All except for two—Gnec and Tut—who gnawed on their nails.

"We must come with you!" Gnec called out to me. "You cannot take the vessel without us."

"Fool!" Tut told him. "We cannot cross the sea. That is why the temple was built here."

"That is a problem," Gnec agreed.

"Do not worry," Tut said. "She will be back. She will need us."

CHAPTER TWO

A POLICE CAR was waiting for me when I disembarked the ferry. The policeman was waiting for me, too, and not because I'd been a bad, bad girl. At over six-feet. Detective Leo Samaras looked like he could wrestle a tree and win.

Was I intimidated?

Sometimes, yes. But only because of how his kisses made my bones turn to mush.

Behind the dark lenses, I knew his warm hazel eyes were watching me.

My eyelids twitched. Winter wind was lashing the island. This time it wasn't a supernatural gale, thankfully. This was a typical Christmas-time spanking.

"Am I in trouble, Detective?"

"Do you want to be?"

"Only if you promise to use the handcuffs."

He winced. "Before today I would have been all in. That was before Pappas happened. The kid tasered his date last night."

Constable Gus Pappas is Merope's rookie. He has a fragile digestive system and a penchant for women's underwear. I wanted to say him tasing his date was an accident, but I couldn't be certain he hadn't developed an electricity kink.

We stood there wincing in solidarity with Pappas's date.

Detective Leo Samaras is my sort-of boyfriend. We aren't official but we're not not-official. Things are complicated. Leo is my sister's high school sweetheart, and although Toula is married and managed to produce the best kids in all the world, there's a piece of her that still has a death grip on Leo's junk. Some days I experience a stab of guilt that I poached her boyfriend, but in reality they broke up more than a decade ago.

Leo smiled all the way to his eyes because that was his usual reaction when he looked at me—except for when our conversation turned towards ghosts, demons, and the other weirdness that was part of my, and now his, life.

I batted my wind-whipped eyelashes. "Did you come all this way for me?"

"Can't think of a better reason to be out in the cold. Bicycle and that bear's cart are already in the trunk. Hop in."

He yanked open the cruiser's back door. The whole vehicle shook as Cerberus leaped onto the backseat. The engine was running and the car was toasty warm. Leo held the passenger door open for me next. I stripped off my gloves and waggled my fingers in front of the vent.

Leo leaned in for a kiss. His lips were soft and they inspired my hormones to make all kinds of appalling and fun suggestions. He put shifted the cruiser into D and placed his hand on my thigh.

"Did you find what you were looking for?"

"I think so."

"Dinnerware?"

"Not this time. This was more like a cool pineapple."

"A pineapple?" His eyes cut to me briefly before returning to the cobbled road. "Really?"

I unzipped my backpack and showed him the goods. Away from its pedestal and in the thin afternoon light, it appeared even less impressive. If they—whoever "they" were—really wanted to hide it they would have built a rock garden and avoided the whole showy temple.

"It really is a pineapple," he said, sounding amazed. "Looks old. You're not planning to ship it out of the country, are you?"

Greek post office staff get twitchy when people bring international-bound packages in for posting. Two-hundred years later, we're still not over Lord Elgin waltzing out of Greece with the Parthenon's marbles.

"My client is local, I promise."

He glanced at the clay artifact again. "And you got it in Greece?"

"On a tiny island past Mykonos."

"The writing isn't Ancient Greek."

"It's not any language that I know about, which is weird."

"Who's the client?"

Yeesh. He had to ask. I made a face. "Adonis Diplas, the new owner of the More Super Market."

His jaw hardened. For a variety of reasons there was no love lost between the men. One, because George Diplas, Adonis's cousin, had recently been arrested for murder. As Greece's most famous TV weather guy, the public had been struggling to accept that George moonlighted as serial killer with an exclusive preference for male victims. Two, Adonis had helped himself to my apartment recently to cook breakfast and twist my arm about finding the Real Killer. The only thing missing from that story was a white Ford Bronco. Anyway, in the interest of full disclosure I'd told Leo about the eggs and bacon. Afterward, he suggested that I beef up security on my apartment. He'd offered to install a video doorbell, and he was the biggest advocate for me keeping Cerberus.

I waggled my eyebrows at him. "Worried I'm going to run off with Diplas?"

Leo snorted. "No, I know we like each other. More worried that he's going to run off with the whole island. He smells like a conman."

Adonis Diplas was attractive, charming, and entirely in love with himself. Like any good petty charlatan, he gotten himself engaged to a woman whose family tree was a stick, and now she was locked away for the crazy kind of murder, not regular vanilla homicide. The More Super Market was an engagement gift to him from the Bakas family, who owned the island's newspaper, and Diplas had moved to Merope to collect.

"Conman or not, he paid me well to find this chunk of pottery, and there are barely any strings attached."

"Strings?"

This was a conversation I didn't want to be involved in because I knew Leo would flip. Not at me but at the other parties involved.

"Diplas knew that I wanted to play Indiana Jones, so he gave me the job in exchange for money and my word that I'd help him prove George Diplas is innocent."

Leo came unglued, in a quiet, non-violent way. His foot tapped the brake. "Are you kidding? You're the one who figured out George Diplas was a serial killer. He almost killed you!"

"I know."

"He confessed to the murders."

"Did he?"

"Yes. And now Diplas expects you to lie?"

"No, I don't think he wants me to lie. He wants me to find out who actually committed the murders ..."

Leo made growling sounds. "George Diplas."

"... because otherwise their grandmother might die from a sudden case of Greek toe cancer."

"My grandfather had that. It went away when I moved back to Merope."

"Everyone's grandparents get that. Yiayia's was just in her *mouni*, that's all." My phone rang. "Diplas," I said to Leo.

He scowled. "Do you have to take it?"

"I really do." I tapped the screen and said, "Come."

Adonis Diplas didn't waste any time with his own pleasantries. "Did you get it?"

What a question. "Of course."

"I knew you would. Bring it to me?"

"Where are you?"

"At work."

"Robbing old ladies?"

He laughed. At least the guy could take a joke. "Taking money from my customers. For some reason I don't understand, Stephanie is wearing bags on her feet, so she can't work right now."

"I get dry feet in winter," Stephanie said in the background. "I am exfoliating with a baby's foot."

I had no idea what that meant, but I hoped the exfoliant wasn't made from real babies.

"I'll be there in a few minutes." I ended the call and stuffed my phone back in the backpack. "George Diplas allegedly followed the path of Jainism, which says that the path to enlightenment is only attainable through a life of nonviolence. That means killing anything is off limits, no matter how big or small."

"Every religion has its hypocrites. Churches all over Greece are filled with criminals every Sunday."

"True. And if that's the case here, I want to know. Or at least Adonis Diplas wants to know, and he's paying me to find out. Plus he sent me on an Indiana Jones quest to find this cool clay pineapple."

"I don't like it."

"The pineapple?"

"Any of it."

I tucked the clay relic back in my backpack. "I don't like it either, but the money is good, and George is being followed by a crowd of ghosts. I'm hoping they'll help and that I can send them to the Afterlife, too. They deserve to get some peace after what they went through."

Leo folded my hand in his. Not another word out of him until we reached the More Super Market, which took a whole two minutes and no change.

"Want me to wait for you?" he asked when we arrived.

"Are you having a slow crime day?"

He grinned. "Wintertime is my summer vacation. By the way, Kyria Yota keeps calling, demanding that we arrest you for stealing a wedding dress."

"I can tell you, without a hint of a lie, that I did not steal that wedding dress."

"But you know who did?"

"Yes, but also no."

"I'm confused."

"So am I." I kissed him quick when I wanted to kiss him long and slow. But I also didn't want to answer any more questions about the wedding dress or its thief, so I kept it short and leaped out before he could grill me harder. Leo lifted my bicycle out of the trunk and reattached Cerberus's wagon to the back, then he drove away after making a date for tonight, provided the island didn't experience a sudden crime spree.

With Cerberus beside me, I flicked out the bike's stand. He sat beside my bicycle and opted to play the sentinel outside while I ventured into the More Super Market.

It's a misnomer, by the way. There's nothing *more* or *super* about the More Super Market. It's barely a market. The store sells dusty groceries and excellent cheese and cold cuts. The island doesn't have an actual supermarket, so for bread, meat, and produce you have to shop elsewhere, in stores dedicated to those specific items. There are other markets, but this one is the second most convenient to home. The Super Super Market—again, not *super* or *super*—was one of those places that held bad memories. Some time ago now, while we were shopping, my fiancé Andreas collapsed and died in my arms from a congenital heart defect. Going back there was out of the question. So the More Super Market it was, with its dust and its quirky employee.

Sure enough, Adonis Diplas was manning the cash register, while Stephanie Dolas lounged on a stool on the customer side with her bagged feet resting on the far end of the counter. She'd pushed her plastic bags into slip-on slippers so that no one could say she was barefoot.

My eyebrows went up slightly. "Is that hygienic?"

"I am wearing shoes," she said, as though that was the answer I was seeking.

Adonis Diplas is one of those guys who looks like he can take a punch without flinching and dish them out hard and fast. He keeps his blond hair hidden under a ball cap most of the time, and smirks like it's his job. Probably the kind of man who would drive dark romance readers crazy by shoving weapons up the heroine's no-no hole. Not me. I was nuts about the boy upstairs, the one who used to date my sister. He would never put a gun in a no-no hole.

Oof. Thinking about them dating in high school hit me in the spleen. Or maybe the gall bladder. Leo was tall and skinny back then, and he lived in black heavy metal t-shirts. At first I hadn't recognized him when he returned to Merope and moved in upstairs, and it wasn't just wardrobe change; since high school he'd bench pressed a few boats.

"On a scale of one to ten, how difficult was it to find the artifact?" Diplas wanted to know.

I sat my backpack on the counter. "Honestly? A one. The hardest part was getting there. There was a second pedestal but nothing on it. Either the other pineapple broke or someone got there before me and only had the strength to carry one. Maybe they were a tall baby or had some kind of wasting disease."

Diplas curled his fingers in a "show me" gesture.

I dug out the clay pineapple and its protective wrapping, laying the padded bundle in front of him.

He stared at the wrapping, as if weighing something in his mind.

After a moment's hesitation, he unwrapped the pineapple. He picked it up, turned it this way and that under the More Super Market's fluorescent lights.

"Hollow," he said. There was a note of surprise in his voice. "You think there is something inside?"

"I've spend precisely no time at all thinking about it."

His thumb brushed against the carved letters. "What about the writing?"

"Not any language I've encountered."

He glanced up at me. "Can you find out what it is?"

"If you're paying, sure. But don't you know?"

His eyebrows took a hike. "Why would I?"

"You paid me to find the artifact, so I figured you'd know things about it." I shifted my weight to my other leg. "Are you telling me you don't know?"

He hefted the clay pineapple and flashed a grin at me. "I know most things, but not that."

"What are you going to do with it?"

He booped me on the nose. "Wouldn't you like to know?"

The cat hair that comes standard with all Greek DNA activated and now I was destined to die from curiosity if he didn't spill the whole story.

"I have so many questions, and I'm not sure where to start. Is this a smuggling thing? Are you going to do a crime? Because I have to say, I'm not down with facilitating crime. And what is this writing, anyway?" I poked a squiggle etched in the clay. "Does that look like an eyebrow?"

"Eyebrows?" Stephanie swung her bagged feet and slippers off the counter. "I know everything about eyebrows. Let me see."

My eye twitched at the idea of Stephanie Dolas, eyebrow expert. Maybe she knew everything about eyebrows, except that you're not supposed to pluck them all out because the early 2000s told you that over-plucking was, like, sick. Which was weird, seeing as how Stephanie was barely out of her teens on paper but firmly in them inside her head. She wasn't old enough to have experienced the great and terrible brow-plucking that marked the beginning of this century, so she'd been doomed to repeat history. These days she had to draw them back on with something I suspected was a crayon.

Before Adonis Diplas could hand her the artifact, she'd yanked it out of his hands.

The following events occurred in slow-fast motion.

Stephanie Dolas, who still had both feet soaking in plastic bags filled with a variety of acids designed to remove dead skin from her tootsies, misjudged the speed at which a person with their feet in goop-filled bags should move.

Her feet slipped inside the bags.

The bags slipped inside her slippers.

The slippers slipped because they were hand-me-downs from one of the Dolas aunts and had no real tread left to grip the sealed concrete floor that graced the More Super Market.

Stephanie fell on her tush, landing in a stack of canned

okra that I hoped was destined for the garbage, because no one should ever eat canned okra.

The artifact, pineapple, whatever it was, became airborne, sailing through the dust mote-dotted air.

Briefly.

Gravity leaped into action and called dibs.

Adonis Diplas and I tried to intervene, but we were slower than physics. The only thing we managed to do was smash our foreheads together. Gravity won because it was gravity. Some people might say it had an unfair advantage.

The pineapple shattered on impact.

Diplas was right, it was hollow. And now the fragments were scattered in big chunks across the market's floor, reminding me of the time Toula smashed my Easter egg because she was eight and she could.

As Adonis Diplas registered horror, and I was leaning forward to help Stephanie up, silver mist poured out from the fragments of the pineapple. A woman materialized from amidst the debris. Tall. Well over seven feet. Bone-thin. Eyes of fire and skin of ice. Nowadays she'd have a problem buying clothes off the rack, but wherever—whenever—she'd come from, she'd had access to a personal seamstress who worked with animal pelts. Hairstyle? None. She was as bald as an apple. Not a ghost. The dead were varying degrees of transparent. This woman was solid, and from her long, lean muscles I'd say she was great at kicking butt. Taking names was probably a bigger problem for her, seeing as how pencils weren't a thing back in the animal-skins-as-fashion days.

Before I could move another muscle, the woman bent down and touched a long finger to Stephanie's chest.

Then she vanished.

Finally, but most importantly, Stephanie Dolas died instantly.

CHAPTER THREE

"Make sure people know I died with my shoes on," Stephanie said, glaring at her baggie-covered feet. "I do not want people to think I was poor."

Diplas crouched down by her body. His hand was hunting for her pulse. He wouldn't find one. Stephanie was gone and her ghost was giving her own body a serious stink-eye.

"That wasn't supposed to happen," he said.

"Of course it was not supposed to happen," Stephanie said. "I had plans tonight. Mama and I were going to watch the new episode of *Greece's Top Hoplite* while I plucked the hairs off her chin and neck."

Diplas was deaf to her ghost words. Not me. The question was whether or not I should let Stephanie know she was as real to me as the dust on the canned goods.

"Start CPR," I told him.

Under normal circumstances, when people transitioned from living to dead, their ghosts were whisked off to the great waiting room in the sky to sit through a forty-day orientation program. After that, they were presented with two options: return to earth to haunt the living, or take the door marked

Afterlife. There were exceptions to the forty-day rule: urgent unfinished business mostly, including, but not limited to, murder. Stephanie had been murdered, and unlike most of the ghosts who came to me to solve their unexpected slaying, I knew whodunit. Problem was, as far as I knew, I was the only eyewitness to the crime.

My Virgin Mary, how the heck was I going to explain this to the police? Leo's ability to suspend his disbelief was already stretched paper-thin. That a weird woman popped out of a broken clay pineapple and poked Stephanie in the chest wouldn't fly.

All of this was zipping through my head as I called Merope's emergency number. I told the dispatcher to send an ambulance and the coroner.

Adonis Diplas flicked a glance up at me as I ended the call. He didn't stop the compressions. "What are you going to tell them?"

I paused for a split-second. "That she dropped dead."

That was true, more or less.

"Do you think they can bring her back?"

"I don't know. Keep going anyway."

My eye twitched. I stabbed it with my finger until the muscle quit jerking. One of these days I'd have to get it looked at. All this twitching couldn't be normal. Maybe I just needed a vacation and a bucket of Xanax. Preferably a sunny vacation spot that wasn't haunted. Finding things was my job; I should take the time to find myself a place that fit the criteria.

Stephanie's ghost was wafting between the shelves. "Why didn't you try to save me?"

My eye twitched harder. We were trying to save her. That's why Adonis Diplas was performing CPR and I'd called the paramedics.

"Is it because you are jealous of my eyebrows?"

I stifled a snort. The only person who'd envy her eyebrows was a certain potato with accessories.

A small ditch appeared between Adonis Diplas's brows. "What are you doing?"

"I'm fine. This is just ..." I shook my head. "I'm going outside to wait for the first responders."

Diplas nodded to a broom and dustpan behind the counter. "Maybe you should clean up."

"Not a chance. It's evidence. The police get upset when you tinker with a crime scene."

"What crime scene? She wasn't murdered. This was one of those random things. Probably her heart or a brain aneurysm."

It wasn't either of those those things, but I couldn't tell Diplas that.

Before I could chew off a fingernail stewing over what I was going to tell Leo about the dead cashier when he inevitably showed up, the ambulance slammed to a stop out front. The doors flew open. Two paramedics jumped out. Ketty Vlaho, whose family owned the local moped rental place, and Dimi Pantazis, a trainee who had recently been transferred from the mainland, strode to the back of the ambulance with brisk, deliberate purpose. Right behind them was Panos Grekos, the island's coroner. He wasn't alone. Scowling several feet above him was his dead mother's banshee. Since she had passed a few years ago, she'd chosen to spend her afterlife screeching at her single son about his pornography addiction. Today she was quiet. She was watching me, wondering if I was going to yell at her again.

"What for did you call them?" Grekos shot a look of disgust at the paramedics. "The dead are my domain. Where is she?"

"Inside," I told him. "And there's a chance she's not dead."

She was dead. That didn't mean healthcare professionals

couldn't wrestle the grim reaper for custody, at least for a few minutes.

"Does she have a pulse?"

"She didn't before Adonis Diplas started CPR."

"Then she is probably dead." He gave me a small shove toward the door. "Quick, before they get to her."

Was he crazy? "Is this some kind of competition between you and the paramedics?"

"Yes."

He didn't elaborate and I was afraid to ask.

We went inside. Despite me telling him to step away from the broom, Diplas had abandoned CPR and was busy sweeping the artifact's jagged fragments into a pile using a small whiskbroom. He was about to sweep them in to the dustpan.

I poked my index finger at him. "What did I tell you?"

He had the audacity to pelt me with his cocky grin. "You said a lot of things."

"Stop sweeping!"

"Why? It's no good. She doesn't have a pulse."

While I was busy glaring at him, Panos Grekos had located Stephanie and was giving her the once-over. He stood and brushed off his slacks.

"Stephanie Dolas is dead. Time of death ..."

There was movement behind the shelves, where the bulk pulses sat in open barrels, collecting dust and anything else customers coughed into the air. A housedress-clad gossip machine clutched her chest and emitted a shriek that was part horror and entirely too much excitement.

"Dead! The Dolas girl is dead! I must tell everyone before someone else scoops the story! Maybe try rubbing alcohol on her chest, eh?" Cardigan flapping, she barreled out of the More Super Market at a speed that indicating her self-reported bunions were a lie.

"And now everyone knows, thanks to Kyria Roula," I said, which was pointing out the blindingly obvious. Gossip was the island's other currency, more valuable than the euro. You couldn't buy food with gossip, but you could buy social status —and what was a hot meal compared to people thinking you were somebody?

Thing was, Kyria Roula, like most of the local mouths, wasn't an unbiased reporter. When she retold the story she'd be adding flair. By the time the tale of Stephanie Dolas's death bounced back to me, it would be unrecognizable. Each new set of ears and mouths added their own frills. The worst part was that Stephanie's family would find out about her death from a random blabbermouth instead of the authorities. If the paramedics couldn't save her.

Damn it.

The coroner and paramedics performed a little dance at the door as they tried to pass each other. Grekos was on his way out to get a body bag and stretcher. "Why bother?" he told them. "She is dead. We no longer need you."

"Have to take a look anyway," Ketty said. "In case you got it wrong."

He glowered at her. "Are you saying I do not know my job?"

"It would not be the first time you have called it wrong lately."

Her accusation hit home and his face purpled. "I will wait here and we will see who is right and who is wrong this time."

Ketty slapped his hand with hers. He leaned on the counter while Ketty and Dimi scooted around to inspect the victim.

I crossed my fingers and hoped for a miracle. From here Stephanie seemed completely dead and her ghost was busy filing her nails with a nail file that she'd acquired out of thin air. She'd moved on quickly from the whole being dead thing.

Death was no more of a burden on her conscience than orphans in Timbuktu. Probably Stephanie didn't even know Timbuktu was a real place.

Panos Grekos's banshee mama wasn't content to stay out in the cold. She had new complaints and wanted to air them.

"*Malakes*! My son is never wrong!" She whipped around to glare at me. "Tell them! Tell them my porn-addicted deviant of a child—*po-po* ... my broken heart is his fault, the *kolopetho*! —is the best coroner in the world. If he says that girl is dead then she is dead!"

Stephanie's ghost looked up in surprise. "How did I die? Did I come to work without a coat again? Mama warned me that would happen."

I ignored them both. My eye watered and I liked to think it was winter's fault, not mountains of stress.

Kyria Greko circled me. "Look at her, ignoring us as if she cannot hear us! *Mounoskeela*!"

I slapped my hand over my watering eye and fought to shut out the dead. Focus on the paramedics, I told myself. Dimi was listening to Stephanie's chest with his stethoscope. He raised his eyebrows at Ketty.

She raised hers right back at him. "Are you serious?"

"Listen for yourself. She is dead. Grekos is right this time."

"You said that last time." She flipped her fingers at him in a *gimme* gesture. "I want to listen."

"Of course I am right," the coroner said. "I know dead when I—"

Suddenly, Stephanie gasped and sat up stick straight.

Panos Grekos swore under his breath. "*Gamoto* ... not again!"

"You owe me, Grekos," Ketty told him with a grin.

Kyria Greko slapped her son around the head, but he didn't so much as flinch.

Stephanie Dolas used the edge of the counter to haul

herself up onto her feet. She staggered to the cash register. Her gaze traveled around the shop. "Who is next? Please form a line. A neat line."

"Stephanie?" I said.

Houston, we had a problem. Stephanie was pushing buttons on the register and counting the cash. Meanwhile, her ghost was staring at her body with a look of horror. I didn't understand all the ins and outs of near death experiences, but shouldn't Stephanie's soul be back inside its body?

Stephanie—ghost Stephanie—stepped through the counter and inspected her physical self. "Is that how I really look?"

As far as I knew, this was unprecedented. Stephanie was a ghost, and yet her body was …

"Is she … *working*?" Adonis Diplas said, sounding dazed. "Is she actually doing the job I pay her for?"

We watched as Stephanie wiped down the counter with a tissue. It was used and covered in mascara, but it was more than she'd ever done in the past. "Wonders will never cease," I said.

"I cannot believe this," the coroner said. "She was dead. I know a corpse when I touch one." He shook his head and hoofed it out of the shop. The bell above the door tinkled.

The paramedics shrugged. "She seems fine," Ketty said.

"Better than fine," Diplas said, still amazed. "I have never seen her work this hard." He adjusted his ball cap. "Or at all."

Ketty and Dimi bailed, and the ambulance bumped away. It was just me in the More Super Market, with Diplas, Stephanie's body, and Stephanie's ghost. Ghost Stephanie was scowling at herself.

"Stop it," she told her body. "You are making us look bad. You better not break any of my nails." Still wearing her foot baggies and slippers, her ghost backed up to the far end of the market and took a running leap at her body and immediately fell out the other side. Stephanie's body didn't so much as flinch.

"Stephanie," I said to her body, "can I check something?"

"You want cheese? I will cut cheese."

"No—no cutting cheese. Can I see your wrist?"

She flopped her arm on the counter. I slid her sleeve up and felt her wrist for a pulse.

Nothing. Not even a blip.

Crap.

That meant ... Actually, I wasn't sure what it meant but it couldn't be good. The timing couldn't be worse. My knowledge base for spooky things was absent, and I had no idea when it would be back.

Diplas leaned over to look at what I was doing. "What are you doing?"

Like I'd touched a hot stove, I yanked my hand away. "Wow, would you look at that time? I have to go. But first, let me clean up the mess."

He watched as I tipped the pottery shards into the cloth and stuffed the bundle in my backpack. "I'll see if I can put this back together."

He didn't look convinced. "It's broken."

"Ever heard of kintsugi? It's a Japanese form of art. You stick the broken bits back together using gold."

"You're going to use gold?"

"I was thinking glue. The point is ..." My gaze flicked to Stephanie, who had located a duster and was moving towards the shelves with a herky jerky sense of purpose. "I don't know what the point is. Do you need this back? It's not much of a gift now, is it?" I didn't know diddly about kintsugi, and I had no plans to return the clay pineapple to Adonis Diplas—not after prehistoric murder lady popped out of it. "I guess I'm still on hook for finding the real killer, so to speak?"

"A deal is a deal."

"I was afraid you'd say that." I hoisted the backpack onto my shoulder and mustered Cerberus, who was inside now and watching Ghost Stephanie trying to talk her body out of performing manual labor that wasn't self care. "Okay. Send me his lawyer's info and I'll see what I can do."

He chucked his chin at Stephanie. "Do you think having a near death experienced fixed her?"

Yeesh. "I don't think you want to know what I think."

What did I think?

Well.

Stephanie's body had no pulse, and yet she was performing menial tasks while her ghost scoffed at her sudden burst of productivity. There was a word for a reanimated body with no soul included.

Stephanie had been divided into two pieces. One was a ghost. The other was a zombie.

CHAPTER FOUR

Yiayia glanced down at the pile of shards while I shook a ring of salt around them. "What did the pottery do to offend you?"

I placed the salt shaker back in the kitchen cupboard. "That pottery isn't just pottery. It is—or was—some kind of hollow receptacle with weird woman inside." A woman who hadn't been spotted since she offed Stephanie Dolas, so I had that to worry about, too. Whoever—whatever—she was, I needed to find her and stuff her back inside her clay pineapple. I gestured at the largest fragment with its unusual writing. "Any idea what language that is?"

My grandmother produced a lorgnette pince-nez out of nowhere and slotted the lenses over her nose. She took her sweet time inspecting the strange markings scratched into the stone. "First we have to decide if this is written in cursive or not."

I snorted. "I'll take that as a no."

"It does not look like any human language I have ever seen."

"What about non-human?"

"I have never seen any non-human languages."

"That was helpful."

She preened. "Thank you."

The sarcasm was lost on her. "I really need to interpret these markings."

She paced the length of my kitchen for several long moments while Dead Cat watched her from the table. "Do you know what this is? I will tell you. This is a time for sexual favors."

"This is the opposite of the time for sexual favors."

She forged onward, undeterred. "I was with an academic one time—several times actually. He could not tie his shoelaces, but he could talk dirty to me in dozens of languages. Some of them I think were not even human. I will see if I can find him. He has to be dead now."

"Wait—*you're* doing the sexual favors?"

"Of course." She patted me on the cheek, leaving the lorgnette pince-nez hanging from her nose. Her hand felt like a patch of foggy air. "I would never ask you to have sex with near strangers to get what you want. That is what I am here for. Casual sex is my favorite part of this job."

"Is that really what you're here for?"

Post-death, my grandmother had ample opportunity to choose the Afterlife over returning to Merope once I'd freed her from her salt jar prison, but she'd decided to stay here for reasons she was playing close to her abundant chest. Not that I wasn't grateful—I loved having her here—but I would have preferred transparency. My life was speckled with too many little mysteries. As a Greek-American woman who found things for a living, and who had way too much cat hair in her DNA, not knowing stuff was driving me bonkers.

She gave me a wicked grin. "A lady never tells."

"You are no lady."

She smacked the air. "A lady never has any fun. Whatever I

am, that is who has all the fun. Being dead does not mean I have to change, eh? At least now I do not need to use protection."

I counted backwards from ten. Not to cool bubbling anger but to remember what we were talking about in the first place.

Oh. Right. Her linguistics expert. "Can you please bring him here to check out this writing?"

"Of course, my love. Anything for you."

"How long—"

She vanished with the crisp pop of new bubble gum.

"—will it be before you get back here with him?"

I was talking to my dead cat and a live dog who wasn't mine.

"All righty then," I said to my hairy co-workers. "First we get coffee, then we get to work. And by *we* I mean *me*."

Dead Cat licked his transparent boy parts. Cerberus flopped down in the living room and did his best imitation of a bear skin rug.

The fact that my apartment building was located directly across from a coffee shop was not a deciding factor when I'd originally leased the place I now owned. Anyone who has ever consumed coffee from Merope's Best knows I'm telling the truth. The origin of their beans is suspect. Were they even coffee beans? Ethically sourced? Did anyone die or suffer or shed tears so that their customers could grimace over cups of coffee-scented muck?

These were all questions that weighed heavily on my mind at 3:00 AM, but right now I needed caffeine to kick-start the thinking engine, and in the absence of real coffee, Merope's Best would have to do. Jogging downstairs from my second-floor apartment to the coffee shop across the street, I ignored the picket line forming between my stomach and mouth. If I was a scab, so be it.

The atmosphere inside Merope's Best was morose, thanks to the death metal Christmas carols. The customers' pained expressions said they'd do anything for a change in music—anything except ask the baristas to tone down the aural assault.

Today was my day to do a good deed. T'was the season, after all.

I approached the counter, where the world's most apathetic barista was already rolling her eyes at me in anticipation.

"I don't suppose you can—"

"No."

"I haven't asked yet."

"No."

"Can I have some coffee?"

She shrugged. "I don't know, can you?"

"Should I make it myself?"

Eye-daggers launched themselves at my face.

"So that's a no?"

"What do you want?"

I scanned the chalk menu for items that wouldn't send me to the emergency room. "Any specials or anything festive and new?"

"We have a cappuccino with a tree in the foam."

A tree in the foam. Pretty. There was a time when foam art was all over social media. "I'll take the extra large if you've washed your hands this week, Medium if you haven't."

She turned away to make my coffee.

Since I'd just buttered her up by ordering, I fired my shot. "Any chance you can change the music?"

"This is my boyfriend's band. He lives in Norway with his wife."

"I don't know if that's a yes or no. Also, aren't you just out of high school? Why are you messing around with a married man from Norway?"

She turned around, pointed to her t-shirt. It read *Shut The Fack Up* in English.

"Is 'fack' an Urban Dictionary thing? Because I don't go there if I can help it. That site knows things that shouldn't be real."

Fack was a common misspelling by Greek vandals and other graffiti artists. I knew what it meant, but I was trying to make conversation over the din. It was that or pass out from the overwhelming scent of industrial strength fake pine. On the upside, it was nice to know that someone here cared about cleanliness.

She dumped a cardboard bucket in front of me. "Your extra large pine tree cappuccino."

"My what now?"

She popped off the plastic lid, revealing a stick with pine needles sticking out in every direction.

"I thought you were going to draw a cute festive tree in the foam."

Her stare said she thought I needed a psychological intervention. "Does this look like Instagram?"

I ducked my head. "Never mind." I grabbed my jumbo pine coffee. "Sorry about the music," I told the other customers. "I tried." They made "what did she say?" faces, because death metal *All I Want For Christmas is You* had dented their eardrums.

The coffee wasn't so bad after I pulled out the stick and tossed it away. At one point I got a pine needle stuck between my teeth, but that was why I regularly invested in dental floss.

Back in my apartment building, I jogged back upstairs. Standing outside my neighbor Lydia's apartment was a small figured dressed like one of Santa's elves.

"I can't handle this," I said to the ceiling. "If there is a God, He needs to forgive me for what I'm thinking."

"You want a piece of this?" Jimmy Kontos asked, pointing

two fingers at himself. "That's understandable. A lot of women—and a lot of their husbands—want some of this goodness. I'm a one-woman man now though, so you will have to live with the disappointment."

That set me back on my heels. "You're giving up on the adult movie industry?"

Leo's cousin Jimmy Kontos was the leading man in a popular series of skin flicks called *Tiny Men, Big Tools*. Apparently he had a huge following. I wasn't one of them, but I'd stumbled onto his set one night and that was when my eye-twitch worsened.

The door across from mine opened. As recently as this year the apartment had belonged to my best friend in all the world, Olga Marouli. After Kyria Olga's murder, her granddaughter inherited the apartment, seeing as how her grandma owned the whole shebang. Every day I thanked the universe that none of Kyria Olga's awful children had moved in across from me. Lydia was quirky, prickly, and owned a lot of clothes that she tended to wear one piece at a time, but I liked her. Today she'd chosen a butt-length sweater with corrective boots that I was sure were designer and not intended to fix any foot problems. Maybe there was underwear under there, but I wouldn't bet on it.

"I told him he doesn't have to give it up for me." Lydia's nose wrinkled. "Does anyone else smell trees?"

"It's my coffee," I said. "The deal of the day at Merope's Best."

Her daytime smokey eyes widened. "And you're going to drink it?"

I swiped a chunk of pine needle off my lip. "If I don't drink it, I'll hear the voices of my ancestors telling me not to waste money."

"I am not giving it up completely," Jimmy said. "Just thinking about making a shift to the production side. That is where all the big money is. You want to do some directing?" He aimed the question at Lydia. "You are good at bossing people around."

"He sees me," Lydia said. "He really sees me."

He reached for her hand. Things were about to get PG13 between the new couple, so I let myself back into my apartment before an "Aww" slipped out of my mouth.

Dead Cat hissed in the direction of my coffee cup. Cerberus gave me a worried look and vanished into the bedroom. The creak of my bed told me that he'd made his big bones comfortable on my blankets. Experience told me he was resting his head on my pillows. Hopefully his new owners, whoever they were destined to be, would have a queen-sized bed to accommodate the big dog and give him the comfy life he deserved. His original owners, the ones who had requested I find him a new home after their passing, had slept in two singles in their living room.

I added a queen-sized bed to the list of requirements for his forever home.

Caffeinated, I sat down at my desk and opened my laptop. Work waited. Oodles of requests. With New Year's Day fast approaching—the day Greeks typically exchanged gifts—the volume of work had increased and the requests were a mixture of unoriginal and crazy. People would rather pay me to find the perfect gift rather than search for it themselves, and I was fine with that. Their delegating kept me stocked in cheese and mortadella.

For the next hour I shopped for sentimental jewelry, the hot toys of the season (I had my own ways of finding them, even when stocks were depleted), and purchased an array of birds for Kyrios Lefteris, who wanted to surprise his wife by reenacting The Twelve Days of Christmas, his favorite English Christmas carol. I warned him about the wisdom of gifting birds, but he refused to be talked down. He said he'd been hoarding newspaper forever to capture all the *kaka*. Every so often I stopped to sip my pine coffee and regret my life choices. Specifically the one where I'd ordered this so-called coffee.

Finally, my inbox was temporarily empty of emergencies, so I settled down to figure out a game plan for all the mysteries bumping elbows in my head.

The clay pineapple. What was the language and who was the tall woman that murdered Stephanie? More importantly: what was she and where was she now?

No idea. I would know more once Yiayia showed up with her linguistics expert, fingers and toes crossed.

Why did Adonis Diplas send me to find that particular clay artifact? How did he know about it? Who was the intended recipient?

I fired off a text message asking him those very things. In return he sent back a whole lot of nothing besides a video of Stephanie's body sweeping the More Super Market, something she'd never done in her life. In death she was downright domesticated.

Stephanie's body had no pulse, yet she was still kicking. To me that spelled zombie. There was no other word in my vocabulary that fit, even if *zombie* wasn't entirely accurate.

I tapped my forehead on the desk. If only the Cake Emporium hadn't vanished. More than anything I needed cake and conversation with Betty Honeychurch. The proprietress of the cake shop was a fount of information about things that went bump in the night and day. All the shop's clientele were touched with the woo-woo stick. To ordinary people, the Cake Emporium appeared as an abandoned storefront, and it wasn't unusual to see strange characters purchasing goodies. The strange cake shop existed everywhere there were people and everywhen in human history. Betty would definitely know more about this zombie-ghost situation.

She also had the ability to read minds.

Betty? I thought as hard as I could. *Are you out there? It's a zombie emergency.*

My phone stayed silent. I could call her, but it would be useless. Since the shop vanished here on Merope, her number refused to connect.

Wherever Betty was, she was beyond my reach.

Unless ...

The UK wasn't part of the European Union anymore, but the geography hadn't changed. I could hop on a plane and be there in a relative jiffy. Actual flight time from Athens to Heathrow was only about four hours. From there I could rent a car and drive to the manor house where Betty lived with her brother Jack. I still had their address in my phone. It was a long way for cake and information, but I could do it.

First, I had to put in some time on the George Diplas job. At the moment Stephanie Dolas wasn't causing issues. She wasn't shambling around Merope, gobbling brains. Far from it. In death she had transformed into the perfect retail employee. As a zombie, I bet she wouldn't so much as flinch after a month of twelve-hour shifts with non-stop Christmas music. Bonus: Her ghost wasn't in my apartment, bugging me about finding her killer.

Lucky, too, because I didn't know what her killer was.

Stephanie's murder needed to wait until Yiayia returned. Then I'd have a thread to pull.

So. George Diplas. The handsome, charismatic, and completely gay meteorologist, who was currently locked away from the world for doing more than his fair share of murder.

One is more than a fair share, in case you were wondering.

Here was the problem that Adonis Diplas was conveniently ignoring. George confessed to the murders. He traveled with his murder trophies. He had tried to kill me. The ghosts of his victims were certain that he was their killer. There was currently no evidence whatsoever that someone else had murdered the victims.

The only person on Team George was his cousin, Adonis Diplas.

But a deal was a deal, and money was money. It couldn't hurt to head to the mainland to talk with George and snoop around his place.

I called his lawyer and arranged visitation. Leo would be the opposite of thrilled. Mostly he'd be worried about my safety.

A knock jerked me out of my tangle of thoughts. Cerberus ricocheted off the bed and galloped to the door. One sniff and he'd assessed our visitor. His raised hackles evolved into wagging and an adorable butt wiggle that nearly knocked over the coat rack.

After stabilizing the coat rack, I peered through the peep hole, to see Leo standing on the other side, juggling two cups of coffee and what appeared to be a cake box.

I flung the door open and relived him of the box before he wound up wearing coffee. The scent of real coffee made me swoon a little. After the pine cappuccino, I wasn't about to turn down genuine caffeine products. If he spilled it, I'd be down on the ground, lapping up the latte with my tongue.

Genuinely happy to see me, Leo smiled all the way up to his eyes. A gang of butterflies moved in to my stomach. "You brought coffee and cake."

"I brought coffee. The cake box was already here."

Weird, but okay. I never looked gift cake in the mouth, and not just because cake didn't have a mouth.

He kissed me until my toes curled, then carried both drinks to the coffee table. His nose wrinkled up. "Is it just me or does it smell like a hospital in here?"

"I made the mistake of going to Merope's Best earlier. Why do I do that to myself?"

"My theory is that we forget in between times how bad their coffee is. It's like Crusty Dimitri's. Jimmy ate a gyro from there last week and it gave him bloody stool."

Way TMI, but also useful information if anyone wanted the scoop on the island's worst eatery. "Is Merope's Best even coffee?"

"Want me to put together a team to investigate? It's the slow season. Pappas and I just arrested a donkey for stealing spinach."

"You arrested a donkey?"

"We made a big production out of it to keep the victim happy and to entertain ourselves. That's how slow crime is right now. Don't worry, we let the donkey go with a warning." He settled down on the couch next to me and slung his arm around my shoulder. The exchange of body heat activated my hormones. "I heard there was some drama at the More Super Market."

I reached for the cup and took a tiny sip to test the temperature. "What did you hear?"

"Grekos called me, spitting fire about how the paramedics are out to get him."

Tread easy, I warned myself. Leo is open minded, but there are limits. He's a person, not a universe.

"Stephanie Dolas passed out. We thought she was dead. He thought she was dead. Then it turns out she wasn't." I stopped abruptly before more words had a chance to weasel their way out. To help myself, I pressed my lips against the cup and sipped.

Leo wasn't distracted by my happy coffee noises. "But?"

Damn it, he'd made me. Denial was the only way through this now. "There's no *but*."

"There's a *but*. I can hear it in your voice, and you're wearing it on your face."

Good thing we were speaking Greek. In English he would have just told me my face was a butt.

"I really need to work on that."

He raised his eyebrows at me.

"Okay, fine." I took another swig of coffee to boost my courage. "Most problems in relationships can be solved with communication, so consider what I'm about to tell you as me communicating and being honest."

He leaned back, his knees man-spreading harder. A flicker of something flashed across his face, too quickly for me to get a bead on it.

I seized on it. "What?"

His chin jerked up then down, signalling no. "You first."

"Grekos wasn't wrong."

"Stephanie Dolas is dead?"

"The paramedics aren't wrong either." I took a couple of deep breaths and let them out slowly while I arranged my thoughts into neat, palatable sentences, which was tough when my thoughts were drunk squirrels at a rave. "Stephanie's ghost is at the More Super Market, and so is her body."

As his brain took a stab at the math, he blinked several times. "I saw her sweeping out the front of the market on the way here."

"You saw her *body* sweeping."

Shallow ditches formed across his forehead and between his brows. "Explain it like I'm five."

Cerberus flopped across my feet. I rubbed his belly with my toes. "Normally when a person dies, you get two things: a ghost and a corpse. The ghost toodles off to Afterlife orientation, and after forty days it either comes back here to haunt a place or person, or they move on to the Afterlife. The body rests in a box for a few days, while family, friends, and often enemies traipse through to pay their last respects or insults, then it's buried. Stephanie's body doesn't want to rest in a box, it wants a full-time job. Meanwhile, Stephanie's ghost didn't go to the Afterlife, and it's not in her body. Are you still with me?" Leo looked dazed. I had to sum this up quickly and without too much weirdness, before he cracked. "So I think her body is some kind of zombie. Anyway!" I snatched up my coffee again and made happy drinking noises, hoping the burst of normality would soften the *zombie* revelation. "Wow. This is great coffee. I should ask for their recipe."

For the next two minutes, Leo sat stock still, except for his face, which was going through the stages of *WTF?* Finally, he reached the last stage: denial. A safe choice. He stood, taking his coffee with him.

"Want to come with me to the *paralia* to check out the Christmas lights tomorrow night?" he asked me.

"Yes, please. I would love to hang out in the freezing cold with you."

His smile was fleeting. "I'll come get you at seven." He moved toward the door. I moved with him.

"Are you going to say anything about Zombie Stephanie?"

Without answering, he kissed me. "Don't forget your cake." The door clicked shut behind him.

Cake.

I had cake.

I barely had my sanity but I was apparently in possession of enough sugar to catapult my mood into the stratosphere before it came plummeting back to earth. Later on, after the sugar crash, I'd have time worry about Leo and his reaction to the news about Zombie Stephanie.

But first, mystery cake.

First thing I noticed was that the cake box was unmistakably from the Cake Emporium. I cut the ribbon that had been curled on the edge of Betty's scissors. I raised the lid. Inside was what smelled like gingerbread cake, delicately piped frosting forming Christmas scenes over the top and sides. I checked for a note.

No note.

Maybe, like a file, the note was inside the cake. That meant there was only one way to find it: eat my way through to the other side. Let me tell you, it wasn't easy being me.

The first few bites vanished quickly. No note revealed itself, so I had no option but to keep on eating.

Twenty minutes later I was swollen with cake and disappointed that Betty and Jack Honeychurch hadn't sent a note with the cake. But I'd had cake, so it wasn't all bad.

Dead Cat wandered into the kitchen to judge me.

"It's not my fault," I said. "The cake was just there and I was desperate."

He pivoted to show me his transparent butt and strolled out of the kitchen again.

Cerberus wasn't nearly as critical. He stuffed his head in the empty box and polished it clean. I didn't have the heart or the energy to stop him. I barely had enough energy to let him drag me downstairs to do his business before bedtime, but I somehow mustered up reserves.

As soon as he was done, we went back to my cozy apartment and all piled into bed. Me, Cerberus, and Dead Cat. Tomorrow was rushing toward me, and I needed to catch the early ferry to the mainland if I was going to speak to George Diplas and his lawyer.

I'd just drifted off when my phone rang.

"Allie Callas's house of mattresses, how can I help you?"

"Are you seriously in bed already?" My sister Toula sounded appalled.

"It's late."

"It's not even nine o'clock."

"I ate a lot of cake, and now I'm sleeping it off. Why are you still up? Didn't Milos and Patra use you up and put you out to pasture?"

"I stay up late even when I'm dead tired. That's kid-free time and I'm not about to waste it. Not that I don't love my kids," she said quickly. "I do love them. But sometimes I want to be a person."

"You'll always be a person to me."

There was a pause while my sister tried to figure out if I was messing with her. Yes. Yes, I was.

I cut her off with a yawn. "Everything okay?"

"I should ask you the same thing. I heard Leo was out drinking alone at the Good Time."

"Tonight?"

"Yes, tonight. Kostas's brother saw him there. Did something happen between you?"

If I'd expected a note of glee in her voice, I was wrong. My own flesh and blood sounded slightly annoyed at the possibility that I'd wounded her former honeybun.

"*Pppft*, no. I told him zombies are real."

There was a long pause that was approximately twenty-two months pregnant, like an elephant. Then: "I don't know if you're joking or not, and it's the *not* that's really bothering me."

Doing my best not to dislodge my companions, I swung my legs out of the warm bed to peer through the shutters. Leo's police car wasn't sitting at the curb. Ergo, he was out somewhere. *Somewhere* being the most decent bar in town for locals during the off season.

For the record, I wasn't plagued by suspicion that he was out drinking with some other woman, one who didn't see ghosts or hold conversations with the two hottie succubi who got their kicks watching Leo eat. Mostly I was concerned that hitting him with the concept of Zombie Stephanie and Ghost

Stephanie had rattled his psyche and now he was trying to steady the ship with ouzo. Ouzo never steadied anything. It only made you *feel* as if dancing like nobody was watching was a good idea.

"I'm on my way."

"He's sitting at the bar. He'll be there until you drive him home and put him to bed. Make sure you leave a bucket by the bed. He's going to need it."

"Future vision pays off."

"It's a curse." The wince in her voice carried across the island and into my ear. Toula was slightly psychic. Her ability to see the future had recently emerged, although there were times when I wondered if Toula had known about her abilities for years and kept them tucked away because she was afraid of being labeled a weirdo. Like, you know, me. She was still struggling with her new identity as a control freak who couldn't control everything. All her chickens had arrived home to roost at around the same time. Wasn't that long ago Milos and Patra announced that they could see the dead like their dear old Thea Allie, and there was nothing Toula could do about any of it. To cope, she marathon-watched a lot of television, while gorging on candy.

I located jeans, a hoodie, thick socks. Okay, today's clothes. I didn't needed to be clean, I just needed to be quick. Maybe I could get to Leo before he required intimate time with a bucket.

Toula read my mind—not literally. It was more like sisters' intuition. "You won't get there in time to stop him from overdoing it."

"Watch me."

"I hate this," she said.

"Maybe if you learn to control it, it might be useful."

"It doesn't feel useful. Mostly it feels terrifying."

Speaking of candy, I heard a telltale rustle of a plastic bag. "Are you eating candy?"

"I can't help myself. My hand keeps moving to my mouth on its own, and every time it does there's a piece of candy in it."

"Have you tried not buying junk food?"

"Do you honestly think I haven't? The problem is I can see the future. I already know I'm going to buy it anyway."

Oh boy. "The future isn't set in stone."

"I have to go," she said, heaving a chest rumbling sigh. "Patra has a school project due tomorrow, and guess who has do to it?"

"Her?"

She laughed. "School projects are homework for parents not kids. Every teacher and parent knows that."

"Didn't you see that coming?"

"I wish."

CHAPTER FIVE

THE COLD CLAWED at me as I set out for the Good Time. Toula was wrong: there was time to stop Leo before tomorrow's head-cracking hangover became inevitable. I peddled hard, dodging potholes and a smattering of the island's ghosts. When my tires reached the cobbled area of Merope's back streets where the Good Time was located, I didn't slow down. The way I saw it this was me taking preventative measures against kidney stones.

A black shadow moved into my path.

My gloves clenched the brakes. The wheels seized up. Adrenaline flooded my body as the back wheel lifted off the ground.

"Whoa there," the Man in Black said, steadying me before I became a lumpy stain on the cobblestones. "I've got you."

I tried to stay cool as my heart slapped against my ribs. "You leaped out of nowhere."

"I assure you, I did not leap."

Now that I wasn't moving, the cold didn't feel as urgent or biting. The Man in Black radiated his own strange aura and potentially his own climate controlled bubble. Tonight he appeared as he always did, in his long coat of midnight and boots that stopped an inch or so from his knees. He was tall, he was dark, he was handsome in that classic romantic literature way. Lots of hard planes, and brooding, and hair that was a touch too long and unruly. Easy to imagine him complaining about how there were no attractive women at the ball.

Not me. I wanted to know why he had leaped out—sorry, not *leaped*—at me in the dark, and at precisely the time I needed to be in a bar, persuading my sort-of boyfriend to put down the glass and face reality. Of course reality was zombies, so maybe Leo was on to something.

I straddled my bicycle and got straight down to what I hoped was the business. "Is this going to be one of those cryptic conversations, or is this about Zombie Stephanie?"

He leveled his dark gaze at me. "What did you do?" His tone had a distinct "old timey headmaster gripping a paddle" edge to it.

"You'll have to be more specific because I've done a lot of things since you were last here. Some of it possibly put me on Santa's naughty list."

"I am always here."

"You live on Merope?" This was news to me.

"The vessel."

"You live in a vessel? Wait. Are you saying you live on a boat?" That made a certain amount of sense.

"The vessel from the unnamed island. You removed it from its resting place. You brought it here. Why?"

He was talking about the clay pineapple. The broken clay pineapple.

My right foot rocked on the pedal. "That's what I do. I find things for money. Why? What do you know about the clay pineapple? Do you know what language the markings are? My grandmother went to find a dead linguistics expert, but she's not back yet, so I'm in a holding pattern. Is Stephanie

Dolas a zombie? She started out the day as a person but now she's a ghost and a body that's really into its job."

His eyebrows rose a fraction. "A zombie?"

"What else could you call her?"

"This person and her health issue are not my concern. Who told you to steal the vessel?"

"You mean who paid me?"

"Yes."

"That's confidential, but I can tell you they no longer have the artifact they paid me to find. It's at my place, broken into several pieces. I'm hoping to do that Japanese thing to it. With the gold, but maybe not real gold. I'm thinking I could afford to use good quality glue. Why? What do you know about it?"

His face contorted. Someone had gas or a serious case of repression.

"Broken," he said as though he couldn't believe he was speaking that particular word.

"Stephanie dropped it before she became a zombie. Is it a zombie pineapple?"

He stared at me, his expression grim. "Where is the vessel now?"

"In my apartment, surrounded by salt."

"If it is broken, it is too late for salt. Where is the second vessel?"

"There's another one?"

"Was it not with the other?"

"There was only one."

His full lips pressed together until they formed a white seam. From the way his nostrils were flaring, it was obvious he was extra moody tonight.

All these riddles. Why couldn't he speak plainly? "If you were to open your mouth and just say what you mean and mean what you say, would something terrible happen?"

His attention snapped back to me. "What?"

My eyes flicked to my watch. Time was marching forward at a ridiculous clip. "Can you just talk like a normal person and tell me what's going on?"

"Do you have somewhere to be?"

"As a matter of fact ... yes."

He seemed to come to a decision. "We will speak soon, Allie Callas."

Without a sound besides his boots echoing on the cobblestones, he swept away, vanishing in a dense, damp shadow cast by a cluster of olive trees.

I was alone.

"Were you talking to a man?" a voice said.

I was not alone.

"No, Kyria Maria," I called out. "I was talking to a pebble in my boot. I did the voice for the pebble as I was trying to shake it out."

"You are a very strange woman."

"I really am."

"Can you find a wife for my son?"

"Isn't your son married?"

"To a donkey's *kolos*."

Kyria Maria's daughter-in-law considered *her* a donkey's butt, too, so they were more evenly matched than they realized. "I'll see what I can do. *Kalinikta*, Kyria Maria."

She muttered her own goodnight and then hurried back home to polish her list of grievances against her daughter-in-law.

Finally, I was on the move again. I hauled ass the rest of the way.

Leo's police cruiser was snugged up to the curb outside the bar, a sprained thumb amidst a mild rash of mopeds and motorcycles. Toula was right, he was definitely here.

The question was: what kind of shape was he in? Not a puddle on the floor, I hoped.

The Good Time was quiet. Most of the island's denizens were tucked away in their houses or apartments, where the fireplaces were hot and the televisions were loud. The bar was dotted with a handful of customers, who were huddled around their drinks with their phones out, creating pockets of cool light in the bar's dim, warm atmosphere. In summer the Good Time would be stuffed to the shutters with tourists, but in winter it was ours.

I didn't have to squint too hard or long to find Leo. Merope's Finest was hunched over the bar, raising and lowering a tumbler to his mouth. The bartender shot me a concerned look.

"He never drinks like this," he said to me.

"Wrong," Leo said, words slurring. "I always drink using my mouth."

I shot the bartender a questioning look. "Keys?"

"Safe." He reached under the counter and dropped Leo's keys on the bar. "Normally I do not interfere, but I think he needs help." After a furtive glance around the bar in case anyone was eavesdropping, he leaned his forearms on the polished wood and did a "come closer" head jerk. "Samaras was talking about zombies."

Oh, brother. "Leo does that when he drinks," I said. "Between us, I think he read his first Stephen King book when he was too young to cope. Scarred him for life."

The bartender's eyes cut to the next warm body through the door. The bottom fell out of my gut. A groan leaked out of my throat and was instantly smothered by the music before it could reach the ears of Kyria Sofia. The priest's alleged sister was dressed like she was on her way to a school board meeting, where she intended to rally against reading, writing, and 'rithmatic. Rigid blond hair—out of a bottle, natch. Twinset. Sensible heels. Nude pantyhose. Wool coat with a ladybug brooch fixed to the lapel.

Tonight she had a new accessory: a small, shaky dog of some variety. Family code only a doggie DNA test could unravel.

Kyria Sofia's eyes narrowed slightly as she combed over the clientele and snagged on me as if I were a persistent knot. The smile she fastened to her face didn't touch her eyes. Her smiles never did. They were as fake as the fillers she'd recently had injected under her skin.

"The whole island is here!" she announced.

The whole island was not here. Merope was home to twenty thousand people and change, and including me there were fewer than twenty at the Good Time tonight. But I didn't correct her because under the surface, Kyria Sofia was a knife, and like all knives, she could easily massacre a reputation or bury herself in a back. I didn't want to join in whatever game she was playing, so I wished her a good evening and smiled. Didn't mean I wasn't dying of curiosity though. Especially since she seemed to have acquired a dog.

A *dog*.

As Scooby Doo would say: Ruh roh.

"I smell peanut butter," Leo said, raising his head. "Does anyone else smell peanut butter?"

My eyelid spasmed. "No."

"I smell peanut butter," he repeated, and rested his forehead on the bar.

Kyria Sofia's church lady exterior was a skin bag stuffed with grubby secrets. She was a relentless social climber and celebrity bootlicker, a charlatan, a vicious gossip, and an avid collector of bestiality porn. And I knew for a fact that she hid the evidence of her animal love in a computer folder labeled Sewing. So far the jury was out about whether or not she could actually sew. To add sauce to the gossip, while she was randomly spying on Merope's oblivious denizens, Yiayia witnessed Father Spiros on the other end of Kyria Sofia's jumbo-sized strap-on. At the time he was dressed like a Great Dane.

All of this meant I was concerned about the pup.

"Cute dog," I said, trying to extract information without being obvious. "Is it yours?"

Ignoring my question about the dog's ownership, the priest's sister pulled herself in to a tight column. "I am just here to remind everyone that Christmas services are coming soon, and my brother expects to see you all at church. Do not spend all your money here. Better to invest your euros in God."

"She does this every week," the bartender muttered.

Her attention slid to me and stuck. "And you, Aliki, you should come, too. My brother would love to speak with you, to share the word of God."

Gulp. That couldn't be good. For one, Father Spiros had the charisma of boiled kale. Also, I was pretty sure Kyria Sofia knew that I knew her brother's holy water was a hoax. The wet stuff the church peddled was as holy as gum on a sidewalk in August.

Arguing with her wouldn't work, though. Not to mention it would be counterproductive. Kyria Sofia was a woman who knew things, and sometimes those things were even true. That meant I had to walk a fine line between doormat and smart-ass.

"I'll do my best," I assured her. She didn't need to know that my best in this situation was third best, at most. Chances were next to zero that I would be at her brother's church on any morning.

She gave me a bright false smile. "You can do better than that. I believe in you. People on this island have much to thank my brother for, yes?"

I couldn't think of a single thing. Father Spiros made me want to beg Carol Ann to stay away from the light.

Nobody in the bar said a word. They didn't need to. Kyria Sofia's face said this wasn't a negotiation. Once she was sure we wouldn't backchat, she pivoted and stalked out into the thickening cold with her shaky canine companion.

"That poor dog," the bartender breathed.

My eyebrows rose up to ask the question. I didn't want to ask it with my mouth in case the dog *was* poor for some other non-sexual reason. Maybe bartender knew it was running low on treats.

The door opened again. In came Stephanie Dolas, armed with a broom and a bucket of cleaning supplies. Behind her body, her ghost was distraught. "Stop it," she begged. "You will break my nails."

Zombie Stephanie ignored her. She was a dead woman on a mission, and that mission was to clean all the things. She began to gather up glasses on the bar, not caring that people were still drinking. The barman gawked as she pushed him aside to sweep a cloth along the already spotless bar.

Leo raised his head. It took him a moment, but his eyes eventually focused on the sight of Zombie Stephanie doing chores that weren't even hers. "The zombies are coming," he muttered. "Here's one right now."

Virgin Mary. I had to get him out of here. In his state that wouldn't be easy. There was way more of Leo than there was of me. Most of my strength was in my legs from riding all over Merope. My arms? They weren't noodles but you could shove one in a pipe and give it a good clean.

"Come on," I said, hauling Leo off his barstool. "Time to go."

His hand had a death grip on the glass. "More ouzo."

"No more ouzo."

"Yes, more ouzo."

"Are you my *mama*?"

A laugh squeaked out of me as I tried to pry his fingers off the tumbler. "If I was your mother, I'd be hitting you with my *pandofla* right now."

"Good," he slurred. "You smell nice and I want to do things to you that I would never to do my *mama*."

"Congratulations. We've established that you're not Oedipus."

He moved in for an ouzo-scented kiss and managed to slide off the stool and onto me. Now we were getting somewhere, although I'd probably be crushed along the way.

"I will drive you home," Leo said.

"As long as you're driving from the passenger seat, fine."

"I can do that."

We moved toward the door. Slowly.

The last thing I saw was Zombie Stephanie running a microfiber duster over the bartender's head.

CHAPTER SIX

THE SUN SHOWED up offensively late, but that was winter for you. Even the sun wasn't keen to roll out of bed on a frosty morning. Me, I was already at the dock, waiting on the morning ferry. Yawning. Suspiciously eyeing this morning's coffee from Merope's Best. It looked like a latte. It smelled like a latte. But was it a latte?

Jiggling as the chilly breeze lashed me, I braved a sip.

"Tastes almost like coffee, which only makes me more suspicious," I told Cerberus, who was leaning against my legs in his canine coat. I'd toyed with the idea of leaving him at home, but it wasn't right to leave him cooped up all day and night. He couldn't just cross his legs if he needed to pee. Truthfully I could have asked Leo or Toula to let him out, but I wanted his steadying company.

Speaking of Leo, he was still sleeping off the ouzo. Last night I'd poured him into bed and set a bucket by the bed along with a glass of water on the bedside table. He'd be suffering soon, but I hoped the water would help.

Cerberus's tail slapped the air. He looked up at me with an open-mouthed doggy smile.

Damn it, I was getting attached to him, falling in love with his shaggy face and his goofy-sweet personality. If I waited too much longer to find him a home, I'd never be able to part with him.

After we got back from Athens, that's when I'd get to work finding him a home. If I could locate people who didn't want to be found, I could rustle up the perfect forever family for the giant dog.

Right? Right.

Several hours later, we stepped onto the dock in Athens, after a brief stop on Mykonos. First thing Cerberus did was locate a palm tree to water. Adonis Diplas had covered costs for a rental car, so I bellied up to the rental counter and waited while the guy found me something that could fit a small bear. The best he could do was a compact. He apologetically handed over the keys.

I set off for the prison, with Cerberus riding shotgun. It was too cold for him to stick his head out the window, so he settled for licking the chilly glass.

Because Piraeus's notorious Korydallos Prison Complex was overflowing with hardcore criminals, Greece had recently cobbled together a new jail for the George Diplases of Greece. Those who were waiting to be sentenced were funneled into the new compound to wait for the judges to get to them—which could take a while. The wheels of justice moved slowly here, and frequently hit potholes, mud puddles, and other obstacles that vanished when someone slid the judges a manila envelope bloated with cash. The new jail was stuck on a bare patch of land, surrounded by rocky outcrops and a smattering of olive trees and beeches. Goats grazed alongside the towering fence topped with a crown of razor wire. Their goatherd was nearby, nose stuck in his phone.

George Diplas's lawyer was waiting for me at the gate. He was shorter than me and straining the buttons of his winter coat, but what he lacked in stature he made up for in enthusiasm and sweat.

"Pavlos Makris," he said, pumping my hand. "You are the private investigator, yes?" He slapped his chest. "I wanted to be a private investigator, too, but my talent is the law. I can barely find my size of underpants at the shop when they are in front of me. My mama used to crochet underpants for me, but now she is dead." He crossed himself.

He wasn't wrong about his mother. She was as dead as dead gets, and she was drifting along behind him like a sarcastic balloon.

At the mention of his "talents," the late Kyria Makri crossed herself and rolled her eyeballs at the pale blue sky. "My son is the world's biggest *vlakas*."

Her son couldn't hear her. "Every lawyer in Greece wanted to represent George Diplas, but he chose me, Pavlos Makris. And do you know why?"

"Because you're the best?"

He laughed like I'd told a cool, fun joke and followed up with an exaggerated wink that made me wonder if he had neurological issues. "No, because I have connections."

"Connections? What kind of connections?"

"Baboulas will kill you if she hears you speaking that way," his dead mother said.

Baboulas? The Boogeyman? Or in this case, the Boogeywoman. Yipes. If that was true, Pavlos was connected to Katerina Makri, Greece's most notorious mobster. What had George Diplas stepped in? You know, besides the multiple homicides.

"I cannot say, but my last name is a clue."

"But you *are* a real lawyer, right?"

His chest puffed up with pride. The coat's buttons struggled to hold on for the ride. "I have an office."

"In a garden shed," his mother added.

My eye twitched. Things weren't looking promising for George Diplas on the legal front. No wonder Adonis wanted me to stick my nose in and poke around. If George was innocent, I might be his only hope. "So, can I speak with your client?"

The lawyer's arms flew up into the air. "Of course!"

He chatted non-stop about the cost of bribing Greek judges as we walked to the entrance. His mouth went on pause and he waited silently while I jumped through all the check-in hoops.

At reception, the receptionist gave Cerberus the hairy eyeball.

"He's my employee," I said.

The receptionist didn't look convinced. "What does he do?"

"He finds good places to eat lunch."

"My father's coworker was a duck," Pavlos Makris said.

His mother's ghost snorted. "The duck was his work wife."

The receptionist came out of his little cage to inspect the big dog. Cerberus was happy to be taken seriously. "Is your ... *employee* hiding any weapons?"

"Do his farts count?"

Proud of his emissions, Cerberus's tail wagged.

The receptionist waved us onward. So that was a no, Cerberus's gas was not considered a weapon. Someone had grown up without pets and had no idea how lethal dog gas could be.

The metal detector was up next. We emptied our pockets and stepped through the frame. Nothing beeped. Finally, we moved on to an antechamber where an ancient woman dressed in black, her back bent, her legs bowed, sat watching a tiny black and white TV. She spat on us to ward away the evil eye and did the sign of the cross.

That was it. We were done with security protocols. Pavlos the Wonder Lawyer got lost twice even though we were following a prison guard, and the guard had to backtrack to find him. Eventually the guard ushered us into an airless room, where George Diplas was already waiting, his hands and legs shackled to the table.

Normally a hearty and hale picture of good health and male prowess, jail time had diminished the meteorologist. He'd dropped weight and muscle. His skin had lost its TV-worthy glow. He didn't know it but he was surrounded by dead men —men he had murdered. Probably.

A light came on in his eyes. "You."

"We meet again."

The meteorologist shrunk back when he noticed Cerberus. Maybe it was my imagination, but I'd swear I saw the big dog lick his lips. Back on Merope, my fuzzy wumpkins had tried to take a chunk out of George's tube steak. In all fairness, George was naked and waving it around like a chew toy at the time

"Sit, sit," Pavlos said, pulling out a chair for me.

George Diplas wasn't done with me yet. His fists clenched on the table. "You are the reason I am here."

I took the offered chair and tapped my thigh. Cerberus scooted into position alongside me, his gaze alert. "No, you're the reason you're here."

Clearly out of his depth, Pavlos shifted from gleeful to nervous.

Diplas's eyes cut to his lawyer. "This is your idea of helping me? I thought you would be bringing someone useful."

"Eh ..."

I narrowed my eyes at the lawyer. "He didn't know I was coming?"

Pavlos Makris' complexion shifted into the hypertension tones. "Maybe I forgot to tell him."

On the table, George Diplas's fists tightened another notch. "What else did you forget?"

His lawyer threw up his hands. "Just a little bit of paperwork, but what lawyer does not forget some of the paperwork, eh? The law has too much paperwork and uses a lot of strange words that I do not think are real words."

"Get out!" George barked.

"Okay, okay. I need to *kaka* anyway."

Without a shred of self-awareness, the sweat-soaked lawyer slipped out of the room, leaving me alone with George Diplas.

Not my first choice. Good thing the guards were just a scream away. Plus I had this big dog who'd like another chance at George's wiener.

"Wow, sounds like you really won the lawyer lottery. No wonder you need help."

"I had a team of the best attorneys in the country ready to take my case, but they vanished. After that, Pavlos was the only one who would help me. Me. George Diplas. After all I have done for this country."

"You point at a map and tell Greeks a day in July is expected to be hot."

His gaze bored into mine. Considered one of Greece's hottest men, his good looks were contingent on his cheerful disposition. When his temperature changed, his attractive features twisted into something darker and unsavory. Nobody in a dark alley wanted to hear the weather forecast from this George Diplas.

"What I do is important."

Adonis hadn't sent me here to discuss meteorology. I was on the mainland to find the truth because George's cousin believed I could find anything—even The Real Killer.

While the weatherman was gritting his teeth in my direction, I hit the brakes and spun the conversation around. "Did you murder those men?"

I expected stoicism at a bare minimum. Maybe some belligerence. A medium-sized tantrum, worthy of a three-year-old whose gyro wasn't wrapped the right way. George Diplas defied my expectations, bursting into a monsoon of tears, big and wet and apparently real. The tears were accompanied by chest-heaving sobs that tugged at my heartstrings.

Oh, brother. If this was him manipulating me, consider me manipulated. I couldn't sit here and ignore a crying man.

I dug around in my crossbody bag for a tissue and offered it to him. His hand reached out tentatively.

Cerberus tensed. His back end trumpeted and he relaxed again. An unholy stench filled the small space. I considered using the tissue to plug my nose.

The door flew open. The guard snatched the tissue out of my hand and stuffed it into his own pocket.

"No comforting the prisoner," he barked. He sniffed the air and gagged.

Up went my brows in disbelief. "It's a tissue."

He squeezed his nostrils shut. "To you. In the hands of a killer a tissue could be a deadly weapon. Have you ever had a paper cut from a tissue?"

"No."

He grimaced. "I have." On an unhelpful note that was short on elaboration, he marched back out. The door slammed shut. Dang it, there was a story there and I wanted to hear that story.

George Diplas wiped his eyes and nose on his sleeve, leaving behind a silvery trail.

"I did not kill those men," he blubbered.

"That's why I'm here. Adonis doesn't believe you killed them either, even though every shred of evidence says you did. But let's say you didn't. Who did?"

"All I know is that it was not me."

The temperature shifted as the dead men jostled around. Their faces were familiar to me now. We'd encountered each other before, back on Merope, and they knew that I could see them. That didn't mean they were helpful. None of them could speak. George—or this mystery killer—had murdered them one at a time by crushing their windpipes. For reasons I didn't understand, the trauma had carried over to their ghost selves.

They assembled around George, glaring down at him. Although he couldn't see them, George shivered.

"Do you have anything I can use to prove it wasn't you? An alibi? CCTV footage? A t-shirt that says *It Wasn't Me*? Anything?"

"That is what you are here for, yes? To find that sort of thing?"

He wasn't going to make things easy. Weird, you'd think an innocent man looking down the barrel of consecutive life sentences would be more cooperative. Maybe he'd already ordered his Rita Hayworth poster.

Lucky for him I wasn't a quitter, especially if the thing I was trying to quit was cake.

I pulled out my phone. "What's your address?"

"Why?"

"So I can search your house."

"What makes you think the police didn't already do that?"

This guy ... argh. "They didn't search your house like I would, and they were looking for evidence to use against you. I'd be looking for evidence to prove your innocence. If you're really innocent."

At that, the ghosts shuffled their feet. There was no sound but they didn't look happy that I was on Team Free George. Who could blame them?

George Diplas rattled off an address in one of Athens'

most exclusive neighborhoods. I jotted it down in my notes and added it to my phone's GPS.

What now? What was I supposed to do? If it walked like a duck and quacked like a duck, then it was probably a serial killing duck.

I scanned the crowd of ghosts, making eye contact with them all. They already knew that I knew they were there. That cat had escaped the bag back on Merope. "Did this man right here kill you all?"

George made a half-assed attempt at erupting out of his seat. The restraints snapped him back into position. "Who are you talking to? I already told you it wasn't me!"

"I wasn't talking to you." My eyes returned to the dead men. They were all indicating that yes, George Diplas dunnit.

Like a brief summer rain, George's tears had already tried up. Now he was gawking at me like I was several lambs short of a Greek Easter. "Is there someone else here?"

The door opened. Pavlos Makris waddled inside, rubbing his hands together. They weren't damp, I noticed. The only visible part of him that was bone dry.

"Only your lawyer," I said.

Pavlos's glance ping-ponged between us. "What did I miss?"

"I was just telling George that I'm going to check out his place."

The lawyer beamed. "Good, good! Can you go today? I would prefer not to have to go to court. I am not very good at trials. The other lawyers play dirty with all their facts and questions. How am I supposed to do all that when I cannot even afford to hire a clerk?"

"At the network we use unpaid interns," George told him.

The lawyer's mouth fell open. "You can make people work for no money?"

"Only the young ones."

Pavlos gazed at the weatherman with rapt adoration. "I want to do that."

"You two are perfect for each other." I stood and organized my things. "I'll do what I can." I aimed that statement at the ghosts. "As for you, I'll call you when I know something useful," I told Pavlos Makris.

"Please hurry," he said. "I cannot wait to make my new unpaid interns do all my paperwork."

CHAPTER SEVEN

On the way back to the rental car, I called Adonis. He was the one paying my fee so I figured I owed him.

"He said he didn't do it, but can't offer up anything that might be helpful in proving that he didn't do it. How am I supposed to find proof that he didn't do it? I can find something. I can't find nothing."

"Sure you can. You can find anything, even nothing."

"I can't find a copy of Sinbad in *Shazam*."

"Because it doesn't exist."

"But I remember it," I said, flipping a wave at the receptionist. "It's out there somewhere, and one day I'll find it, even if it happened in a parallel universe." As the words came out of my mouth, an idea formed in my head. I made a note to ask the Man in Black if *Shazam* had, in fact, been filmed and distributed in another reality. "How do I get into George's house? Does he have a key under a rock in the garden? An unlocked window?"

"You'll figure something out," he said entirely too cheerfully. "Got to go. Stephanie is mopping the roof and I need to see if she can check on the shingles while she's up there."

On that unhelpful note, he ended the call.

Back in the rental car, I blew out a sigh and slumped over the steering wheel. Cerberus leaned against me and burped. The scent of doggy treats wafted over me.

I rolled down the window slightly. "Okay. Let's ride."

He made happy chuffing sounds and settled down in the passenger seat with the seatbelt strapped around him.

Being Greece's most popular weatherman had made George Diplas a fortune. He owned a fancy villa with a view of the sea, but it wasn't quite close enough to be considered a beachfront location. There was no real yard, with only a foot between the narrow sidewalk and the steps leading up to the front door. Still, it was an expensive and heavy front door, with a polished brass knocker. The neighborhood was haunted by an assortment of slaves from Greek antiquity who shook their fists at me as I knocked on the front door.

No one answered. Probably because George was busy doing prisoner stuff.

I eyed the windows. Reached out. Gave one a little push. Did my best to look like a decent woman who didn't break and enter, I glanced over my shoulder and scanned the street. Nothing to see except chickens running around like they'd dodged a fox.

"You're my lookout guy," I told Cerberus.

Afternoon. The neighborhood was quiet except for the chickens. People were at their jobs or in their homes. No one to watch me—

"What are you doing now?"

My hand snapped away from the window. I wheeled in the direction of the voice. "Nothing!"

My accuser was a dumpling in a thin blue housedress dotted with grey flowers. She was holding a whiskbroom and dustpan.

"Are you trying to break into the handsome man's house?"

"No! Yes! Maybe."

She sniffed. "Try the bathroom window. That one is never locked."

I went around back. She drifted alongside me.

"Why are you helping me?"

"The man who lives here is handsome but rude. He never speaks to me."

"You do know you're a ghost, don't you?"

"Of course I know I am dead. I was at my funeral. Do you think I am a *vlakas*?"

At her own funeral. Well before the forty days of Afterlife orientation was up. That made her a murder victim or someone with similar unfinished, traumatic business.

"There." She gestured with her broom.

The bathroom window. Barely wide enough to accommodate my shoulders and hips, but I could make it work. This wasn't my first dance at the bathroom window rodeo. At least this time I wasn't dressed like a store brand sex worker.

I shot a grateful smile at the dead woman. "Thanks. I could help you, you know."

"That is what you said."

"What?"

She waved off my question. "How can you help me, eh?"

"Sometimes I help spirits who've been murdered or who have unfinished business. I'd be happy to help settle that business."

Her expression remained passive for a moment, then she nodded. "That sounds like a good deal to me. Go inside, take care of your business, then we will talk, yes?"

"You want to come in with me?"

She shuddered. "In there? Never."

"Is there something wrong?"

"Eh, I do not want to give you spoilers."

Yipes. What was that all about?

Before scrambling through the open window, I made sure my salt shaker, pepper spray, and hand-held fan were all within easy reach. A good girl scout, prepared for almost anything that might rush at me. Except cops if the house had an alarm system. For that I'd have to rely on charm and my connection to Merope's police department.

You've got George Diplas's permission, I reminded myself. *If the police show up, waving their bonking sticks, tell them they can talk to the house's owner. Who is in jail. For multiple murders. That'll get them off your back.*

"I'm going in," I told Cerberus. He cast a doubting eye at the tiny window and trotted off to sit by the back door.

I boosted myself up and in through the window. It was a tight squeeze but I managed to only nearly dislocate one shoulder. My hip took a beating on the way through. Someday this would bite me on the butt when I discovered I'd need a hip replacement.

But not today. Today I was a successful home invader.

I performed a wonky handstand on the toilet, conveniently located below the window, then slowly rolled onto the floor. Go me. Any minute now the Impossible Mission Force would be blowing up my phone, begging me to take on a mission.

Now that I was in the house, I shifted into information seeking mode.

George's bathroom was stark white. Marble everywhere. White towels sat folded in perfect stacks on the custom cabinets' shelves. Someone had built pyramids out of toilet paper rolls. Probably not aliens. Touches of gold didn't do much to break up the visual monotony, and I got the feeling the room was for show. Even the little basket beside the toilet was empty.

Not wanting to tackle his house alone, I headed for the

back door to let Cerberus inside. He was pawing at the ground, like he was trying to dig his way in.

"Easy, boy."

He bounded in, then sniffed me all over to make sure I was still me. After a thorough inspection, he decided I passed muster.

To work.

Where to start? I wasn't sure what I was looking for. Something that proved George's innocence, because that was the job. But what?

You can find anything, more than one person had told me recently. Even Adonis Diplas believed in my ability to find something, even if that something was nothing.

They weren't wrong. I did have an uncanny ability to find things where others had failed. But was it some sort of gift or just something I was good at because I was persistent and possessed excellent Google-fu? The jury was still out.

I closed my eyes and picked a direction at random. That led back into the bathroom so I gave it another shot and found myself in another bathroom. This one was jet black with silver accents and gave me a serious case of the willies. A bathroom had no business being that dark and shiny. The shower curtain was black velvet, for crying out loud. My gut told me there was nothing in this room, except maybe Anish Kapoor hiding behind the shower curtain.

A voice dragged me out of the bathroom and back into the hallway. "Are you from the magic box?"

I followed the voice down the hall, glancing at the photographs on the walls on the way. George Diplas adorned his walls with the weather. Specifically professional shots of tornados, monsoons, tsunamis, and other wild weather phenomena.

The voice had emerged from what appeared to be the master bedroom. That seemed like a viable place to hide evidence of innocence or its evil twin, guilt. So that's where I went.

The bedroom door was open.

Wow. It wasn't lost on me that scores of Greek women would do anything to be wearing my boots right now, because my boots were in George Diplas's bedroom. They didn't know his equipment pointed due male. Probably that wouldn't slow them down anyway.

George's bedroom was made for happy penis times. Silk bedding. Cuffs attached to the headboard of a round bed in the center of the room. A swing that didn't belong in any children's playground. A jumbo bottle of lube that was this close to being classified as a barrel on the bedside table. The flatscreen television mounted to the wall between the built-in bookshelves looked downright quaint compared to the rest of George's playroom.

And it definitely looked normal next to the fairytale little old grandpa lounging in the bed with the bedcovers hiked up to his neck.

"What?" he said. "Haven't you ever seen a nice, old and completely benevolent real human watching tiny people in a magic box before?"

Cerberus growled, deep and low, the sound vibrating through my body. The sweet, sunny dog had turned apex predator.

Without acknowledging the creature in the bed, I stepped backwards and closed the door before Cerberus launched himself across the room. He turned and rushed into the kitchen.

I called Adonis. "Does George have a roommate?"

"No. Why?"

"Houseguest?"

"No."

"What about your grandfather?"

"He's dead. What is going on?"

"Nothing," I said and ended the call. Cerberus reappeared at my side. I gave him a quick chest scratch. "Just remember, you're backup. Don't attack unless I need you to."

He gave me sad puppy eyes, but he sat his bottom down to patiently await my shrieks.

I opened the door again.

"You again," the old man in the bed said. "What do you want?"

"Is George here?"

"No, that worthless meat bag is not here. Last I heard he was locked in one of your—I mean our—human prisons. Why?"

"And you are?"

He made a sound like a twelve dogs having a puke-off, then said, "You can call me whatever it is you—we—humans call males like me."

"I'm just going to call you 'Red Riding Hood's Papou,' because honestly, I don't think you're really George's grandfather."

He shrugged under the covers. "Whatever."

What was I looking at? Hard to say. On the surface it appeared to be male but the skin kept rippling in a way that reminded me of the wallpaper in season three of the *X-Files*, the episode with the cockroaches.

"You're not a ghost."

"Wow, somebody give the human woman a prize for having eyes. No, I'm not a ghost. Ghosts aren't anything. I'm everything."

Outside the bedroom window, I spotted the dead woman spitting in the direction of George's bedroom.

"She keeps doing that but it won't work on me," the old man said.

"Because she's a ghost?"

"Because I'm stronger than the evil eye."

"What are you doing in George's house?"

"I am his grandfather, he invited me in. We had some good times. Now he's locked up and I am watching the magic box."

"Did these good times include murder?"

"What?" He clutched invisible pearls. "No. Do I look like a murderer? I am a nice old man. Why do you keep asking that anyway?"

"And you're a ..."

"Grandfather." He—it—dragged the word out slowly, like it was tethered to a plow and being pulled by a three-legged ox.

My butt he was a grandfather. "Are you a demon?"

"What? No! What ever gave you that idea?"

"You're a demon."

He threw up his hands. "Okay, you got me there. I'm a demon. The demon to end all the demons. The uber demon."

A demon. Lovely. "I don't suppose you're anything like a succubus? I know a couple of those." My heart was deciding how hard to bang.

Its laugh sounded like a clogged toilet. "Succubi are nothing!"

Ghosts were nothing. Succubi were nothing. Life experience told me this was an ego trip. Everything that wasn't it—whatever *it* was—was nothing.

"And you're here because ...?"

"I am taking a vacation, catching up on the news of the mortal world, and watching these tiny people trapped in these other worlds. I have not yet figured out how to get to them, but when I do I will crack their worlds open with my bare hands."

Who knew the demon had hands. It had myriad protrusions now, none of them particularly hand-like, and definitely no opposable thumbs. The human grandpa facade was slowly falling away.

I didn't fancy spending time explaining television to a demon. My mind was focused on finding out how the demon wound up inside George's house.

Tread carefully, I reminded myself.

"How, precisely, did George invite you in?"

"Stop asking questions or I will scream."

"Did he do some kind of ritual or was it an accident?" I narrowed my eyes at it. "Did something go wonky with Microsoft Word? Because if anything could summon a demon, that definitely could."

The demon let out an ear-piercing scream and hoisted the bedcovers up to its chin. "Stop asking questions! I just want to watch the magic box!"

"Why?"

It shrieked again.

"Something you need to know about the mortal world: If you scream like that, especially in a fancy neighborhood, you're going to attract attention. And I'm starting to get the distinct feeling that you don't want attention."

My phone bipped. Text from Leo.

> Leo: Where are you?

My fingers hovered over the screen for a moment, before plunging onward with the truth.

> Me: In George Diplas's bedroom.

Dots appeared. Disappeared. Appeared. Disappeared. Reappeared, then:

> Leo: So that's a no for the Christmas lights, then?

Crap. The Christmas lights. We were supposed to wander

around in the cold and freeze together while eating corn roasted over hot coals. No way would I be back in time, and after this trip I'd need a Silkwood shower and a nap.

> Me: Tomorrow night?

> Leo: Tomorrow night.

I shoved my phone into my pocket. The demon was watching me. At least I think it was. And if I didn't know better I'd say it was scared.

"Are you scared?"

"What? Me? No! I am a *daimonos*! I am not afraid of anything!" Its human skin rippled and tore. He went up in a cloud of glitter, and when it settled he was fully his demon form. Yeesh. Eight or so feet of boils, goo, pus, extra limbs, and topped with the complexion of a burnt Chicago-style pizza.

I tried to keep my expression steady. My heart was running in circles, looking for the exit. "Holy water?"

"Okay, yes, holy water. See these scars?" I couldn't see any scars with that mess going on. "Holy water." It gave me a sly look. "Do you have holy water?"

No holy water in my arsenal, but the demon didn't need to know that. What I did have was salt, though. Could I use it to contain the demon? Possibly. Although really, did the demon need containing? He—it— didn't look like it was in a hurry to get out of bed and get the day started.

"How long have you been in bed?"

"Why?"

I rustled around in my bag and pulled out the handy container of table salt I kept on me these days for emergencies of the supernatural variety. They happened more than you'd think.

"Just curious. Need any snacks? A grocery run?"

"Are you speaking of food?"

"I am."

While the demon pondered my sudden burst of generosity, I shook salt around the perimeter of the bed. Lucky for me George had one of those round beds that sat in the middle of the room like the 1970s had never grown up. The demon didn't seem to notice or care what I was doing, although it did scowl when I briefly blocked the television.

"In that case I would like fifty babies, seven virgins—male or female, does not matter—a whole bull, and a bucket of butterfly wings, because you let my chickens out."

"They were already outside when I got here." My stomach lurched. "Do you want *tiganites* with that?"

The demon made gagging sounds. "Keep your fried vegetables, but tell me, does the city still have all those philosophers wandering around, spouting philosophy at anyone who wants to be bored to death?"

"Only when the bars close."

"Bring them to me then. All that philosophy softens the meat, and I get enjoyment from devouring people who will not shut their mouths for five seconds in a row."

"You don't like talkers, huh?"

"Only when I am doing the talking. I have been talking for millennia, since long before your kind crawled out of the ocean, dragging their meat carcasses across the dirt."

The potentially useless salt circle was done and this conversation was going nowhere in a real hurry. Thus far I'd found no evidence either way when it came to George Diplas.

"The man who lives here, do you know him?"

Teeth appeared. Jagged. Sharp. Too many rows and too close together. "I know him. But you are asking the wrong question."

"What's the right question?"

"Come back again when you know it."

"Can't you just tell me?"

The demon zippered what I guessed were its lips and made a big production of throwing away an invisible key. If it ever left the bed it could have a decent career in pantomimes.

"Okay, fine. Eyes on the demon," I told Cerberus. Didn't have to tell him twice—or at all. The mammoth dog had been locked on the demon since we walked in.

One section at a time, I worked my way through the house, hunting for anything that might absolve George Diplas. There was nothing. He could be any regular rich guy, with a penchant for kinky sex and photographs of weather. There were no bodies in the basement. Which was good, seeing as how the house didn't have a basement. As far as I could determine, all his murder trophies were currently in police custody.

After a prolonged search, I came up empty handed. At times I got the feeling I wasn't here alone, that someone else was breathing the same air. But I never saw anyone, not even a ghost.

"Leaving now," I told the demon.

"Lock up on the way out, and tell no one I am here. Do not forget the philosophers when you return."

Cerberus and I went out the back door. I turned the doodad and locked it behind me. The bathroom window was still unlocked, in case I needed to ask more questions.

The helpful ghost was waiting for me outside. She was sweeping the yard with a broom that wasn't really there.

"Did you get what you needed?"

I hesitated. "I'm not sure."

"Okay." The broom vanished. "Time to do my thing for me."

Fair was fair. She had helped me and I owed her. "What do you want me to do?"

She grinned. "I thought you would never ask."

CHAPTER EIGHT

Nature abhorred a vacuum and gravity abhorred a flying pie.

I knew this because gravity jumped up and snatched the *milopita* out of the air and dragged it down the victim's body, slopping the rest over her black slippers. And I'd just gotten the thing up in the air, too. By throwing it. Just like my new ghost pal asked.

To make things confusing to everyone except Greeks, a pie could be a pie or it could be cake. The confection crumbling over Kyria Ekonomou's footwear was pumpkin pie. I'd bought it at the neighborhood *zacharoplasteio* for ten euros with the ghost woman egging me on.

Kyria Ekonomou wiped the cake off her face with the back of her hand, then she kicked off a pumpkin-covered slipper.

Ruh-roh. Now I was done for. There was no way I could outrun a flying *pandofla*.

"It wasn't me!" I said in my defense. "Well, it was me. But I threw the *pita* as a favor for someone else."

"Who?"

I glanced at the ghost.

"Tell her it was from Mitsa because she is a *mounoskeela*."

"I can't use that word," I muttered.

"Why not? Is your mother here to put pepper in your mouth?"

She had a point. My mother was presently on a cruise ship, but still, if she ever found out I was using that kind of language, I'd be in time-out.

"Mitsa," I said, reluctantly speaking up. A promise was a promise, and she had helped me scramble through an unlocked window. "Mitsa made me buy it and throw it. Because you're a ... a ... *mounoskeela*. Her words, not mine." I added the last bit quickly so she'd know this wasn't my idea.

She reared back with the slipper.

I ran, but not fast enough. The slipper clipped my ear as I yanked open the rental car's door for Cerberus and threw myself in behind him. Things got hairy and slobbery for a moment as we swapped seats. I turned the key and rolled away, Kyria Ekonomou throwing rude hand gestures at me in the rearview mirror.

If I came back to the neighborhood I'd have to wear a disguise.

It wasn't until I was boarding the Mykonos bound ferry that I realized I should have searched for the Cake Emporium's Athens' store while I was in town. Something told me I'd be back in Athens soon. Finding the cake shop and the Honey-church siblings was high on my to-do list. Even if they didn't have answers they'd have insight.

Cerberus nosed my bag and I realized my phone was jittering in its pocket. A frantic text from Leo.

> Leo: You okay??

Not frantic by most people's standards, but this was Leo we were talking about. Captain Cool. Two question marks was a serious freak-out for the chill detective.

> Me: Fine. Why?

> Leo: Earthquake in Athens.

Greece lived on a network of fault lines. Earthquakes were nothing new. Still, it was sweet of him to worry.

> Me: The question is are you okay? What do you remember about last night?

> Leo: A beautiful woman put me to bed and didn't stay.

> Me: Maybe next time.

> Leo: Tomorrow night—you, me, the Christmas lights.

I smiled.

> Me: It's a date.

The next morning I was waiting when Adonis Diplas opened the shop. Not alone, either. Stephanie Dolas—both of her—was spit polishing the window frames. Her ghost had given up complaining and was peering in the neighbors' windows.

As soon as we were in the door, I shoved my phone under his nose. Specifically the photo I'd sneakily taken of the demon in George's bed.

"Talk," I said.

"I am talking."

"About this." I waggled the phone.

"An empty bed?"

I glanced at the screen. George's whacky so-called grandfather demon was huddled under the covers, but all Adonis was seeing was a pile of rumpled covers. Damn it. Foiled by the lack of woo-woo in Adonis's DNA.

"Are you okay?"

"Fine," I muttered. "Do you know what else I found in his bedroom?"

"Relics of his debauched sex life?"

"Besides those."

"Cookie crumbs in the bed?"

I stared at him. Hard. There was no reason to think that Adonis knew about the demon, but something still reeked of week-old fish in the sun.

"Nothing, that's what. I didn't find anything. Not anywhere in the house." But still, there was that feeling of not being alone, aside from the demon.

"I told you if anyone could find nothing, if would be you."

"Words have ceased to have meaning for you, haven't they?"

He reached across the counter and booped me on the nose. "I have faith in you."

Faith was in plentiful supply in my own brain, but there were limits. As I kept saying to him, I couldn't find something if there was nothing to find.

There was the demon angle, though. George Diplas undeniably had a demon living in his home, and I suspected it had something to do with the murders, even if it was playing cheerleader while George did the strangling.

But Adonis couldn't see the demon, and I wasn't about to

scar the man's psyche by opening a window into the woo-woo world.

"Is George allowed to get phone calls?"

"I guess. You would have to ask his lawyer."

Yipes. That was a whole other issue. "Have you met your cousin's legal team?"

"No. Why? You want a Coke?"

I waved away the Coke he was offering. What I needed was coffee. Anything less and I was going to run out of steam soon. "Do you know anything about his lawyer?"

"Generally speaking, I try to avoid lawyers."

"Because you're not on the same side?"

He laughed. "Lawyers are on one side: theirs. What's the problem with George's lawyer?"

"Does the name Baboulas mean anything to you?"

Adonis dropped his Coke. The bottle hit the floor and rolled toward the door, spraying foam. The door opened. In came Zombie Stephanie with her bucket of cleaning products.

"I'm going to take that as a yes. Pavlos is a family member—and probably a Family member. And for some reason they're interested enough in your cousin that they scared off his original legal team and installed whatever it is that Pavlos Makris is. If I had to guess, I'm not sure he can even spell *lawyer*, and not because of a learning disorder. I think he's just as stupid as a bag of hair."

"You are adorable. Want to get married and have twelve or so children?"

"You're engaged, and I've got a boyfriend and standards."

"The standards are a definite obstacle."

I snorted. Me and Diplas? Never going to happen. Not even if I was single and the world's men had died off in a horrific worldwide event that started with "Hold my beer ..."

"Don't let the Bakas family hear you talking like that.

They'll make all of this" —I waved my hand in the direction of the market's shelves— "go away."

His grin packed up and boarded the next train out of town. He was back to business—business being his cousin's homicide hobby.

"Call George's lawyer, see if you can speak to him. Maybe figure out what Baboulas has to do with all this, too. That's what I'm paying you for."

He had a point. I just wasn't sure if it was a real point or a falsely indignant point. Reading Adonis was tricky. Not too far below the surface, he was a conman of some flavor, and I had no intention of being one of his marks. But what if I already was?

"Okay, I'm following a tiny lead," I told him. "It's the only one I've got, because right now there's nothing to indicate George is innocent. The only ones insisting he didn't do it are you and him—and he's just saying that now that he's locked up."

"And we are right, you will see."

I didn't see. But money was money and I would keep digging until I hit a wall or a cool fossil and ended up in the news.

"Cheeeese," Stephanie said. She'd finished cleaning up the Coke and now she was holding a lump of feta the size of a baseball in her outstretched hand. Brine dripped between her fingers. "Cheeeeese."

"Take the cheese," Adonis said. "Things get messy if you don't take the cheese."

Yeesh. Stephanie Dolas had been cleaning all kinds of things with those hands, except her hands.

"Thanks, Stephanie. I'd love some cheese."

She dumped it into my outstretched hand. Adonis went over to the deli and brought me a sheet of waxy paper. When I was done wrapping the feta, he slapped a sticker on the seam.

Stephanie's next mission was to clean up the mess she'd just made. She grabbed the mop and began slopping water over the cheese brine. Cerberus whined. He gave me puppy dog eyes.

"Don't get between Stephanie and her mop," I told him.

The bell tickled, signaling the arrival of a new customer. Kyria Dola bustled in with her reusable shopping bags. At the sight of Zombie Stephanie mopping the floor, she dropped her bags and crossed herself.

"It is a sign from God Himself! My daughter is finally ready to find a husband!

Ghost Stephanie drifted through the closed door. "*Gamoto*," she said.

The next item on my to-do list on this gusty morning was to buy an assortment of goodies from one of the island's *zacharoplasteios*. They were tasty, I was sure, but they couldn't help missing the Cake Emporium's magical zing.

Even my former boss, Sam Washington, was disappointed when he opened the door. He craned his neck at the box in my hands like he was trying to see where I'd conjured up this pile of substandard sadness.

"That smells good but it doesn't smell like it's from your magic cake shop that doesn't exist."

"It's a consolation prize, I know, but it was the best I could do under the circumstances."

"Did you make up for the quality with quantity?"

"You know I did."

Sam rolled the wheelchair backwards to let me in. "I guess you and your bear can stay. What's up?"

After we hugged, I set the cake box in the kitchen while Sam was busy giving Cerberus cuddles. "George Diplas."

"The weather guy? The one who was arrested for killing my brothers?"

Sam was all about men. He'd fallen in love with Luther Vandross at a tender age and the passion had never worn off. Even Vandross's death hadn't dimmed my old boss's devotion. "George's cousin hired me to prove his innocence. The thing is, as far as I can tell, George is up to his elbow in the cookie jar. He did it. I can't find anything that says otherwise."

"So you want me to help this clown get off?" He held up his pointer finger. "And I don't mean in a good way."

"No, I just want to know if he did it or not. I want the truth."

"And your client?"

"I want to believe he wants the truth, too. It's possible he has an ulterior motive, but I'll cross that bridge when I get to it."

"Well, I guess we'll see about that. What kind of angle are you thinking?"

I forwarded him my list of dead men and their places of origin—a list I had thanks to Yiayia. She'd grilled the dead men and made them write their biographical information on ghost paper, which was apparently a thing. I'd transferred everything to real paper and my phone's notes. "I need to know if George Diplas really was in town when each of these men was murdered. On the surface it looks like he was, but I just need one shred of doubt. I'm going to need times, not just dates. Also ..."

Up went his eyebrows. He ran a hand over his shaved scalp. "Ooh, this sounds bad. Just hit me with it, Callas."

Expecting Sam to flip, I told him about George's lawyer and the Baboulas connection. To my surprise, he broke out in a grin.

"That's more like it," he said, cracking his knuckles. "Pappa needs a challenge now and again to stay sharp."

"Aren't you worried about Baboulas?"

"Nope."

"Is it because you're already in a wheelchair?"

He busted out laughing. "Heck no. Let's just say I know some things about Katerina Makri that she'd rather keep quiet. Wouldn't win her too many friends in the Bad Guy Club."

"Consider me intrigued."

My old boss zipped his lips. "A gentleman never tells, but I'll find the connection. All right. Seeing as how you brought cake to fuel the machine and given me a challenge, the least I can do is give myself a kick in the pants. I'll let you know when I've got something, if there's anything to get."

"Good man."

"I'm the best, Callas. Don't you forget it."

If Luther Vandross's ghost ever dropped by for a visit, I'd definitely put in a good word for Sam. It was the least I could do.

CHAPTER NINE

THE DEAD MAN SAID, "Did you tell your *yiayia* I want a do-over?"

I hit the brakes. Skidded to a stop on the road. Cerberus's cart left the ground for a moment and landed with a thud. I wasn't used to the extra weight back there yet. Once I steadied us, Cerberus hopped off and padded over to give my hand a nose boop.

Vasilis Moustakas, a low-level flasher in life and in death, had paused in the middle of the road. Traffic didn't care. It couldn't see the old man or his walker anyway.

I wheeled my bicycle to the sidewalk and watched a motorcycle buzz through the elderly ghost. Kyrios Moustakas stumped over to where I was crouching, petting the big fluffy puppy. Cerberus was a spectacular shield for my conversations with the dead. Everyone assumed I was talking to my dog, even though he wasn't technically my dog.

"Tell her yourself," I said. "I won't be your booty call facilitator—or hers."

"I do not know what that is, but I like the sound of it. Do you want to see …"

He kept on talking, and maybe even waggled his wiener at me through the opening of his pajama pants—his chosen post-death outfit—but the pajama pants and his privates went unnoticed because something else had caught my attention. Further down the road, a man was yelling at himself.

Sort of.

More like his ghost was berating his body. The body of Thanassi Koutetis, teacher, plodded along the sidewalk, while his ghost was a short distance ahead, drifting backwards, waving his arms and begging his body to stop and listen.

"I have to go," I said, straddling my bicycle. "Want to get back in the cart?"

Cerberus chuffed a no.

Vasilis Moustakas waved his walker at me. Fortunately it was the only thing he was waving, which made a nice change. "Tell Foutoula about that thing I said."

"I will." Did I have clue one what I was agreeing to? I did not. I was fixated on Thanassi Koutetis. Both of him. The resemblance to the Stephanie Dolas ghost-zombie situation was uncanny.

With a thump, I rolled over the curb and coasted up behind the teacher. Thanassi taught history at the island's high school, and as far as I knew he wasn't dead. And yet here he was, in pieces.

"Thanassi, what are you doing?"

His ghost jerked to a stop. His body kept going, right through him.

"Something is wrong," Ghost Thanassi said. "*Yia sou*? Can you see me?" He waved his hands at me.

Bad. So bad.

Something strange and nefarious was happening here, but what? Had the strange female figure from inside the clay pineapple turned the history teacher into a zombie-ghost combo meal, too?

I needed answers. Problem was, I didn't want to talk to ghosts to get them.

"I know you can see me," Ghost Thanassi said. "Do not pretend you cannot. Ghosts talk. We know things."

For crying out loud. "Can't any of you keep a secret?"

He baulked. "Why? We are dead. What else are we going to do besides gossip?"

I made a quick decision that I knew I'd regret. Now that I knew Stephanie wasn't an isolated incident, I needed to start gathering intel.

Ugh. Why me?

"Okay. Fine. Come to my place. We can talk where people won't assume I'm crazy."

He gestured at his body. "I cannot leave him ... me."

"Where is he—you—going?"

"The same places I always go. The library or the school. I have not yet missed any of my classes."

"You're still teaching?"

He looked almost proud. "As if I can stop myself. I go from the school to the library and the library to the school. Nowhere else."

I coasted slowly alongside Zombie Thanassi. At least this way I was talking to what appeared to be a person. Eyes were on us, guaranteed. "What happened? How did you get this way? Was there a woman involved? Or something that looked like a woman?"

"I woke up this way last week."

Last week. Before Stephanie dropped the clay artifact. One data point. "Nothing strange happened?"

"No. I went to sleep in one piece and woke up in two." His expression was distraught. "What is wrong with me?"

I heaved a sigh. "I'm not sure, but I'm trying to find out."

"Find out fast, eh? Come find me when you know something. I will be at—"

"The library or the school?"

"At least I know you are listening to me."

I didn't have the heart to tell him that even if I discovered a reason why he'd been separated into two hims, there was no guarantee I could squish the bits together. He wasn't a sandwich.

More trouble was waiting for me at home. As I closed in on the apartment building where I lived, I spotted our dead gardener, hands jammed down on his hips, watching a fisherman fishing in the courtyard's tiny fountain. The fisherman's ghost was flapping his arms, using his outside voice to berate himself.

"*Vre, malaka*! What for are you fishing there, eh? This is a *putana*'s fencepost!"

Technically it was a fountain, but he was right, this situation was a woman of transactional affection's fencepost. Meaning it was out of control.

I kept my head down and forged onwards to the small and cramped lobby. This whole zombie-ghost thing had just bounded to the top of my to-do list, ahead of proving George Diplas's alleged innocence. There was little I could do before I heard back from Sam anyway.

"You!" The fisherman caught up to me. The floaty bit, anyway. The solids remained behind, calmly fishing in two inches of water. "You have to help me! I know you can, Aliki Callas. Everybody is saying you can fix this."

"Nobody is saying that." I kept my voice low as I stowed my bicycle in the lobby. "I don't even know what *this* is."

"That teacher from the school told me you can help. I know I am a ghost and that means I am dead, but if I am dead, why is my body fishing with the bits of me that should be in the ground by now?"

If I didn't fix this soon, every ghost on the island would be in my house, and I'd had enough of them lately. The news about what I could do was spreading faster as my available time dwindled. Fundamentally, I was an introvert—albeit an extroverted introvert. That meant I was good chatting to people for a while, but then I needed to hole up in my second-floor Hobbit hole and do Hobbit stuff. Alone. No ghosts allowed. Except Yiayia, Dead Cat, and Cerberus, who was very much alive.

Still, I needed more data so I could do whatever needed doing—whatever that was. That meant socializing.

I tucked the wagon behind my bicycle and turned around. Cerberus was waiting in the stairwell for me. "What's the last thing you remember? Before you ... split up with yourself."

The dead fisherman picked a booger while he thought about it. "I was chasing a turkey. That m*alakas* comes to my home every day and does *kaka* all over my yard. Varvara refuses to keep it contained, so I told her next time it came to my house I would catch it and eat it."

"Something must have happened. Did you have any enemies?"

"Are you saying I was murdered? I was not murdered. Who would kill me? I do not have any enemies except that turkey."

"Did you have any unfinished business—I mean, major unfinished business?"

"I did not catch the turkey."

"I don't think runaway turkeys count. Did you see an unusually tall woman with no hair by any chance?"

"If I had seen a woman like that she would be my wife now."

"Did you pay your taxes?"

"Taxes!" he spluttered. "Now you are accusing me of not being Greek. Greeks do not pay our taxes. If this is how you find things, I do not think you are doing a very good job."

Wow. Rude. And this guy wanted my help? If I wasn't

doing a good job—and this wasn't a job because jobs paid—it was because I had next to nothing to go on and a trio of ghost-zombies who were skimpy with useful information.

"Then go home, and tell yourself to stay out of my fountain"

As I trudged up the stairs with Cerberus bouncing ahead of me and the ghost trailing behind me, I called Leo. "I know you don't want to hear about zombies, but I've got three zombie-ghost combos and counting."

"How many dead bodies?"

"Technically zero. They're just dead on the inside, where it counts."

"The law only cares if they're dead on the outside, too."

Fair point. The law was all about hands in cookie jars. Right now there were hands flapping around the jar but the cookies were untouched.

Rats. All those cookie thoughts had led to cookie wants and needs. Not a *koulouraki*. A genuine American chocolate chip cookie. Chewy. Chocolatey. Still warm.

"We should probably be having a completely different conversation."

"So let's do that." The tense note in his voice mellowed. "I had a dream about you last night."

"Was I partially undressed at the most?"

"Yes, and you were promising to stay away from George Diplas." His voice dropped down into the low, horny registers. "Are you partially dressed and promising to stay away from George Diplas?"

"Sweats and fuzzy socks."

"So close."

"And I just got back from visiting George Diplas last night."

"The police won't be happy. I'm not happy."

"Ah, but his defense attorney will be. Although I'm not

sure Pavlos Makris is what anyone or anything other than a tree stump would call a keen legal mind. Between us, I suspect he got his diploma out of a cereal box."

"Probably shouldn't ask this, but how did it go with George?"

"George says he didn't do it and there's a demon sleeping in his bed."

"So he's going to plead insanity?"

"What?" Cerberus, the dead fisherman, and I piled into my apartment. I locked the door. "Not that I know of."

"If he's claiming there's a demon in his bed ..."

"No, there was literally a demon in his bed. An ugly one, too. It was pretending to be his grandfather, like in Little Red Riding Hood."

There was a long pause—the pause of a man trying to decide if today was a good day to take up scrapbooking or hoarding. While he struggled to come to terms with what I'd told him, I shrugged out of my coat and performed my usual coming home ritual. By the time I'd kicked off my boots, he'd managed to find words.

"I don't know what to say. Is George Diplas a serial killer or not?"

"Maybe. Stay tuned."

"Allie ..."

"Look, this is what I do, apparently. I find things. If he's innocent, I'll find out. If he's guilty I'll find that, too."

He blew out a long sigh. "This one doesn't feel right. Gut feeling. And I don't want you involved. Diplas already tried to kill you once."

"Are you trying to protect me?"

"Yes."

"I like it."

"So you're going to drop the Diplas thing?"

"I never said that."

"Allie ..."

"Leo ..."

"Woman," he growled, "you're a handful."

"Not usually, but lately—like since I re-met you, actually—things have been weird. This isn't normal for me or my life. Most of the time, my job is me doing small stuff. Shopping online. Going to auctions. That sort of thing." I changed the subject. "Want to come over and make out?"

"I'll be right there."

I ended the call and turned around. The dead fisherman was at my window, watching his body fish for coins in the fountain.

There was a soft, bubblegum-esque pop and Yiayia materialized with her hand clutching the tie of a man I could only describe as an exhausted professor. The thin, stooped man had been grading papers for decades and someone had put him away wet. Very obviously one of Yiayia's paramours. The fatigue was a giveaway. So was the grin.

"My Virgin Mary," he said, "will you not let me rest first, woman?"

Yiayia waggled her eyebrows suggestively. "Rest when you are dead."

They both laughed, which made two of them.

Death jokes. *Sigh*. They were fifty percent more groan-worthy than dad jokes.

"This is the man I was telling you about," Yiayia said, releasing his tie. "He can interpret what is written on those pieces of pottery."

"Perhaps." He shifted into snooty academic mode. "There are no guarantees, although I am familiar with most forms of archaic writing. Now, show me the writing, please."

I led him into the kitchen, where the fragments were still surrounded by salt. While he squinted at the clay bits, I pulled my grandmother aside. "Does your friend have a name?"

"Yes, but I forgot what it is and I do not want to ask him because I do not want to encourage conversation. When he starts talking ... ah-pah-pah!"

Fair enough. In my head I called him Professor, whether that was true or not.

Because the shards of pottery were solid and Professor was dead, he couldn't pick up the pieces to inspect them. To compensate, he whipped out a handy magnifying glass from his coat pocket. Nice that he had come prepared. Or maybe he was one of those ghosts who always carried a few tools of the trade.

"Hmm ..."

Yiayia flicked her gaze at me and shrugged.

"Hmm ..."

Now seemed like a good time to ask questions. "Any idea what it is?"

"It is old."

"Anything else?"

He straightened up for a moment and swung around to peer at me through his handheld lens. "Do you know what is Proto-Greek?"

It rang a bell. "The language Ancient Greek evolved from?"

He made an affirmative hum. "This" —he point at the shards— "is from before Proto-Greek. Proto-Greek evolved from whatever this is."

"Can you interpret any of it?"

"I believe it is an old recipe book. That is a fish and this is a fire, and that over there is water." His transparent finger jumped around the pieces, pointing out blobs and scrawls. "Probably a recipe for fish soup."

"Why would they write a recipe on an old clay pot?"

"Where else would they write their recipes? Did they have

paper? No. No paper. They could not even go to the shop and buy my books."

"You wrote books?"

"Of course I wrote books." He peered down his nose at me. "I was very famous when I was alive, in certain circles."

"What circles?"

"The round ones, mostly."

I shoved my finger against my eyelid before it started hopping around like an angry cricket. "So you're sure it's a recipe?"

"I said what I said."

"There's nothing about something inside the sealed pineapple?"

"No contents, only ingredients. Although now that I think about it, maybe this artifact was an ancient can of soup and the writing is the list of ingredients."

Yeah, I didn't think that was it. But he seemed sure, and he was an expert on something. Probably himself.

"So no, say, unusually tall people packed inside?"

"I do not see people in the ingredients."

"Are you positive?"

This was his chance to admit that he was in over his head and making it up as he went along, but instead he doubled down. "Yes. There are no people of any size in this can of fish soup."

"Can this fish soup turn people into zombies?"

His watery eyes blinked at me. "What kind of soup do you young people eat today? There is no such thing as zombies. How can you make soup out of a thing that does not exist?"

"People think ghosts aren't real and yet here we are."

He didn't look amused by my observation. "That is different. Ghosts are people. Dead people, yes, but still people."

"Zombies are people."

"Where does she get these ideas?" he asked Yiayia.

She grabbed his butt. "Listen to her, eh? Then I will let you do that thing I like."

That got his attention. Apparently he liked doing that thing my grandmother liked, because he and his magnifying glass returned to the shards. He came at them from a different angle this time.

"Not a word about zombies. Or a symbol. I still say this is an ancient can of soup with the ingredients or recipe etched into the surface. But this language predates most of my knowledge. As far as I know there is nobody who can help you with this—nobody living."

Nobody living. Fortunately I wasn't limited to the alive-and-well resource pool. "What about somebody dead?"

"I—" He was this close to replying when his comeback died on entry. "That is a good point. Everybody who can understand this is dead—long dead. Maybe one of them can help you."

My gaze flicked to my grandmother. "Yiayia?"

She gave me a helpless sort of look. "I do not even know where to begin finding a spirit that old, but I could ask around."

Cerberus gave a single warning bark. A split second later someone knocked on my door.

I excused myself to let Leo in. He made an impressive entrance with a long kiss that tingled all the way to my toes. When we surfaced for air, he pulled back and looked me over.

"You weren't lying about the sweats or the fuzzy socks."

"Are they a turn off?"

"Nothing is sexier than a woman who is comfortable."

"You say that now, but you haven't seen me when I'm in complete pig mode."

"I can't wait."

My eyes flicked to the kitchen, where Yiayia was propositioning the dead professor. Some things could never be unheard.

"Everything okay?" Leo said.

"Ghost stuff. I'm getting some outside help with reading the inscription on the pineapple. Way outside."

"A ghost?"

"A ghost."

He held up a bag. "Hungry?"

My stomach growled. "I can be bought, and you just bought me for the next hour, at least."

There was a big, dramatic yawn that didn't come from Cerberus or the dead man at the window, watching his body fish. Leo had brought food, and food meant succubi. The two demon women got their kicks watching Leo eat.

Which made three of us.

In the beginning I'd called them Bleeder and Choker, because that's how they presented themselves when they were trying to persuade me that Leo was a serial killer. They were peeved about a living human woman putting her paws on their Pokemon collectible. Nowadays they were called Jezebel and Tiffany because their real names had the ability to flay skin off the inside of a human ear. We tolerated each other, more or less. Jezebel and Tiffany presented themselves as supermodels who had been filtered through various apps until their beauty was in the vicinity of the Uncanny Valley.

It was hard not to compare my fuzzy socks and sweatpants with that, but somehow I managed.

Leo carried the food into the kitchen. The succubi followed. The moment they entered, the professor jerked upright.

Tiffany struck a pose. "What are you looking at, ghost boy?"

The professor muttered and went back to staring at the shards.

"You two are demons," I said. "Maybe you can help me with something."

The professor went "*Meep*" and vanished with a pop.

"Help? Help isn't really our thing." Jezebel boosted herself onto the counter, flashing a mile of taut thigh. "Unless it's helping ourselves."

"We're great at helping ourselves," Tiffany confirmed.

Over at the counter, Leo's eye was twitching as I chatted with what appeared to him to be thin air.

"The clay fragments on the counter," I said. "Can you interpret the writing?"

Jezebel leaned over to look, then she sat back up again. "Yes."

"Well?"

"Oh. You want me to tell you what it says?" Her smokey eyes cut to her pal. "I think she wants me to tell her what it says."

My patience was thin and dwindling. "That would be great."

She thought about it a moment. "No."

"Please?"

"No."

"Why not?"

"No means no."

Great. Now she was using sane and decent logic against me.

"Demons," Yiayia muttered. "I am going to watch TV. Ask the sexy man to turn on my shows for me, eh?"

I passed on her message to Leo, who looked relieved to be leaving the kitchen.

Tiffany squinted at the writing. "I know what it says."

"Is it a recipe or a can of fish soup?"

She looked at me like humans were even dumber than she'd first thought. Then she scoffed and boosted herself up alongside Jezebel. It was a miracle they could move in their bodycon dresses. "What does he see in this one?"

"I do not get it," Jezebel said.

I pinched the bridge of my nose. Squeezed my eyes tight. Tried not to scream. Reigning in my frustration wasn't easy. All I wanted were some answers that were true. I had three zombies, three ghosts, one runaway woman who'd been stashed inside the clay pineapple, and no answers that didn't involve fish. So sue me, I wanted to throw a minor tantrum.

I released my nose. Opened my eyes. Swallowed the shriek.

"Just one question. Does it say anything about zombies?"

They looked at the fragments again. "No."

Calm, quiet: "Any idea where I can find someone who can interpret this and is actually willing to tell me what it says in its entirety?"

"Ask the ones who made the vessels," Tiffany told me.

"Oh, okay! Who made them?"

They looked at each other and shrugged. "We do not know."

"But you're demons."

Jezebel clutched pearls that had suddenly appeared in loose ropes around her neck. "That is xenophobic. Just because we are demons, does not mean we know all the other demons. Do you know all the other small, pathetic, fleas that are people?"

She had me there.

Leo returned to the kitchen and the available space shrank. He was big and I was suddenly overtly aware of his him-ness.

"Is it still weird in here?" he asked me.

"So weird."

"Want to go hide in your bedroom and fool around until the weirdness goes away?"

"If you think that will work, I'm in."

CHAPTER TEN

THE SUCCUBI BOLTED when another man in their collection decided to eat lunch. Yiayia was busy watching her daytime shows with Dead Cat. Cerberus was draped across the floor in front of my door like the world's biggest draft stopper. Leo and I were warm from being wrapped up in each other. He went to the window and peered out.

"There's a man fishing in the fountain."

"Yeah, and his ghost is looking out the other window, watching."

"But ..."

"I know. That's three so far. Three ghosts separated from their bodies. All three bodies are sort of plodding along, operating according to their own internal programming. Stephanie Dolas is cleaning everything. This one is fishing. Thanassi Koutetis is still teaching. I don't know how good he is at it now, but being a zombie isn't slowing him down. It's not slowing any of them down." I rolled my head on the back of the couch to enjoy the view. The view was his butt. "Stephanie died. Actually died. Then she came back even though she doesn't have a pulse. I really want to know if Thanassi and this guy died, too."

"You're sure she died?"

"Panos Grekos said it himself. Then she sort of jumped up when the paramedics checked her out."

"So they revived her?"

"Yes but also no. Like I said, no pulse. I checked it myself." An idea formed in my head. "Can you ask Panos if these other two died as well?"

"Are you afraid of him?"

I winced. "It's not that, exactly. It's his mother."

"Is she haunting him?"

"She's a banshee, and she knows I can see her."

He chuckled, low and deep, and kissed me on the forehead. "I'll talk to Panos. Anything to stop an outbreak of zombies on the island."

"I need to know what they all have in common. There has to be something."

"They died and came back."

"Yeah, but more specific than that. Otherwise the island would be overrun by zombies."

He paled. "On my way. Lights tonight?"

"Yes, please."

The dead man kept on fishing. Didn't so much as flinch when Cerberus shoved his nose between his cheeks and sniffed.

"Rude," I told the big dog, without an ounce of conviction. Cerberus picked up on my lack of sternness and bounded around the courtyard. Out on the street he peed on a few things and then he was happy to go back upstairs where the warmth was.

Angela called as I was shrugging off my coat.

"Hi," she said.

"Hi."

"Hi."

"Are we going to do this all day or are you going to give me a name?"

Angela Zouboulaki was one of my most frequent clients. Normally she gave me a man's name and I was expected to investigate him to see if he was worthy of being the next Mr. Angela. Skeletons in the closet were okay; it was wives she was more worried about. Lately the multimillionaire had experienced a run of worse than usual luck. When she tried to switch teams, I finally caved and told her to date her butler Alfred, who was so in love with her that he regularly hid in the butler's pantry to wait out his anxiety attacks.

She sighed like her cosmetic surgeon told her Botox was now a banned substance. "Allie, that is my problem. I do not have a name to give you. I have given up men."

"We've been over this," I said, kicking off my boots. "You can't just decide to be a lesbian. That's not how sexuality works."

"Come see me."

"Sure. When?"

"Now."

I shoved my feet back into my boots. "Can I bring my dog?"

"I am allergic."

"To dogs?"

"To the things that go with dogs. Fur and *kaka*."

"Sorry," I told Cerberus. "You're on babysitting duty. Don't let Yiayia do anything I wouldn't do."

"I have already done everything you would not do," Yiayia said. "Some of it twice. If I joined OnlyGhosts I would be a millionaire. Let me tell you, if you are going to do terrible things, best to do them for money."

I shoved my finger into my eye socket to stop the frantic twitching and struggled into my coat, one-handed. It wasn't easy but I prevailed. I really did need a neurologist, or maybe more magnesium.

Or less weirdness.

My phone rang again.

"You can babysit tonight," Toula announced.

Yipes. In the old days she used to ask. "Isn't that supposed to be a question?"

"Why? I already know you're going to do it. Why beat around the bush?"

"I liked you better when you couldn't microdose the future."

"I'll be there at six."

"Wait—Can you see if Leo and I are taking them to see the Christmas lights?"

There was a pause I couldn't interpret. "The future is hazy," she said. "Ask again later."

"Leo and I already made plans."

"The future is less hazy now, so I suppose later is here. Yes, you can take them to see the lights. Leo will keep them safe."

"Wow. Your confidence in me is the opposite of confidence."

"It's not that, it's ..."

"What?"

"I'm not sure."

"Is this a woo-woo thing or mom anxiety?"

"Yes."

"Milos and Patra will be safe and fine, okay? Leo will be with us and so will Cerberus."

"That behemoth of a dog that belonged to the Kyria and Kyrios Vrettos?"

"He's the size of a bear with the personality of a golden retriever, aren't you, baby boy?" Cerberus rolled over to lap up my attention. I buried my hands in his fur and rubbed his tum-tum.

"Oh my God, you got a dog."

"I did not get a dog. I'm his foster mom until I find him a good dog."

"You got a dog. Or the dog got you."

"See you tonight," I said.

My inner cat stabbed the red dot and made my sister shut up. Honestly, she could have used her powers for good, but instead she was using them to be annoying. Sisters. And I couldn't even complain to Mom and Dad because our parents lived on a cruise ship now.

Yiayia tore her gaze away from television. "Was that Toula?"

"She's even more annoying now that she gets glimpses of the future."

"I love your sister, but ask her to see if she ever gets the stick out of her *kolos*."

Angela Zouboulaki, widow, divorcee, one percenter, lives on a pricey slab of land with a killer view of the Aegean Sea. Her yard is gravel, broken up periodically with stark white statuary and fountains. Her house is a white box. An opulent and large box, but a box.

Her butler, Alfred, opened the door. Could have been my imagination, but the stiff British butler's face was an ounce less sour today. Someone had smiled recently and it showed.

"Mrs. Angela is expecting you," he said. He stepped aside so that I could enter the grand foyer and swap my boots for slippers. Angela kept a basket of new slippers by the front door so that anyone entering her home would leave dirt and other cooties outside without breaking Greece's social contracts. Bare feet were a no-no, even in your own home.

"How's it going?"

"I cannot complain, Miss Allie, and that vexes me. I do so enjoy my petty grievances."

I raised my eyebrows at him. "Are you and Angela …?"

"A gentleman never tells. However, I am not a gentleman, I am a butler, and since you are responsible for certain recent … changes, I will tell you that Mrs. Angela and I are gradually becoming companions. Any day now I expect she will ask you to complete a full background check on me."

"Alfred," I said, "she already did when she hired you."

"Ah." He stood a little taller. "Very good, Miss Allie. This way, please. Mrs. Angela is waiting."

We traveled down long corridors devoid of color, to Angela's drawing room. Most Greek houses had one room set aside for entertaining guests. That's where Greek women kept their valuables such as the good couch and family photos in fancy frames. Angela kept hers stocked with a minibar and expensive art by artists who painted with shades of white. Angela was white's number one fan.

Which was why I reeled when I realized the white couch now featured rust-colored pillows.

Angela bit down on her stuffed lip. "Are they too much?"

For a moment I was speechless. Angela never did colors in her house. She preferred to be the only break in monotony. This was unprecedented.

"Wow."

She threw her hands in the air. "It *is* too much!"

"It's two colorful pillows."

"I know!"

"I like them."

A line tried to appear between her brows, but the Botox refused to yield. "You do?"

"They suit you."

"Are you sure?"

I sat on one of the pale armchairs, hoping my clean clothes wouldn't leave any marks or lint on the fabric. "I do, but does it matter what I think? You're Angela Zouboulaki."

"I *am* Angela Zouboulaki." She rose off the couch and began to pace the room in her fluffy slippers. "I own half this country."

"And in all your ... forty years—"

She whipped around. "Thirty-five!"

More like fifty-something, but who was counting? Not Angela.

"—excuse me, thirty-five years, has anyone else's opinion ever mattered?"

Her nostrils flared. "You are right! Alfred suggested I add a little color, but I *only* went along with his idea because I liked it."

"Exactly!"

Now that her confidence had roared back, Angela returned to doing what she did best: making expensive plans. "We should celebrate ourselves, Greece's strongest women. Have you ever been to the Asteri Spa?"

"Not recently." Or ever. Touch my feet and you were liable to get kicked in the face. Involuntary reflex.

"We will go. My treat. A girls' trip. Alfred will drive us."

Fifteen minutes later we pulled up to the spot where the Asteri Spa used to be.

CHAPTER ELEVEN

"This is a problem," Angela said.

A problem implied a small inconvenience like the salon going out of business. *Catastrophe* was more accurate. The Asteri Salon had been swallowed or replaced by a salon-sized hole in the ground. The hole's edges were jagged and raw. It was filled with fire and reeked of rotting eggs. If I listened—and I was trying not to listen—I could hear low, muffled screams from the bottom.

This was bad.

"I think they're closed," I said, trying to be calm. Not easy under the circumstances. "Maybe there was a death ... in the whole business."

Alfred threw his body between Angela and the bubbling hell pit that had swallowed the Asteri Salon. "Run, Mrs. Angela! Save yourself!"

Angela brushed him aside. "It is just a big hole in the ground. A sink hole. It smells like my first husband's *kolos* after he ate hot peppers."

"That's the brimstone," I said, like I was an authority on hell and volcanology.

The burning—pun totally intended—question was whether the pit was a natural phenomenon or paranormal. Angela and Alfred could see the hole, so it wasn't a ghost thing. But there were more things in heaven and Earth than Horatio could dream of. Shakespeare said it himself.

My inner scientist suggested a test. And lucky me, here I was with a container of salt handy. I never left home without it.

"What are you doing?" Angela wanted to know.

"Seasoning."

That got me an approving nod. "That is the most Greek thing I have ever seen in my life."

Alfred's anxiety wasn't happy. "Mrs. Angela, please, come back to the car. Let me take you home where it is safe."

She ignored him.

While she was ignoring poor Alfred's pleas, I poured an approximate tablespoon of salt into my palm. In a wide arc, I flung the salt in the hole and flicked the last few grains over my shoulder. Superstition was stitched into every Greek cell, whether we admitted it or not.

What happened?

A whole lot of nothing. The molten maw continued to boil and steam.

So much for science. Wait—was it science? Did the supernatural world follow the rules of their own science, or were they still confined by our box of natural laws?

I needed to know these things.

There was movement beside me. The Man in Black had arrived on the scene with his usual pronouncement: none. He was gazing into the hole, his forehead rippled with proof of his concern.

"Send your friend home," he said without shifting his eyes away from the hell hole. "It is not safe for her here."

Angela giggled like the girl she was approximately fifty years ago. The Man in Black may or may not have been a man, but he passed as a human male, and that was enough for Angela's loins to quiver. "Are you going to introduce me to your friend?"

"I would if I knew his name."

Next to Angela, Alfred was simmering. His face was set its usual polite butler mode, but there was a definite stiffness to his flared nostrils. His upper lip was practically cardboard.

The Man in Black flicked his gaze at me. I cleared my throat.

"Time to go," I told Angela. "Alfred is right. This isn't safe. You should go. Alfred can protect you."

Alfred's chest puffed out at the compliment.

"What about you?"

"I'll walk."

Angela's forehead tried its best to wrinkle up and failed miserably. Botox doing the heavy lifting again. "Alone?"

"My ... uh ... friend will walk me home."

She shrugged. "Okay."

And that was that.

Alfred scooted around to open the rear passenger door. Angela bypassed him and angled into the regular passenger side. He stood blinking for a moment, certain that something had happened but not quite sure what.

"Go with it," I told him.

"I am not sure I know how. There are rules and natural laws. I am a butler and sometimes Mrs. Angela's chauffeur, but nothing has prepared me for this."

"Just have a conversation with her."

"About what?"

"Normal things. Interests, hobbies, work."

"I did buy a new type of starch that is working better than I hoped."

"Maybe stick to hobbies."

His shoulders squared. "That *is* my hobby, Miss Allie."

Yeesh. Poor Alfred. Maybe I needed to find him a smalltalk course.

"The weather is always safe," I told him.

That worked. With a curt nod he folded his lanky body into the limousine's driver's seat and turned the wheels toward home.

When I returned to the pit, the Man in Black was crouched down, giving Cerberus cuddles. Cerberus, who the last time I saw him was snoozing in my apartment.

"He's looking for a forever home," I said. "Need a new hunting dog? I don't think he'll hunt much except sticks though."

"He already has a home."

"What? No."

The Man in Black gave me one of his penetrating gazes. I got it. I was penetrated. "He has chosen wisely."

That was just his opinion. I couldn't keep Cerberus. Not in my apartment. It wasn't fair to keep him cooped up.

But was he cooped up? He was always out with me, wasn't he?

I changed the subject before I wound up admitting the Man in Black was right.

"So what is it?" I nodded at the hole. "Portal to hell?"

With a final rub, he rose up off the ground. "In a manner of speaking."

"And the spa?"

"Still here, but out of phase with your time and world."

"Do you think you could try speaking in paragraphs? Because something weird is going on. Weirder than usual. And I have to tell you, I don't normally freak out, but I'm starting to freak out. There's a hell pit here, and the island has zombies, but it also has ghosts to go with those zombies. I had no idea dead people could splinter off into ghosts and zombies."

"There is mischief at work."

"There is, and the only person who can help me speaks in single sentences that are frequently non sequiturs."

He looked at me.

"That's Latin for 'it does not follow,' meaning that your words regularly have no relationship whatsoever to my questions."

"This world has recently experienced many instances of another dimension intruding. How long has this hole been here?"

"I rest my case. As far as I know, since today. Nobody is gossiping about it, so it's definitely brand new. I didn't know a thing about it until Angela and I came to get our nails done."

His eyes slid to my hands. I shoved them into my pockets.

"I'm busy and I use my hands a lot. Perfect nails don't really fit with my lifestyle."

"That is nothing to be ashamed of."

"Who said I was ashamed?"

His gaze flicked back down. "Your hands are in your pockets."

"Yes, because it's freezing."

"Really? I had not noticed."

"So are you going to tell me what kind of mischief, as you put it, is happening here?"

He took his sweet time answering. "I do not believe your zombie-ghosts and this hole are related. This is a weak spot, worn or created between dimensions, and zombies are merely bodies that have been reanimated by necromancer."

"And the ghosts?"

"Humans are made of two parts, the flesh and the soul. An accomplished necromancer can raise the flesh and soul together. Whoever is responsible for the your situation is no master of their craft."

Craft. Like they were knitting a scarf.

"So who is this necromancer?"

"I cannot see into all the hearts on your island, Allie Callas. But you must find them and convince them to reverse what they have done. Mortal bodies are not designed to stumble around this earth without their souls."

"Because they'll eat brains?"

He stared at me, his eyes dark and unfathomable. "No."

I waited. He wasn't forthcoming with explanations. "Okay then. I guess I'm off to find a necromancer, a murderer, and an obnoxious amount of sugar. And you're going to …?"

He was gazing into the hole. "I will be here."

"Doing …?"

"Observing."

"Does this have anything to do with the broken pineapple?"

He said nothing,

Cerberus and I left him to his mysterious hole. On foot. Because my bicycle was back at Angela's place. I didn't mind walking, but the stiff sea breeze was using me to strengthen its pitching arm.

"How did you get out?" I asked Cerberus.

He grinned up at me and bumped my hand with his head.

"Did you at least lock the door behind you?"

In response, he hiked his leg and watered a post that was obviously too dry.

My head was full and I had no place to dump the contents. Civilized and industrious zombies were loose on the island, along with their ghosts. A strange woman had burst out of the broken pineapple, killed Stephanie, and hadn't been seen since. George Diplas may or may not have killed a bunch of men, and a demon was living in his house. Betty and Jack were still absent and the Cake Emporium was not only closed but gone.

Was it still gone?

Yep. While I was lost in thought, my feet had seized control and brought me to the narrow alley where the Cake Emporium used to sit. Wind whistled a dirge as I stood in front of the empty retail space.

I pressed my nose to the window, my heart a clenched fist, longing for the days when Betty used to fill the storefront with seasonal decorations crafted with sugar. Before the store vanished, she'd created a winter scene, complete with a sugar lake and tiny sugar ice skaters. Now there was nothing inside except maybe some dust that was waiting to be stirred by a new tenant.

With my eyes closed, I tried once again to reach out to Betty Honeychurch.

Nothing happened.

CHAPTER TWELVE

As soon as night showed up, Toula threw her kids at me and hit the gas pedal.

"She's in a hurry," Leo said, watching the minivan hurtle down the narrow street.

"Mama and Baba are going to Butt Town," Patra announced. At six years old, my niece hadn't developed a filter yet, and as a Greek, chances were high she never would. Milos —eight—was more circumspect. He tended to think before he farted.

Both kids collapsed on the ground in a damp puddle of cackles. They didn't know about Butt Town or what went on there. All they knew was that butts were funny in any language.

Leo was grinning. "I've got nothing."

"I'm never making eye contact with Toula ever again." I gave him the side eye. "Did you two ever ..."

He choked. "No."

Cerberus cast a baleful glance at the kids on the ground, then looked to me as if asking for permission.

"Go ahead," I told him.

One at a time, he hauled the kids up onto their feet by their coat collars.

"Where is Butt Town?" Milos asked.

Patra said, "In Fart Land."

"Diarrhea World," he countered.

And they were off again, laughing their heads off. Cerberus bounded around them, grinning.

"Toula better hope it's not," I muttered. Then, raising my voice: "Let's go see the lights."

"Please," Leo muttered.

We piled into Leo's police car, with Cerberus squeezing in between my niece and nephew. The promenade's lights weren't far, but Leo didn't want us to walk in the cold.

Half the island was out and about to see the Christmas lights. Merope's municipal building had a big tree that wasn't exactly Rockefeller Center size, but would pack a wallop if it fell on someone's head. True to Greece's roots, the boats along the dock were festooned with lights in neon colors. Kyrios Xaris, a local farmer, was grilling corn cobs over glowing coals. Other business owners were selling roasted chestnuts, spiced nuts, *koulouria*—the soft pretzel's Greek cousin—and *souvlakia*. Crusty Dimitri's had dragged their cart out, too. They were selling mystery meat with hands that hadn't yet performed their yearly hand washing. Christmas carols struggled to be heard over the chatter. Greek voices tended to drown out ambient sounds.

We wandered along the promenade with our coats and winter woolens beating back the cold. Patra and Milos danced ahead of us with Cerberus playing nanny on his long leash.

That's when I spotted a flaw in the holiday season charm and groaned.

When you have an island of twenty-thousand people, an inevitable amount of inbreeding happens over the generations.

Cousins sometimes accidentally married cousins. Cousins sometimes purposely married cousins.

Then there was the Bakas family.

Since the family that founded the local newspaper first discovered the printing press, their gene pool had dwindled to a dry, cracked patch of dirt. Bakases only married Bakases, and it showed. Tomas Bakas, the paper's reporter and senior editor, appeared malnourished, weak-boned, buck-toothed, with ears that could lift him into the air if only he had the muscle tone to flap them. Chins had been bred out of the Bakas line entirely. Probably that's why the family had arranged the marriage between Adonis Diplas and Tomas's cousin Effie: they wanted their chins back. Obviously with Effie locked up for the award-winning combo of insanity and murder, Adonis wouldn't be siring Bakas babies anytime soon—or ever. They'd never get their chins now. Not unless they arranged more outside "help."

Like a common cockroach, Tomas was lurking around the Crusty Dimitri's cart. His eyes widened when he spotted me. At least he had some self-awareness.

I sidled up to him. "What are you doing here? Aren't you supposed to be locked up for the good of humanity and the news?"

"They let me out because there was a shortage of rats to eat."

"Ah. You swapped information for freedom."

He had the audacity to look offended. "Men like me must use what little talent we have."

"And they say the Bakases are dumber than a sack of rusty hammers."

"They do say that," he admitted.

We watched one of the island's denizens roll up to the Crusty Dimitri's cart to place an order. Someone's outhouse was going to get a workout later.

"So what are you doing here?" I asked the man who had thrown me to his crazy cousin.

"What does any newsman do? I am hunting for a story."

"Turn up anything interesting yet?" I had both eyes on Milos and Patra. Cerberus was glued to them like at least one of his ancestors was construction grade adhesive.

"I heard that somebody stole a wedding dress from Kyria Yiota."

"Huh. Weird. Can't imagine who would do that."

"She thinks it was you, but she says you are too stupid to rob her successfully."

The memory of the snapping mousetraps still stung. Her mockery was nothing compared to those. "Anything else interesting?"

He hesitated.

I elbowed him. "What?"

"I heard that Stephanie Dolas died and then she came back, but she came back wrong."

My eyes sought out Stephanie in the jumble of bodies. Wasn't difficult to find her because she was the only one vacuuming the cobblestones. The vacuum wasn't plugged in, but that wasn't slowing her down.

"She looks fine to me," I lied. Everyone who knew Stephanie Dolas knew that she probably had no idea how to work a vacuum cleaner or a feather duster.

"That is not Stephanie Dolas."

His powers of observation were astute for a man whose family tree was a wreath. "Oh, Great and Terrible Tomas, tell me, who is it then?"

He cast furtive glances sideways and over his shoulder. "I think she has been replaced by a robot or aliens. Possible the Turks are responsible. I am working on an exposé."

Astute, but not bright.

"You think Turks replaced Stephanie with a lookalike Stephanie? Why?"

"Why not? And she is not the only one who is acting strangely. There are others."

Now he had my attention. "Who?"

He tilted his head indicating that he wanted me to shuffle away from the open ears. Leo and I exchanged glances. Mine said, *Can you watch the kids?* His said, *Sure, so long as I don't have to hear about Toula and Butt Town again.* Mine replied that no more Butt Town was fine with me, that we were on that same page together.

"Okay, so who?"

"Thanassi Koutetis, Kyrios Heleoitis, and Mariana Spiropoulo."

Mariana Spiropoulo. Her I didn't know about. That she'd passed was unsurprising, seeing as how she claimed to have been born during World War I. The only shocking thing was that she hadn't shown up on my doorstep yet. Possibly because my apartment didn't have a doorstep. I didn't even have a nice mat outside the door. Maybe I needed one.

My eye twitched. Tomas seized on my moment of bodily weakness.

"You know something."

"Who me? No. I don't know anything about anything."

"You know," he said, his expression smug. "Fine, if you will not tell me, the *Merope Fores* will hire you to find out."

The *Merope Times*. The island's only newspaper. The rest of our print news was imported from the mainland.

"Do you remember what happened the last time the paper hired me?"

"Yes, but this time there was no murder."

I wasn't sure about that, but I didn't say so. Stephanie was definitely murdered by something from another realm.

Bakas said, "People are talking about Stephanie ..."

"I, for one, am shocked that people on Merope are gossiping. It's so unlike them."

"... and I want to give them the real scoop about what is happening with Stephanie and the others."

"The real scoop or the scoop that you're making up as you go?"

"Sometimes that is the same thing."

I begged to differ, but I didn't do it out loud. Why couldn't Tomas just go away?

"I don't want to do this," I said.

"I thought you could find anything." His voice took on a wheedling tone that made me want to sprinkle LEGO throughout his house for his unsuspecting feet to find. "That is what people say."

"Just because I can find it, doesn't mean I want to deliver information into your hands."

"Fair," he said. "Okay, I will just tail you. If I stay close enough then I will know everything you know."

"Why, you little—"

"Allie." Leo cut me off before the rest of that sentence popped out. "I have to go. I'm sorry. This is not how I wanted tonight to end."

Me either. As much as I loved Milos and Patra, I was hoping their parents would get to Butt Town and back in a hurry so that I could snuggle up with Leo.

"Everything okay?"

He moved me away from Tomas, who was doing his best to eavesdrop. With ears that size he could pick up sounds from the bottom of the ocean if he concentrated. "There's something happening at Ayios Konstantinos."

"Did news finally break that the holy water is a lie?"

He chuckled. "People would run Father Spiros off the island."

That wouldn't be the worst thing to happen on Merope.

Maybe then the Church would send the island a priest who couldn't play the featured creature in an 80s horror flick.

"What is it?"

"Don't know, but I have to go find out."

I twisted the front of his sweatshirt in my hand and dragged him down to my level for kissing. His lips said he wanted to stay. His phone said he needed to run.

"Are you kissing?" Constable Pappas's voice stepped out of the speaker.

I pushed Leo away gently. "You should go before Pappas gets horny."

"Too late," Pappas said.

Leo stuffed the phone in its holster. A peck on the forehead and he melted into the crowd.

I mustered my nephew and niece and appealed to their bottomless stomachs. "Hmm ... I wonder if anyone around here likes corn?"

"Me!" Milos jumped up and dabbed. "But it makes Patra fart, so I should get hers."

"Corn makes Milos fart, too," my niece told me.

"Everybody farts," I said. "So you can both have corn and blame it on Cerberus."

Cerberus didn't look like he minded being blamed for gas and other odors. He accompanied us to where Kyrios Xaris was grilling corn.

The corn was sweet and salty and slightly charred in places. Corn was delicious at the best of times, but this was magic. We gnawed and wandered for a few minutes, and when we were done with our cobs, I bought each of us a small paper bag of roasted, salted chestnuts. Every so often, someone would stop me to ask if I could find something for them. I took notes and promised them I'd get back to them as soon as my hands weren't a salty mess and I didn't have two dwarfs in tow. That's what they were pretending to be now. Dwarfs.

Apparently they'd been reading the Artemis Fowl books, and Mulch Diggums, a dwarf, was their favorite character. As far as I could tell dirt went in one end of Diggums and directly out the other through a flap in his pants. Bad things happened if you stood behind a dwarf when he unhinged his jaw and opened his butt flap.

No news from Leo yet. Whatever was happening at the church must be engrossing. I hoped it wasn't another murder. Homicide was an activity that used to be limited to the summer season on Merope, but this year autumn and winter had seen more than their fair share of killers.

At the base of the giant Santa Claus with a hooked nose, Lydia and Jimmy were bickering about something.

"Trouble in paradise?" I asked.

"I'm trying to tell him that his movies should have closed captions," Lydia said. "He disagrees." Her style tonight was a faux fur coat and booties with nothing else to keep winter out, unless the lashings of glossy red lipstick or the plate-sized hoop earrings counted.

"Actually, I agree with her, but I love it when she gets feisty." Jimmy Kontos, porn star, blushed.

"Really?" she said.

"Really."

"Okay," Lydia said, thinking. "On the count of three, Apple or Android?"

Patra giggled. "Are you going to eat dirt and open your *kolos* flap now?" she asked Jimmy.

I clamped my hand over her mouth. "Patra."

"I love those books," Jimmy said. "I made a series of shorts loosely based on them once."

"Tell me you weren't Diggums," I said.

He blinked at me like my brain had suddenly fallen out of my head. "Course I was. How many dwarfs do you think live in Greece? Ones who make" —he eyed the kids— "the same kind of movies I make? Only one. Me."

I'd opened my mouth to guess a number somewhere between one and three when an unholy screech tore through the night.

Ear piercing. Primal. Mad about something worse than having to parallel park on Merope's side streets during the Christmas light presentation.

The crowd parted. Truthfully, every face registered fear. My hand was already diving into my bag for something I could weaponize. Whatever was coming at me was moving fast. My mind went directly to the tall woman who had materialized out of the artifact and poked her finger of death at Stephanie Dolas.

A-ha. Salt.

Yiayia appeared out of nowhere, doodahed up like Mrs. Santa Claus. "Allie, that is a bad—"

I flung a handful of salt directly into the face of a furious Kyria Yiota. She clawed at her eyes, howling.

"You *malakismeni mounoskeela*!" she screamed at me. "First you steal from me like a common *tsigana*, and now this!"

Well, heck.

"A warning might have been nice," I said to my grandnother.

"I tried," she said, "but I was busy doing my best to avoid Vasili Moustakas. He keeps waving his *poutsa* at me."

"Not in front of the children." I tried to cover their ears but it was too late. Hazard of having a niece and nephew who could also see the dead.

"That old man with the pet worm is funny," Patra said. "The worm must be old because it's really wrinkly."

"Worms don't get that old," her brother told her.

"They do if they're ghosts, too," she said.

Kyria Yiota was armed not for bear, but for whatever was small enough to lose in a game of *Pandofla*, Head, Scissors. She thrust her foot at her daughter. "Take off my shoe!"

Her daughter dutifully complied, although her face said she'd be okay with her own personal sinkhole right about now. "This is not a good idea, Mama."

"Did I tell you to speak?" Kyria Yiota snatched the shoe out of her daughter's hands and slammed her stockinged foot on the cobblestones. She wheeled around and aimed the shoe at me.

Yikes. I was about to catch footwear to the face and there was no time to duck. The shoe sailed toward me. My face scrunched up in preparation.

I braced myself for the pain.

For the humiliation.

Why couldn't Toula have foreseen this? I could have worn a catcher's mask.

And then ... nothing.

CHAPTER THIRTEEN

THERE WAS A *WHOOSH*, followed by a *thud*. I opened an eye to see the best boy in all the world with Kyria Yiota's shoe clamped between his teeth.

Cerberus grinned at me. His tail swished back and forth. Somebody *knew* they were the best boy. He dropped the shoe at my feet like he'd brought me a gift. I didn't want to touch it. I knew where that shoe had been.

"Who's my sweet baby puppy-wuppy?" His tail swished harder. "Okay. Milos, Patra, Cerberus, on the count of two, let's run. One ... two ..."

The kids took off in different directions. It took an act of Cerberus to herd them back together and get us all moving away from Kyria Yiota, who was pitching death threats at my back.

"This is fun!" Patra squealed.

Milos was less enthused. To me it looked like he'd recently discovered that exercise wasn't fun. At eight years old, he was an adult.

Our feet thumped the cobblestones until we rounded the

corner and left the main street. We stood panting in the shadow of the produce store.

Then I heard it.

A new screech.

This time it wasn't Kyria Yiota. The bloodcurdling vocalization was furious and filled with frustration.

Milos and Patra froze. Cerberus's hackles stood at attention.

The sound was coming from Ayios Konstantinos.

Leo was there.

"Cerberus, protect."

As usual, the big pup seemed to know what I meant. He gave a quick woof and took the rear as we trekked up the street to Ayos Konstantinos. When the holy building emerged from the night, he placed his massive body between the kids and the church.

The police were onsite, for all the good that was doing. Leo, Constable Pappas, and a couple of the other officers were standing on the narrow sidewalk, attention focused on the church's blue dome.

Raging on top of the church, the strange woman from the clay pineapple had ripped off the cross and was using it to punctuate her screams. The police appeared to be puzzled, as if they were looking at something but weren't sure what.

"What do you see?" I asked my niece and nephew.

"Some lady waving her arms," Milos said. "She looks mad about everything."

Made sense. Probably police couldn't see her, just the cross whipping back and forth as she seethed.

Patra giggled. "Maybe her children are naughty little fuckers, too"

I choked. "Where did you hear that?"

She shrugged. "From the man who lives at the school."

"Lives as in he's alive and otherwise homeless, or lives as in that's the place he's haunting?"

"The second one."

"He's a dead *xenos*," Milos told me. "He hates kids, but if he hates kids why is he at the school?"

I made a mental note to go have a word with the ghost at the island's elementary school when I got the chance. In the meantime, I had an angry woman—or whatever she was—to deal with.

The problem was the cops standing outside the church. Three of them had their phones out, recording the shenanigans. The fourth one was Leo, and he just looked worried as I hurried over. When he realized I was there, his expression shifted to one of relief.

"Someone called in a disturbance, but I think this is more of a you thing than a police thing." He rubbed his hand over the back of his neck and gave me an *I can't believe I'm asking this* look. "Is it a poltergeist?"

"You can't see her?"

He jerked his chin up once for no. "Just the cross flying around by itself. We've got other problems, too. There's a sinkhole where the Asteri Spa used to be."

I winced.

He zeroed in on my wince. "What is it?"

"Less of a sinkhole, more of a hell hole. But I think it's temporary. The salon is still there. It's just out of phase with our reality."

He raised his face to sky. Closed his eyes. "The police academy never prepared me for this."

"Me either, and not just because I didn't go to the police academy."

He curled his arm around my shoulder and pulled me to his side. We stared up at the church's roof together. "Was Merope always this weird?"

"It's getting weirder lately."

"I thought so."

High on the dome, the woman was howling at the heavens, spitting out words I couldn't translate from ground level.

"Watch Milos and Patra," I told Leo.

"What are you going to do?"

"Find answers."

"Allie ..."

I glanced around. Spread my arms out either side of me. "See anyone else that can fix this?"

"I was going to tell you to be careful.

"I'm always careful."

The truth was this felt like my fault. I was responsible for the clay whatsit coming to Merope in the first place. All those Indiana Jones movies should have taught me that stealing artifacts always turned spooky, but apparently I was a slow learner. Now it was up to me and no one else to make it right. At the very least I had to gather intelligence so I could form a real plan, rather than making it up as I went.

He kissed me quick. "I don't like this but I trust you."

With that out of the way, he told the other cops to head to the hell hole that used to be—and still sort-of was—the Asteri Spa. Then he went to join Cerberus and Toula's kids.

The heavy doors to Ayios Konstantinos were closed but unlocked. I laid my hands against the wooden slabs and pushed. I tried to look cool, like Aragorn in *The Two Towers*, but then my foot shot out from under me and I slid along the church floor on my backside.

No sweeping soundtrack to accompany my movements. Just cackling from the church's caretaker, Kyria Aspasia.

From the floor I said, "Did you just mop?"

"Nighttime is the best time for mopping. No one is here."

"That's what I thought." I groaned as I hauled myself up

off the cold, damp marble floor. "There's a problem on the roof."

"You mean the demon that just ripped off the cross and is now waving it like the Greek flag at a basketball game back in the 1980s?"

"Very specific, but yes. Is it a demon?"

"Maybe. Who can say?"

I glanced around. "Where is Kyria Sofia?"

"With the other chickens."

"She's not here?"

"Do you know what she cares about?"

"Fame and animals?"

The church's caretaker shook with laughter. "And money. She will be happy when she hears about this. What happens when you damage a building?"

"You get an insurance payout. But wouldn't that go to the Greek Orthodox Church?"

She shrugged. Her hump moved with her. "Maybe." She gestured at the ceiling with her mop. "Now you go up and see what is happening, eh?" A gnarled and liver-spotted hand rifled around in her pocket and pulled out a small bottle filled with clear liquid. "Here, take. This is real holy water, not the *skata* we have here."

"Will it work?"

"Eh, who can say? The ladder is in the back."

Heights didn't thrill me. They were too high, for starters. My keen instincts told me I'd be a pro at falling but a rank amateur at landing. A deadly combination. A pounding heart and screaming instincts didn't stop me from locating the ladder and scaling up to the roof. To appease them, instead of standing on the dome, I chose the flatter part. My chances of survival were better there.

I was good at finding things, right? If that was the case, I could find a way to cool the temper of the woman on the dome. She had bees in her bonnet and didn't seem like she was going to quit raging any time soon. I got it. That's how I felt when Netflix canceled *GLOW*. I was still mad about it. This gal had been cooped up in a clay pineapple for gods only knew how long, so maybe this was an emotional release. A therapist would call this a healthy outlet.

If only I could understand her.

"Leo!"

From across the road, he looked up.

"Eat something!"

"Eat?"

"Yes, eat!" I mimed eating. Badly. Honestly, it was shocking that Leo still wanted to kiss me with these acting skills.

"No food!" He looked at the kids, but they were out of snacks, too.

Surely I had something he could eat that wasn't lip balm or an old receipt. Time to find out. I yanked open my bag and poked around. Alas, my bag was a snack-free zone tonight, unless you were a dog. Cerberus's chicken and liver treats were sealed up in a plastic bag, ready to be dispensed when he was an extra good boy.

Desperate times called for liver-flavored measures.

"Ignore the packaging," I called out. "Just eat them. Please."

I threw the bag down. Leo caught them with one hand. Under different circumstances I'd be turned on by his athletic prowess. Instead, I had to mentally commit the moment to memory to be enjoyed later, when he wasn't about to eat dog treats.

He inspected the bag. "These are ..."

I waved my hand at him. "I know. They're all I've got."

"They're liver."

"And chicken. Chicken is delicious, and they're more

chicken than liver, actually. I know because I read the ingredients."

"And why do I have to eat them?"

"Trust me. It might be a matter of my life or death."

That did it.

He tore into the bag and popped one into his mouth. His jaw worked as he chewed. First time in history any living creature had ever taken that long to eat a dog treat.

Cerberus stared at Leo, unblinking.

Right on cue, the succubi appeared. No pop. No shimmer. One second there was nothing and then they were there. They sighed and made happy noises as Leo struggled to eat the treat.

Relief washed over me. "Great!" I said. "Exactly the succubi I wanted to see. Help?"

All that got me was pealing laughter.

"Why should we help you?" Jezebel said.

I hooked my thumb at the woman on the dome, shaking the cross at the stars. "I can't understand a word she's saying, and I feel like she's making a good faith effort to communicate."

"So you wish to ask us for a favor?"

Yeesh. When they put it like that ...

I glanced back at the woman. If she threw the church's cross it could hurt one of Merope's people—or worse. She'd already taken out Stephanie, even though Stephanie was back, more or less. Two of her. The point was I had a responsibility to my people. And because none of them, except Milos and Patra, could see her, that meant I was the only one who could do something. Even if it meant being on the hook to a pair of succubi whose hobby was watching my boyfriend eat.

If he was my boyfriend. We weren't really official. It was one of those conversations we hadn't gotten around to yet.

"Hey Leo, are we boyfriend and girlfriend?"

He paused chewing a second dog treat. His eyebrows rose up slightly. "Of course we are. You mean you didn't know?"

"I wasn't sure."

"You're mine," he said. "And I'm yours."

The way he said it was romantic. My heart did that swelling thing and my cheeks burned. But now wasn't the time. I had an island to maybe save.

"Okay," I told the succubi. "Yes. I'm asking for a favor."

"If we grant you a favor, you will owe us one in return. A favor of equal value."

"Agreed."

"Say 'I solemnly swear—'"

For crying out loud. "Really?"

"No, we are just messing with you. What do you want?"

"An interpreter." I gestured at the seven-foot woman. "She's upset about something, possibly the way the church is decorated, and I'd like to be able to communicate with her."

"We already told you to find the ones who speak her language."

"Okay, yeah, I'll do that. But in the meantime I need to talk to her."

The succubi exchanged a glance and then shrugged. "Okay," Jezebel said.

Great. Wonderful. Now we were cooking with fire.

"Come on up," I told them.

Their Uncanny Valley faces registered confusion. "For what?"

"So you can interpret?"

"Unnecessary," Tiffany said. "Her kind can speak any language, but you still owe us a favor."

"What? No way!"

"You agreed to give us a favor in return for helping you, and we helped by giving you information."

Damn it, they were clever. Probably that's why they were demons and I was a lowly mortal.

My head tilted, and that's when I realized the seven-foot woman was steamed about being stuck on Merope. She didn't want to be here. What she wanted was to go home.

"I have one job," she was yelling. "One miserable job, and now I cannot do it! I want to go home! Somebody call me a Pegasus!"

"You're a Pegasus," I said.

She stopped. Turned. Her blazing hot gaze roamed over me before settling on my face. "You! I have seen you before."

I waved. "Hi. I'm Allie Callas. And you are …?"

Her nostrils flared. "I have no name. I am my purpose. That is what I am for. What do I need with a name?"

"So I can call you something?"

"You do not need to call me anything." She turned in a full circle, her eyes nervously prowling the dark landscape. "I must return home."

Home. The island where I'd found the clay artifact. "You mean the island?"

"Is that where they placed me?"

"That's where your pineapple was, uh, found." This wasn't the time to admit that Adonis Diplas had paid me to locate her pottery house and remove it from the island. Not when she was so distraught and I was a fragile meat sack filled with a skeleton and several gallons of water.

"An island." She seemed to be tasting the idea as much as the word. "Clever. A shrewd choice. Far away from land and all its people."

"I heard there were people on the island. Well, ghosts actually. Dead people."

"Dead?" Her voice sharpened. "How?"

"Old age? They died thousands of years ago. It's 2023."

She tossed her head. "Time means nothing to me. Only

my purpose."

"So what I'm understanding is that you want to go home to the island—"

"Need. Want is for things that are optional. My purpose is not optional."

"—and you don't have a name. Okay, I can take you home."

"How? Do you have a boat?"

"Not exactly, but I have access to a boat."

She flung the cross off the roof. It landed on the ground with a ground shaking clatter. "Take me there, mortal!"

"I'll take you there, but I have questions first."

"There is no time!"

I pointed at her. "You said time means nothing."

Her nostrils flared several times as she tested my logic. "Very well. Ask your questions, then we must leave at once."

I didn't tell her that the next ferry off Merope was hours away. There would be time—ha—for that later. First I needed answers.

"You killed a woman when you popped out of your clay pot. Why?"

"She is dead?"

"In a manner of speaking."

"An accident. I assumed I was released to smite my enemy. That is my purpose, my function, my only reason for existence."

And I thought my job was challenging at times. "Why did you turn her into a zombie?"

"What is this word? I do not know."

"A zombie. The walking dead. Her body is moving around, performing normal tasks, but her soul splintered off so now she's a zombie and a ghost."

The fire that was her eyes dimmed. "I did not do this."

"What about the other zombies here? Why did you kill

them?"

"I have taken no other life but that one, and that was an accident. My purpose is not to kill mortals."

"What is your purpose?"

"That is my business alone." She glanced around. "Where is my vessel now?"

"You mean your clay pineapple?"

"Yes."

"It broke. That's why you popped out and how you came to be standing on a church roof."

She blanched. "Broken! I cannot cross the water without the company of my vessel."

"It's okay, I have super glue and I know how to use it."

Fingers crossed that super glue worked on clay.

"*You* have my vessel?"

"I've been trying to find an interpreter to read the writing on the side."

"In Case of Emergency, Break Vessel."

"That's what it says?"

"Yes."

That son of a motherless goat. Grandma's fancy-pants professor was making it up. Can of fish soup, my pasty white bottom.

"What emergency?"

"Pray you never find out," she said darkly, which was really something because all her words bore charred edges.

"Okay, off the roof. I'll take you to your vessel. It's at my place."

"Truly you will take me there?"

"Truly."

"I will fly behind you."

Good enough. With the disaster averted, or at least transmogrified into an entirely different disaster, I climbed down off the roof and returned the ladder.

The church's caretaker made a sound like she was glad I hadn't fallen off the roof.

"Did the demon fix the cross?" she asked.

"I don't think she's actually a demon, but yes, in a manner of speaking."

Kyria Aspasia's hump shook with silent laughter. "I am sure that Sofia will find a way to make a profit from this, eh?"

"Speaking of you-know-who, did she get a dog?"

She crossed herself. "What dog? Theos, Christos, and the Panayia, that woman must never be left alone with an animal."

"She had a dog with her the other night at the Good Time."

"That is very strange and very bad because she does not have a dog, unless you include Spiros."

Yiayia's tale about Kyria Sofia, the strap-on, and the Great Dane costume waltzed back into my mind. Yikes. Probably I'd never recover.

"Something to worry about another time," I said and took off towards the church doors.

Leo, Toula's kids, and Cerberus were waiting a small distance away from the cross protruding from the ground. The clay artifact's occupant was hunkered on the edge of the church roof for my instructions.

"This way," I called out to her.

Milos was gawping at me with something that looked like admiration. "Wow, Thea Allie, you can talk to her?"

"I can now. I had some help that wasn't entirely helpful."

"From the two sexy ladies who like Leo?" Patra asked.

Milos elbowed her. He was blushing.

"They're sexy?" Leo said.

"They're not fans of dressing appropriately for the season," I told him.

"I'm going to dress just like them when I'm twelve," Patra announced.

"Over your mother's dead body," I said. "Everybody into the car. We're going home."

"What about the funny lady on the church?" my niece said.

"She's going to follow us."

"She must be a fast runner," Milos said in awe.

"Her big plan is to fly."

The kids and Cerberus all twisted around in the backseat to watch the pineapple's former occupant leap off the roof and take to the air. She didn't have wings or any sort of aircraft. She sort of hung suspended in the night sky like a Harrier until Leo bumped the gas pedal. Then she began to move with us, staying within fume-sucking distance.

Toula was waiting outside my apartment with Yiayia.

"Careful," Yiayia said. "Toula has a *kolos* stick again." She winked at her great-grandchildren. Milos giggled. Because she hadn't learned to wink yet, Patra held down one eyelid and blinked with the other.

My sister closed her eyes and rubbed her temples. "You are calm, you feel at peace, and the world is soothing. Everything is cotton candy."

Patra flung her arms around Toula's waist. "Thea Allie bought us corn and chestnuts, then we went to church and the funny lady threw the cross on the ground. And the man with the wrinkly pee-pee wanted to kiss Yiayia."

Ruh-roh.

Toula's gaze smashed into mine. "We have to go now so that I can scream into my pillow," she said in a faded voice. "Maybe two pillows."

"Two pillows are better than one," I assured her.

With a tight grip on her kids, she vanished down the stairs, leaving me with Leo, Yiayia, and a nameless being who could fly and lived in a clay pot. The hallway's mellow light revealed her to be younger than I'd first thought. Logically I knew she was older than Greece, but her skin said she was barely out of her teens. It was the eyes that told tales about her real age. They were full of fire—eyes that had seen things and had spent forever trapped in an itty bitty space and being mad about it all.

Cerberus didn't hate her, though. He was leaning against her knees, gazing up at her like a dog in love. Interesting.

"Do you want a dog?" I asked her.

"You have seen my vessel. Does it look like I can fit an animal in there?"

So that was a *no* then.

"The beast has already chosen his companion," she added.

"Wait until you see my place," I told her. "It's not much bigger than yours."

Her eyes flashed.

Leo hooked a thumb at the stairwell. "I should be going …"

"You can stay if you want."

"This one is pure of heart," the woman said. "He can stay."

"She says you can stay," I said to Leo.

"Who?"

"The woman from the pineapple." I shook my head. "You can't see her, so it probably looks like I'm standing here, talking to myself."

"Looks a little bit that way," he said. "Are you in any danger?"

"Tell the human male I will protect you with my life," the woman said.

Yiayia fanned herself with an elaborate fan worthy of a Southern belle, one of those accessories she managed to manifest out of nowhere on demand. My grandmother had mastered the art of being dead and made it her *skeela*. "Oh-la-la. Whatever this one has going on, I like it."

Yiayia wasn't just promiscuous, she was flexible, like a pipe snake.

I passed on the message. Leo relaxed, but not much. His muscles were still bunched and coiled, prepared to go into cop-mode.

"I'll be upstairs if you need me."

I stood on tiptoe and pressed my lips to his. "Talk to you soon."

He nodded once and headed for the stairwell.

I unlocked my door. Cerberus went in first, then me, followed by my new guest, then Yiayia.

"Nice *kolos*," Yiayia said. "She works out."

The lady of the pineapple zeroed in on the dead man at the window. "Who is this?"

"He's watching over his body. His solid half loves to fish. He's not having much luck in the fountain, but nevertheless, he's persisting."

"A protector. This I understand. Show me my vessel."

I swapped my boots for slippers and hung up my coat and bag. The kitchen was our next stop. Her jaw tightened as she soaked in the sight of her vessel's fragments. That couldn't be a good sign.

"And you say your *super glue* will fix this?"

"Super glue can fix almost anything. Then you can hop back in and go back to sleep until there's a real emergency."

She looked at me as if I'd lost my brain on the way here. "I cannot just 'hop back in.' I am not a djinn. There is a ritual."

Of course there was. Supernatural matters were never simple.

"That could be a problem."

"If there is a ritual, my Allie can find it," Yiayia said. "That is what she does. My little *mounaki* finds things. She has a supernatural talent for finding that which has been impossible to locate through other means."

Nice that Yiayia had faith in my skills. Bad that she was exaggerating my abilities to a being with hardcore power. "She means computers. I have access to computers. There's nothing supernatural about them. You just turn them on and type stuff in, and then answers come out if you know what to ask."

"That is what my granddaughter thinks. If it exists, she can find it in this world and maybe others."

No I can't, I mouthed.

"Get your super glue," the woman from the pineapple said.

Like everyone else on the planet that lived in an apartment or house, I had a junk drawer. That junk drawer was in the kitchen. I yanked mine open and instantly located an unopened tube of glue.

"See?" Yiayia boosted her transparent backside onto the kitchen counter. She could do that now that she was dead. In life she would have been complaining about her hip, her feet, her legs.

"I have eyes—eyes that directed me to the glue."

"That is what you think," my grandmother said.

I got to work glueing fragments together with the occasional input from the vessel's inhabitant. My backseat crafter. I didn't complain, though. I moved the pieces according to her instructions and waited as she pored over the mess. Stephanie broke the clay doodad, but this was my fault. I responsible for the lady of the pineapple being here in the first place. She should have still been on the island, coiled up inside her cozy home, waiting for someone to smash her vessel in case of an emergency. Instead she was here, away from her island and out of her bed, with no emergency in sight.

Morning was on its way. I had to get her back to the island and find a way to stuff her back into her vessel. Otherwise who knew what would happen?

Not me. Because she refused to tell me.

CHAPTER FOURTEEN

Dead Cat was my alarm clock. At the first sign of roosters crowing, he leaped onto my head and made "I am a brave hunter" chirping sounds. He wanted a rooster and he wanted one now.

They were safe. The living ones, anyway.

Wrapped in my comforter, I rolled out of the bed like a human burrito. "Go forth and catch a rooster—if you can."

I unfurled my post-thirty body and tried to figure out if anything new hurt today. So far I was feeling fine. Tired, but fine.

The lady of the pineapple was there waiting, arms folded. She wasn't blinking. Who knew, maybe she didn't need to blink.

"It is time," she said in a commanding tone. "Get my vessel and we will go."

"Can I shower first?"

"Shower?"

"Wash myself."

Doubt clouded her expression. "Is there ... time?"

In the wee hours, I'd explained that we would have to wait

for a ferry to transport us. As someone who didn't own a boat, I couldn't take to the sea whenever I pleased. I did my best to explain time and how it mattered when it came to public transportation in the modern era. If we went to the dock too soon, there would be a whole lot of water and no ferry. She'd nodded once and went to stand in the corner of my bedroom to watch over me. I offered her the couch or the other half of my bed, but she said she preferred to stand, given that she'd been stuck in a clay pot for thousands of years—maybe longer.

"The ferry won't be here for another hour, so there's plenty of time for a shower and breakfast. Do you eat?"

She adjusted her animal skin outfit. "I derive sustenance from the magics that created me."

So. Breakfast for one it was.

I boiled my skin for a few minutes under the scorching water, brushed my teeth, slathered moisturizer over my face, and wiggled into clean clothes that could stand up to the cold air that would be rolling across the sea. Breakfast was honey drizzled on a chunk of bread that saw peak freshness three days ago.

The super glue had long set, so I handed the clay relic to the lady of the pineapple, and she tucked it under her arm like a football.

The only thing missing was coffee.

"We have to make one very important stop on the way."

"Will it take long?"

"We have time." I did a once-over of her outfit, which was a skimpy arrangement of animal skins. Non-restrictive for fighting but bad for fending off winter. "Do you want a coat?" There was a lot of her lengthwise, and my coats wouldn't be more helpful than a shrug. "Maybe a blanket?"

"I do not feel the cold."

Handy skill to have.

With Cerberus padding alongside us, I steered the lady of

the pineapple downstairs and across the street to Merope's Best. I needed coffee, but this would have to suffice.

I opened the coffee shop's door and waited as she ducked inside. The death metal carols had been replaced with jazz, and the mixture of living and dead customers didn't look any happier about the selection. The barista couldn't have cared less. Merope's Best didn't hire employees based on their personalities or ability to wield a milk frother. As far as I could tell, the only required qualities were apathy and an ironic t-shirt collection.

The lady of the pineapple slammed to a stop just inside the entrance. Her nose rose into the air, like Cerberus when someone nearby was grilling a whole lamb.

"What is that?" she asked, awestruck.

"They call it coffee, but I wouldn't swear on my life that it's real coffee. It's more like coffee substance."

"It smells ... intoxicating."

"You can smell it?"

"Of course."

Poor thing. She'd have been better off being able to feel the cold. "Would you like to try some?"

"You mean ... consume this coffee?"

"Yes. You drink it. But that might be a problem with the whole not being corporeal thing you've got going on." I waved my hand over her invisible-to-others body. "If you could even hold the cup, the coffee would probably spill everywhere."

"A simple remedy." Her eyelids fluttered. "There. Now take me to this coffee."

The screaming was the first sign that the lady of the pineapple had flipped an invisibility switch. Now everyone inside Merope's Best was getting a good peek at the island's newest *xena*.

She looked bewildered. "Why are they screaming?"

The animal skins, the seven-foot height, the crazy eyes, to

name a few things. But I didn't want to hurt her feelings, so I played dumb. "I don't know."

"Why are they running away? Is coffee bad?"

"Merope's Best coffee has been known to make people scream."

"True story," the barista said. He was completely unfazed. Of course, this was a guy with enough holes in his head to strain spaghetti. "Pain and fear is the goal of every new beverage we think up. I wanted to do a Chernobyl cappuccino with a squirt of pureed turnip and radium foam, but apparently our owner is scared of lawyers."

"Wow." There were no other words. What could anyone say to that?

The barista inspected his newest customer. "With that whole vibe you are giving off, I bet you would love a *skata na fas*. They are trending on social media thanks to us."

"Is that even true?" I asked him.

He made a face. "Look it up if you do not believe me."

I checked my phone. Damn him, he was right. Merope's Best and their weird barely-coffee was becoming a trend. Come summer we'd be drowning in tourists. I'd be forced to line up to get my morning cup of brown slop. Not cool.

"That's the worst name ever for coffee," I muttered.

"Thanks," he said. "It's one of my creations. Coffee and hot chocolate poured over a brownie ball and sprinkled with nuts and roasted corn."

"We'll take two," I said.

"With caramel drizzle?"

"Extra drizzle on both."

"Nice." His eyes slid back to my companion. "Where did you get the red contact lenses? Your eyeballs look like they are on fire."

"I was forged inside a volcano."

"I was forged in Athens," he said, like this was a sane and normal conversation.

"Yes," the lady of the pineapple said. "I can smell the defeat in your blood. Your people's people are why I was created."

He leaned on the counter. "Are you seeing anybody?"

"I am seeing you right now." She pointed to me. "And her."

"You're bi. Nice. Me too."

The other barista dumped two coffees on the counter. "*Skata na fas*," she said.

I handed the lady of the pineapple her cup and kept the other one for myself. It smelled safe, but you never knew with Merope's Best. Sometimes their coffee had bonus greenery. At least they were over their Christmas lattes today. Nobody wanted pine needles stuck between their teeth.

She stared at her cup like she didn't know what to do about coffee. Understandable, seeing as how she had been literally living inside a blob of clay for gods only knew how long.

"Like this," I told her, raising the cup to my mouth. I showed her the tiny hole for sipping and put it to my lips. She did the same. Her eyes widened as she took her first tentative sip.

"By the gods, it is as hot as the volcano in which I was forged!"

She wasn't wrong. The coffee was undrinkable at this temperature, unless you wanted to flay the skin off the inside of your mouth. Didn't stop her, though. She sucked down the coffee like it was room temperature.

"It has chunks," she announced when she reached the bottom.

Yeah, Merope's Best coffee-substance regularly contained chunks. Sometimes they were identifiable. Today it was brownies, thankfully, although there was a moment there when I felt what I suspected was the promised kernel of corn.

We had arrived at the docks. People were waiting for the ferry. They eyed the woman and shuffled away from us.

"She doesn't bite," I announced.

She jiggled her hand. "Sometimes I bite."

"But you won't bite these people, will you?"

Her gaze scraped across the smallish crowd. "No. None of you pose a threat to that which I am sworn to protect."

Among the group was Kyria Roula—the same Kyria Roula who was there when Stephanie keeled over in the More Super Market. She was wearing the same dress, the same cardigan, the same bunions peeking out the side of her sandals. Sandals in December weren't an uncommon sight. She and the other older women on the island compensated with knee-high stockings.

"Who is your friend?" she asked me. Her eyes were aglow with curiosity. There was fear, too—fear that someone else would beat her to the gossip.

My mind spun through myriad lies before picking the most likely to be true. "This is an old school friend from America."

Kyria Roula looked the newcomer up and down. "She is very tall."

"She plays basketball."

"And is she staying with you?"

My basketball-playing BFF from America held up her vessel. "This is my home."

Calculations scrolled through Kyria Roula's head. Connections were forged and cemented. Conclusions were leaped to. The gossip took shape. Before long it would shape-shift into something else, but for now Kyria Roula had her story. New chasms appeared on her forehead as the obvious problem struck her: the ferry was imminent and she was supposed to hitch a ride. If she boarded the boat, someone else might beat her to whatever story she'd fabricated about my tall new pal and her pottery abode.

Then a lightbulb went on in Kyria Roula's head. This was the technological age. Like most other people on the island she was armed with a cellphone. On this cellphone she was a permanent part of a group chat. Gossip dispersal depended solely on how fast she could type with her thumbs.

Fast, apparently. Even teenagers weren't that speedy, and they were born with phones in their hands.

Not ten seconds later, Toula called me.

"You never said you had a friend from home visiting."

Given that we'd spent our formative years in the US, it would always be home, philosophically speaking. Never mind that both of us had decided to stay here after we graduated. Toula because she met Kostas and me because there was no real reason to leave. Maybe I'd change my mind someday. It was nice to have options. But today wasn't the day for change.

"News travels fast." I raised my eyebrows at Kyria Roula. Her gaze skittered away along with the rest of her, as she and her phone hurried to the other side of the dock. "It's not like that," I told my sister. "It's a work thing. The woman is a client, sort of."

"I knew it had to be something like that. You don't really have friends."

"Wow, rude." Kyria Olga, my best friend in the world, had recently been murdered. I missed her every day. There was Sam, of course. Although we were more mentor and mentee, because of how we'd started. Then there was Angela, who was really trying to have a female friend. "Got to go," I said to my sister. "But while you're throwing stones around, make sure your walls aren't made of glass."

"I have friends!"

I stabbed the screen and made my sister go away. Some

days we got along. Other times her insistence on infantilizing me drove me round the bend and I couldn't resist poking back at her like the little sister I would always be.

The ferry pulled up to the dock. Everyone stood back while we boarded. Which was nice, really. Usually the widows rushed at the gangplank like it was the Thermoplylae Pass and they were Spartans. It was pleasant, for once, to avoid flying elbows, or, my personal favorite, a shoe skidding down my shin before crushing my foot. We found seats on the deck, and when everyone else boarded they left us with the top deck to ourselves.

"I need to ask you something," I said, warming my hands on my coffee.

"Ask."

"There's a hell hole where one of our salons used to be. Did you do that?"

"No."

"Do you have weapons?"

"Why do I need weapons when I have myself?"

Girl power. "Good point."

Her neck swiveled until those fiery eyes were staring at me. "Weapons, do you carry them?"

"Pepper spray, a stun gun, a tiny vial of holy water, and salt."

"And the creature? Is he not also a weapon?"

The creature wagged his tail.

"Cerberus? He's a dog."

"No. I speak of the other who watches over you. The one in black."

"The Man in Black is watching me?"

"When he is able."

"I don't think he's a weapon so much as he is a confusing and muddied fount of information. He speaks in riddles and comes and goes as he pleases. Do you know him?"

"No. But I have seen him watching over you, and I sense that he was like me, once."

That got my attention—hard. The Man in Black was mysterious, vague, and completely resistant to sharing information about himself. He reminded me of a guy I dated briefly just after high school. Nigel was British, and he was here on Merope for business—or so he told me. He hadn't corrected me when I asked if he was a secret agent. By that point I was working for Sam as a sidekick slash servant. Then Sam broke the news that Nigel's wives had hired him to find Nigel, whose name actually *was* Nigel. Even for a criminal he was dumb. Not that I thought the Man in Black was a bigamist and a compulsive liar. He was just ... opaque. The man had the density of lead. I already suspected he couldn't be human or fully human. He came and went like a panther, which shouldn't be possible in his tall riding boots. When my life was in danger, he frequently appeared. He'd stolen the wedding dress from Kyria Yiota on my behalf, without tripping her forest of mousetraps. And he knew things—things he refused to share with me. So the fact that this woman-shaped being had just tossed a nugget of highly coveted information at me made my head spin. I was ravenous for more.

"Once? What—who—exactly are you?"

"I was forged to protect. I have told you this already."

"But ... why were you stuck in a clay relic and he isn't?"

"I do not know these things."

With that out of the way, she moved to the corner of the deck and stared out to sea.

"Here is my friend!" the fisherman on Mykonos said. "You want to rent my boat again, eh?" Euro bills danced in his eyes.

"I do," I said. "I really do."

"Where we go this time, eh?" He plucked the envelope of notes out of my hand and crammed them into the pocket of his rough gray pants.

"Same place as last time."

"For what? I do not understand. But your money is good and I liked your *yiayia*. Foutoula and I had some good times ..."

In life, Yiayia had experienced a lot of good times with a lot of people. My grandmother had enjoyed spreading the wonderfulness of her.

"If we leave now, we can be back in time for lunch," I told him.

He grinned and cast off from the dock.

The pineapple's resident had gone invisible again. To the fisherman, anyway. I could still see her with her vessel tucked under one arm, staring out to sea. I did notice, however, that the fisherman's eyes seemed to avoid the patch of space she was occupying, as if she'd hit him with a "don't look at me" whammy.

Two hours later the unnamed island appeared on the horizon. My companion rose from her seat. As she did, the boat listed slightly. The fisherman's weatherbeaten forehead crumpled up. "Strange things happen at sea, yes? She does as she pleases with us all."

The two dead men that hadn't boogied into the light last time were waiting on the shore. They watched the boat roll in, the lady of the pineapple with one foot on the prow. At the sight of her, they fell to their knees.

What was that all about? I was desperate to ask but didn't want the fisherman to think I was three Mythos bottles short of a six-pack. Not when I needed a ride back to Mykonos and would probably need his services again in the future.

"We are saved," they called out. "They have come back for us."

From the granite stare on the lady of the pinapple's face, that was the opposite of true. Someghost and his pal were about to get an ass whuppin'.

With the grace of one of the big cats, she leaped off the boat, her legs slashing through the water until she reached the beach. The fisherman, thankfully, was too busy gauging how close he could maneuver his boat to the shore without scraping its bottom. I jumped out after her, glad that I'd put on my waders again. Without them I'd be hanging around in wet, freezing clothes.

By the time I was on dryish land, she was already flaying them with her tongue and Cerberus was peeing on anything that didn't move.

"You! You allowed my vessel to leave the island!"

Bowing. Scraping. "We had no choice, our most precious tool. We lost the use of our mortal bodies eons ago when we died. We could no more stop the thief than we could hold back the tides." Gnec's eyes connected with mine. "Wait! There is the thief now."

Everybody stared at me, except the fisherman whose head was bent over his Nintendo Switch Lite.

"About that," I said, scrambling to cover my bare butt. "Actually, I've got nothing. Yes, I was paid to bring the funny pineapple back to Merope, so that's what I did. Was it stealing? Yes, but also no. If it had obviously belonged to someone I would have left it here." In my head I was cursing the day I ever heard the name Adonis Diplas. Stupid Bakases and their family stick.

"You were only able to take my vessel because of their incompetence," the lady of the pineapple said.

Gnec's mouth fell open. "She can see us! The thieving one can see us!"

"I knew it," Tut said.

Gnec shoved him sideways. "You knew nothing."

"Yes, I can see you," I said. "I could see you and the others the last time I was here, but I didn't say anything because ghosts can get annoying fast. You regularly seem to have a to-do list for me, and I have to limit my pro bono work or I won't be able to afford to pay my bills."

"Those were our slaves," Gnec said. "Since they left we have been forced to spend all our time together. Tut is very stupid."

"Gnec is angry because I will not say that thing he likes."

The woman from the pot held out her decorative yet tiny home. "You must perform the ritual and place me back in my vessel until I am needed."

The dead men's faces fell.

"Ah," Tut said.

"As much as we would like to do that, we cannot," Gnec told her.

"That is your function," she said. "What else are you for?"

"We are ghosts. We cannot perform a ritual without hands and solidity." Gnec waved his hands through the air to make his point and failed completely. More success when he kicked the sand and his foot went straight through the grains. "And there are other problems."

"One problem, really," Tut added.

"One problem," Gnec agreed. "A huge problem."

"What problem?" I asked them.

Gnec splayed his hands. "The other vessel is not here."

CHAPTER FIFTEEN

The lady of the pineapple stared at the men with her volcano-forged gaze until they started to twitch on the shore. Which left me to ask the questions.

"Not here? How? When? What other vessel?"

I already knew the other pedestal was empty on my first visit, but that didn't mean I didn't want answers.

Nobody said anything. The woman from the vessel was too busy being intimidating, and the two proto-Greek stooges were too busy withering under her gaze. I marched back through the foliage to the ancient temple. Two pedestals. No stones.

While she continued to berate Gnec and Tut, I searched the scrub around the temple for signs of the second vessel. Anything would be helpful. Shards. Footprints. A signed confession or an IOU from whoever removed or broke the first stone. Maybe their phone number.

What I got was nothing except scores of broken pots, rocks, and branches. None were a match for the clay vessel. There was nothing to find—not here, anyway. I trudged back to the beach.

"Did you find the vessel?" the lady of the pineapple asked me.

"Not a sign. It's probably on display at the British Museum by now. We're never getting it back unless we berate them ceaselessly on social media."

Three sets of eyes blinked at me. They were from antiquity and I was a child of the nineteen nineties. Explanations were a waste of time right now, so I reiterated my previous question.

"When was the first vessel stolen?"

The dead men looked at each other than looked at me. "We do not experience time the way we did when we were alive," Tut said. "Could be a thousand years ago, could be last month. We cannot say."

"Was it opened?"

More exchanged glances. Under different circumstances they'd be a substandard comedy duo.

"The vessel was still intact when it left here," Gnec told me.

At the rate they were dispensing information, this was going to take forever.

"Who took it?" I asked.

"A man." Gnec looked proud of his answer.

"What man?"

"A man." He registered shock that his answer wasn't sufficient. "What does any man look like? He arrived on a boat and departed with the vessel the same way." He changed the subject. "Do you know why we did not depart to the Afterlife with the others?"

"You have unfinished business," I said.

"What unfinished business?"

The woman stopped pacing to fling words in his face. "You failed to protect the vessels, you fools! That is the unfinished business! They must stay together for the safety of all!"

Gnec had the decency to hang his head. "Ah. That. We were afraid of that."

She turned to me. "If the other vessel is out in the world, it could be opened at any time."

"Do you think it's open?"

She looked to the sky and inhaled. "I cannot say for certain. The world has changed and dark forces are everywhere."

"I think that's the satellites bouncing information all over the planet. That and smog. Humans today really like their cars and toxic factories."

"When I was searching for a way home, I saw a man on your island dressed as a donkey. A woman was doing things to him. Terrible things. She had a big piece of wood and—"

"That's just our local priest and his sister who probably isn't his real sister."

She turned her back to the sun. "You spoke of a burning hole at your home."

I nodded. "It appeared yesterday. The Man in Black told me the spa is still there, it's just out of phase with my world. What is it?"

"It is a sign!" Gnec threw his hands at the sky. Tut did the same.

"The other saw this hole?" she asked.

"He did."

"I have changed my mind. The other vessel must be open. The hole of fire is a sign that we are all doomed if I do not find the vessel that these fools neglected to prevent from leaving."

On that dramatic note, she stalked toward the interior of the island where the temple lay hidden from outside eyes.

"I told you it was a sign," Gnec said.

"Look what you did." Tut was watching her leave and shaking his head. "Her whole purpose is at stake now because of you."

It took me a moment to realize he was talking to me. "I don't even know what her purpose is!"

"To protect Greece, of course. There is no higher purpose."

My hands formed beseeching claws in the air. "Can I please, for the love of the Virgin Mary, have more information?"

Gnec sighed and settled on the beach. He arranged his animal skins so he wasn't flashing a mile of wrinkled scrotum. "Two vessels were created. One to contain great evil and the other to contain a guardian, its opposite. Then after we made her in a volcano, we performed a ritual to preserve them both in their vessels for all of eternity, if necessary. In the event that the vessel containing the evil was opened, the other would automatically release the guardian to defeat the great evil. And then you came along and stole the guardian vessel!"

The optics were terrible.

"Granted, I *did* take the guardian's vessel from this island, but because I was being paid to do a job. Had I known that it contained a supernatural being who was created specifically to protect Greece from whatever it is she's protecting it from, I would have left her here to do her job. But the way I see it, the other vessel was—is—already gone. So she needs to be wherever it is."

He scratched his head. "That is a problem."

"Exactly." I paced for a bit. "What's your role in all this?"

"We are—"

"Were," Tut said.

"—the caretakers of the island and the temple. We were sent here after the ritual with our slaves to prevent anyone from stealing the bad vessel or its counterpart, the good vessel."

"But now you're both dead and no backup is coming, and the horses have escaped the paddock anyway."

"If that means it is too late, then yes," Gnec said. "No reinforcements came, nor will they ever come. The world has forgotten about us and the secrets we were protecting."

"Except they didn't forget about you, because someone else took the bad vessel and maybe purposely left the guardian vessel behind, and then someone else sent me here to steal the guardian vessel. That means someone knows something—and they definitely know more than me, which is annoying. I don't know who or how."

Not entirely true. I knew who had hired me. Adonis Diplas, shady yet attractive character. Since before he'd stepped foot on Merope I'd suspected he was up to no good. And now look at ... well ... *everything*. My island had a hell pit, for crying out loud. As bad as things had been on Merope, we'd never had our own portal to hell until yesterday.

What did he want with the guardian vessel?

Couldn't be anything good.

And if he'd hired me to steal the good vessel, did he know who had the bad one? Ten euros said he did. Probably some filthy rich buyer who'd promised to fill Adonis's pockets.

Ugh. I was going to have to shake him down hard. He wouldn't pony up information for nothing.

Too bad my phone wasn't getting a signal here. I really wanted to hear that turd-blossom twist in the breeze as I interrogated him. Oh well. Watching him squirm and lie in person would be even more satisfying. When that was done, I'd punt him off Merope and into the Aegean Sea.

Tut's hand fluttered to his chest. "They know about us? I am flattered."

All my self control went into not rolling my eyes.

The lady of the pineapple, protector of the country, marched out of the trees and back across the scrubby terrain. Her expression was thunder and her eyes were spitting sparks. Literally.

"The vessel is gone and mine is broken, although now it has been fixed with super glue." Head clutched in her hands, she collapsed onto her knees. "I have failed."

I patted her on the shoulder. "Buck up, little camper. I've got a lead, someone we can shake down for information. But you might need to be invisible at first and then make an unsettling and shocking appearance when I give you the signal.

She peeped at me between her splayed fingers. "What is the signal?"

"I don't know. Do you have any ideas?"

Gnec did jazz hands. "This is a good one."

"I'm not doing jazz hands suddenly and unexpectedly during a fact-finding mission."

"How about this?" Tut did spirit fingers. These two had really missed their calling in musical theater.

One at a time, I pointed to them. "When you finally make it to the Afterlife, make sure you look up Bob Fosse. I feel like you'd get along." I reached out and helped the guardian up off the pebbles. "Okay, the signal will be me turning to you and saying 'now.' Does that work?"

The fires in her eyes flared. "That is more of a command and less of a signal."

"Okay, I'll think of something on the boat home."

With Cerberus bounding ahead of us, we waded back to the waiting boat, where the fisherman was yelling at his game. Gnec and Tut stood on the shore, looking like their best pal had just died. In reality their best pals had died thousands of years ago.

"We must come with you. We know everything about the guardian and the other vessel."

I waded back.

"Sorry, no can do. Salt water."

They put on their sad faces. "There must be some way."

There was a way, now that I thought about it. Ghosts

could be transported across bodies of salt water if they hitched a ride on a talisman of some kind—say, one of their possessions.

"You're sworn to watch over both vessels, right?"

"We performed a ritual and everything. The great evil's description and the guardian's magic words were burned into our bodies." He bent over and lifted his animal skin, revealing a saggy cheek.

Yikes. "Then you should just be able to piggyback on the remaining vessel."

"We cannot do that."

"Well, do you have any belongings still here?"

"My comb has been destroyed by time," Tut said.

"And my lyre," Gnec added.

"What about your bones?"

"Time ate them, too. You will have to come up with a solution or we will be forced to remain here."

I slid the backpack off my shoulders and dumped it on the sand. Inside was the one thing that might work. I'd grabbed it off the coffee table before my last trip to the island and hadn't gotten around to putting it back where it belonged. Yiayia's pink Himalayan salt jar.

With a bit of wiggling, the flat cork popped out. Was there room inside for two? I was about to find out.

"Hop on in. The view is terrible but it's a free boat ride."

They didn't look remotely offended. "We have traveled in worse," Tut said.

Gnec bobbed his head. "At least it does not smell like fish."

I held out the jar.

Like magic—probably it *was* magic—the jar sucked them both up.

"Are you okay in there?" I said into the mouth of the jar.

"As long as Tut does not fart I will be fine." There was a pause. "Too late. Let me out."

I slapped the cork in before he made a hasty exit. The little voice in my head said both ghosts could be useful. We'd need them when we found the other vessel, especially if the contents had leaked out. Which, given that my island was sporting a lovely hell hole, I assumed they had.

We rode back to Merope in silence. The guardian stood poised like one of the big cats—calm to the casual observer, and yet on high alert. Nose in the air, she jumped off the ferry ahead of me and held up her hand to keep me behind her.

Cerberus gave me a what-the-heck side eye.

I was slightly alarmed. "What's wrong?"

"I am trying to scent my enemy."

"Do you smell him?"

"No, but somebody here smells like feet."

"A lot of people here smell like feet. You get used to it."

She nodded once and let me off the ferry. Meanwhile she was invisible again and I was having to pull of my usual talking-to-thin-air without looking batshit crazy stunt. Given that there were about five other people disembarking and I had my phone out and pressed against my ear, and a dog at my side, I have to say I was pretty much succeeding. Go me.

"Where is the one who compelled you to steal my vessel?"

"At the More Super Market. He was there when you accidentally killed his cashier."

"Then we will go to him now."

CHAPTER SIXTEEN

WITH A TOOTHBRUSH IN HAND, Stephanie Dolas was scrubbing the windows outside the More Super Market.

"*Yia sou*, Stephanie," I said to her body.

Her ghost sighed and rolled her eyes. "This is *malakismeni*." Her gaze landed on the guardian. She tilted her head. Nibbled a hangnail. "I recognize you. Are you somebody famous?"

"No," the lady of the pineapple said.

"Too bad. Even as a ghost I never meet anyone famous."

"Fame is nothing. All that matters is balance in the universe."

Stephanie stared at her. "If you say so ..."

I pulled the guardian aside before I entered the store. I couldn't keep calling her the lady of the pineapple. She needed a name, even if it wasn't hers. Given that she had no name, she might enjoy having one of her own.

"I was thinking about the name situation and how you don't have one."

"I have no need of a name."

"You do. You really do. You're a person ... guardian ...

being with your own thoughts and feelings. You need a name that's you."

Cerberus was prowling around on the end of his leash, sniffing for bits of food. He wasn't picky. Food adjacent would do.

"Your face says you have a suggestion."

"As a matter of fact, I do. In my head I've been calling you the lady of the pineapple. Using the first letter of each word, that spells Lotp. That's a typo, not a name, so how about Lottie?"

"This Lottie, is it a good name?"

"If you like it, yes."

"Lottie." She repeated the name several times before nodding. "I will respond to this name you have given me."

"Okay, let's do this, Lottie. Wait for my signal. The signal will be me waving my arms and calling out to you."

The bell over the door tinkled as I pushed inside. Because Stephanie Dolas was a one-woman cleaning service now, Adonis Diplas was on checkout duty. He didn't look fazed. Dirtbags never did.

He set down his cellphone. A grin sprawled across his face. Another woman might find it charming and downright sexy. I was hip to his conman ways. I wasn't sure how yet, but I could smell trouble wafting off his genes.

"Allie Callas. Did you follow that lead about George yet?"

"Adonis Diplas. Not yet. I have questions."

"Want to ask them over dinner?"

"Over this counter will suffice."

He leaned back. Folded his arms. "So it's that kind of talk then."

With a small thud, I set the broken and super glued stone on the counter.

"You fixed it."

"It's *kintsugi* with super glue."

"Nice. So you're handy as well as an expert at finding things."

I pointed to the clay vessel. "You sent me to the island to find this. Why?"

He shrugged. "Told you. It was a gift. That's what you specialize in, don't you?"

"I find all sort of things, including trouble."

"Are you saying this broken pot is trouble?"

I sidestepped his question. "A gift for who?"

"It's personal."

"A woman?" I thought about it a moment. "Are you cheating on your poor, incarcerated fiancee?"

"Not a chance. You're looking at the most devoted man on the planet."

I doubted that. Devoted to his own agenda, maybe. Still, nobody was whispering about how he was sneaking in and out of anyone's bed. The gossip mill didn't know what to make of him because he hadn't given them any material thus far. To them he was just the *xenos*—the outsider. He was Greek, yes, but he wasn't one of Merope's own. Even Toula and I barely passed, and generations of our family—both sides—were from here. We were descended from the original core settlers.

"Then who?"

"I'll tell you who if you tell me why."

Oof. That was a problem. He'd struck upon the one thing I couldn't do. "It's confidential."

"Then so is the intended recipient."

This was getting me nowhere. I changed directions, hoping for a hit. "How did you know where it would be?"

"I can't say."

"What do you know about the clay pineapple?"

"I know that it's got you riled up. I can help ease that tension if you like."

"Ugh. I've got a boyfriend."

"Not talking about sex. We just got some new snacks in."

My stomach demanded that I hear him out. "What kind of snacks?"

"Imports from your home country."

"Be more specific."

With a head tilt, he rounded the counter, leading me to the freezer in the corner where the More Super Market kept ice cream. Now the freezer had a new product: Smucker's Uncrustables. Uncrustables were made of chemicals, white bread, peanut butter, and jelly that may or may not actually contain any real fruit. Did my stomach care? No, it did not. My digestive system and tastebuds wanted PB&Js and they wanted them now.

Before Adonis could utter a word, I had a box tucked under each arm and a sandwich in my mouth.

He stared at me in amazement. "You're supposed to defrost them first."

I growled at him. Nobody told me how to eat a peanut butter and jelly. I was there when the old magic was written. I slapped some money on the counter and marched out of the store.

Lottie was waiting, invisible to everyone else. "Did you get the information?"

The door fell shut behind me. "I did not get the information, damn it."

I turned around and walked back in. Adonis Diplas had gone back to scrolling on this phone. Only his eyes and brows rose up to greet me.

"Forget something?

"Something? No. Everything."

"Are we back to this again?"

I dumped the sandwiches on the counter. "Yes, we're back to this. Because you distracted me with food."

"And it worked."

"I, for one, am shocked that a conman is good at dodging the truth and tricking people."

"Look." He set the phone down on the counter slowly. "I hired you for a job and then paid you for it, as per our agreement. You then completed the job. Our obligation to each other ends there, unless you have information about George, which I've also paid you for."

"I find it weird that you haven't asked for the vessel back, given that it's fixed."

His jaw pulsed, ever so slightly. Anyone else might have missed it.

"Now," I called out, waving my arms.

He looked confused. "Now?"

The door flew open. There was a kerfuffle as Lottie got tangled up in the bell over the door. Eventually she managed to extricate herself by tearing off the bell. She dropped the crumpled mechanism at my feet.

"This device attempted to defeat me, but it was no match for my strength."

"Wow. Thanks. It's not every day someone saves me from a bell."

She nodded once and turned her flaming gaze on Adonis Diplas. "Is this the one?"

"That's the weasel."

Adonis wasn't rattled. At least not on his face. Who knew what was churning beneath the surface, where things like anxiety and fear lived? Given that he was some kind of petty conman, I wasn't surprised that the man could act.

He nodded once. "Adonis Diplas. You look like a kasseri kind of woman. Maybe a nice manouri."

Her gaze swung to me. "What is this one talking about?"

"Cheese." I swung my index finger at him. "Don't you dare try to distract us with cheese. It'll work."

Lottie's eyes lit up. More lit up than usual. "Is your cheese anything like your coffee?"

Now Adonis Diplas registered surprised. "You gave her coffee?"

All I had to say were two words. "Merope's Best."

"So not real coffee then."

"I enjoyed your human coffee," Lottie said. "And now I wish to try this cheese."

He shot me a questioning glance. I shrugged. "Load her up on samples, but don't think you're off the hook. We want answers."

Lottie made angry growling noises. "I will make him suffer if he does not give us answers. I was created with a full spectrum of ways to cause pain and suffering. This one will squeal like a small piglet if I ruffle his hair. I see the vanity crouching inside him."

"I don't like my hair being touched," he admitted. "Let me get that cheese."

We followed him to the small deli counter, where a tub of feta soaking in brine had recently been opened. Other unopened tubs were lined up at the rear of the counter. Greeks ate a lot of feta. Good thing it was relatively cheap here, compared to the US. The cold cabinet contained a variety of other Greek cheeses, a block of cheddar, and an assortment of salamis and cold cuts. Adonis reached for a wheel of pale kasseri and a white ball of manouri. Lottie glared as he produced a knife for slicing.

"One wrong move and I will use your weapon to gut you. I will dance wearing your guts as ribbons."

"I'm just going to cut the cheese, unless you would prefer to eat it straight from the wheel."

I bit back a snicker. My inner seven-year-old was present.

She took the offered cheese. Sounds came out of her

throat. The kind you usually hear in porn. Someone really liked cheese.

Wait until she heard about pizza.

The conman raised his eyebrows. "Good?"

"I have no words," Lottie told him.

"More?"

"More."

Adonis Diplas was a lot of things, but he wasn't stingy. Both of us scored more than our fill of free cheese—and I could eat a lot of cheese. While he was cutting he said, oh-so casually, "Why don't you tell me what this is really about. Maybe then we'll get somewhere."

I gestured at the other counter with my cheese. "That clay pineapple?"

"What about it?"

"It is my vessel," Lottie said.

"Your what?"

"Vessel," I said. "A container used for holding things."

"And it was holding you?" he said to the seven-foot woman.

"Yes. For a long ... time."

He looked to me for an explanation.

"She has issues with time."

"How long?" he asked me.

"From what I gather, since people."

"That's a long time." He slid her another slice of cheese. Pungent feta this time. "You look good for your age."

"How I look is irrelevant." Lottie accepted the cheese. "All that matters is my purpose."

"Purpose?" His gaze flicked between us. "What purpose?"

"To keep the nation you know now as Greece safe from my quarry."

Back to me: "Who is her quarry?"

"Evil."

"The nature of the evil matters not. I must find the other vessel, and return evil to its prison if it has escaped."

"So you're going to stuff it back in the jar thingy and not kill it?" I asked.

"It will be worse than death," she said with her mouth full of cheese. "Then we will return to the island for the rest of eternity."

"And this," I said to Adonis, "is why we need to know everything you know about the vessel."

"What happens if the evil in the other, uh, vessel gets out?"

"Chaos. Destruction. Death." Lottie licked her fingers. "That is just the beginning. Before it is done it will devour your whole world."

"Maybe you can distract it with your cheese," I said to Adonis.

He drummed his fingers on the counter, then picked up the knife. "Does this have anything to do with the burning pit where the spa used to be?"

My jaw dropped. Cheese fell out of my mouth. Cerberus rushed to my rescue and ate my cheese. "You know about that?"

"Everyone knows about it. It's a burning pit. People are already camped out there, cooking over the flames."

I groaned. Of course they were. These were Greeks. "Are they dancing?"

"What is a party without dancing?"

"There's not supposed to be any dancing or a party! It's a literal hell pit!"

"How about you tell them that," he said. "Let's see how that goes."

I mustered my indignation. Partying at the hell pit, for pity's sake. Anything could happen to them. "I intend to."

Laughing, he shook his head. "I have to see that."

"Then lock up your store and let's go."

His eyebrows shot up almost to his hairline. "Wait—are you serious?"

"As serious as the seven-foot whatever she is standing next to us."

"I am very serious," Lottie said dryly.

I raised my eyebrows at Adonis like, *See*?

"All right." He rinsed the knife and slid it into the plastic holster attached to the counter. After washing his hands, he snatched his winter coat off the stool behind the cash register. "Let me tell Stephanie to take over."

Yikes. Was that a good idea? What if she suddenly went full zombie? "Uh, she's okay with customers?"

"That near death experience was the best thing to ever happen to her work ethic. Before she was a bare minimum employee. It was all I could do to get her to stop rolling her eyes at customers and keep gossip to her free time. Why?"

"Near death. Let's go with that."

"Not following."

"Never mind." I scooted to open the door. Adonis slapped it shut.

Lottie growled at him. Cerberus shoved his whole body in the space between us. Adonis released the door, but his expression said he wanted it to stay shut so he could squeeze an answer out of me. This guy wasn't dumb, and I really wanted him to be dumb.

"I killed the girl," Lottie blurted.

Well, so much for keeping the cat in the bag.

His face said it didn't compute. "You ... what?"

Lottie looked to me to explain.

"When Stephanie dropped the pineapple—vessel—and it shattered, Lottie here popped out."

"Lottie," he said, sounding dazed.

I forged onwards. "Stephanie was the closest living being,

and Lottie mistook Stephanie for this great evil, seeing as how she's only supposed to come out if the other vessel breaks." I looked at Lottie.

"That is correct. Afterward, I traveled around the island looking for a way home."

"Wait, wait, wait." Adonis held up his hand, but not too high so I wouldn't mistake it for a *moutsa*. "So Stephanie *was* actually dead?"

"Was ... is ... who can say?"

"You're not saying much of anything, actually. If she's dead, then ..."

I stared at him. Meaningfully. And with a hefty dose of *Didn't you watch The Walking Dead? Or Resident Evil?*

"No," he said.

"Yes."

"No."

"Yes."

"She's a ..."

I made a *keep going* motion with my hand.

"... zombie?"

"Yes, but she's the good kind. I think. Instead of eating brains, she's cleaning."

"Her work ethic *is* amazing," he admitted.

"She's not the only one running loose on the island either right now, so that's another issue I'm dealing with right now."

He looked confused. "Why are you dealing with it?"

"It's a long story."

"I've got time."

"No, you don't. I've got to go see a bunch of people about the perils of cooking over a hell hole."

"Are there perils?"

"They could fall in. Plus who knows how many carcinogens that thing is spitting out. Probably California is already printing warning labels."

He shrugged into his coat. "Let's go check it out."

"Wait—you still haven't told us anything."

"Haven't I?"

"Lottie's vessel. Who was it supposed to be for?"

"Haven't you figured it out?"

I thought about it a moment. "George."

"My cousin George. He has a pest and needs an exterminator." He nodded at the guardian of Greece. "And that right there is the exterminator he's looking for."

CHAPTER SEVENTEEN

The air came out of me in a whoosh. "George opened the other vessel?"

He indicated *yes*. "The way George tells it, it was an accident. His cleaning woman broke the other pot."

George Diplas. The murders. The ghost men. The demon sleeping in his bed. He was the culprit. At the very least he was George's sidekick.

I turned to Lottie. "I know where great evil is hiding out."

"Then we must go!"

She was right. We needed to get back to Athens ASAP. But I couldn't just blow off my other commitments. "First I need to shoo everyone away from the fiery pit. I can't let anyone get hurt."

"There is no time," Lottie said.

"I think there's plenty of time. The first and only time I saw your friend he was snuggled up in bed, watching soap operas."

"He is not my friend, he is my quarry."

"Your quarry loves daytime television, so he's not going anywhere in a hurry. I got the feeling he's terrified of something, I know that much. Now that I think about it, it's probably you."

"He would be a fool if he were not afraid of me. I was created to kick the oozing mess he sits on."

Good times were happening at the hell hole. Never underestimate the Greek ability to throw a spontaneous party, especially when there's a free cooking source involved. Half the island had turned out for what appeared to be several parties smooshed together. There was food, there was dancing, there was Leo and Constable Pappas trying to erect yellow caution tape around the hole and failing miserably because they were no match for old men with lamb and suckling pig carcasses to cook.

Leo gave me a woebegone look. "I can't get them to leave. This place is not safe but they don't seem to care."

"I can scare them away," Lottie said.

She was visible now and Leo was struggling not to stare.

Constable Pappas was openly gawking at her. "I think I am in love," he muttered. She glared so hard it was a miracle his face didn't catch on fire. He sighed, undeterred. The constable wasn't good at taking hints. You had to write the hint on a stick and beat him with it, and knowing Pappas he liked that, too.

"You find things," Leo said, nuzzling my hair in front of everyone. "Find a way to get them away from here."

He was wrong, this kind of thing was out of my wheelhouse. I dealt with the tangible. He was asking me to work miracles. Almost nobody can dislodge Greeks from a party.

Still, it was Leo. For him, I'd try.

I checked out the crowd, and before long a pattern emerged. They were mostly older. A lot of yiayias, widows, men who liked to complain about the cost of living. The kind of people who whined when someone else received a good deal, but who would shove a friend under a bus to get to a discount.

An idea came to mind. A way to move immovable Greeks. Which isn't easy. Once they've committed to a party, they become one organism. Persuading them as distinct entities wouldn't work, so I had to move the whole devoted beast.

Leo wanted me to find a way to move them?

By all the deities, I'd found one.

Diplas was going to hate it, which meant I was already madly in love with my own idea.

I raised my eyebrows at Adonis Diplas.

He had the decency to look nervous. "What?"

"You'll see."

"I don't like this," he said.

"I don't like you," Leo muttered.

They both stood there for a moment, the air between them saturated with testosterone. I had the feeling they were dogs, taking turns peeing on the tree, and I was supposed to be the tree.

I didn't want to be a tree.

Moving on. First step was killing the music. I needed to be heard.

I marched over to the 1980s boombox that was surprisingly in loud working order. Wow. Technology really used to last. This thing was a dinosaur. I shoved down hard on the STOP button.

The music died.

Everyone looked at me. Instead of being mad about it, they were wreathed in smiles.

"Aliki Callas! *Ela*! We made a party!" several someones called out.

I waved away a dozen invitations. That was Greece for you. People wanted to share the fun.

"Do you wish for me to lift you so that everyone can see you?" Lottie said. "I am stronger than all these people combined."

"I'm good," I said.

Leo handed me the megaphone from the police car's trunk. He helped me scramble onto the hood. I chose my words carefully, for maximum effect.

I glanced at Adonis. His lips were pressed in a tight, white seam. That didn't stop me from flinging one arm into the air. "There's a huge sale happening at the More Super Market right now! Feta is fifty percent off!"

Adonis Diplas said words. Bad words. Words you wouldn't yell across a church. They were quickly drowned out by the thundering sound of Merope's people abandoning their parties. Times were hard and everyone wanted cheap cheese and groceries.

My phone rang. Toula.

"Are you near the More Super Market? They're having a sale. Grab me some more Merenda?"

"If I can fight off the hordes, sure."

She ended the call.

Within seconds, it was just Leo, Pappas, Adonis Diplas, Lottie, Cerberus, and me at the hell hole overlooking the sea. Today was doggie Christmas for Cerberus. Tangles of drool hung down from his chops as he decided which rotisserie to attack first.

"You are a miracle worker," Leo said. He shot a glance at Lottie, then dropped a kiss on my forehead. He and Pappas got to work setting up the tape.

"Are you fucking crazy?" Adonis Diplas said. "Do you know what you just did to my business?"

"I'm sure you'll figure out a way to profit. People like you usually do. Besides—I owed you one." I gestured at the bubbling, burning hole. He made a face like he needed to poop and sprinted in the direction of the More Super Market.

"Good riddance," Leo muttered.

I raised my eyebrows at him. He shook his head and went back to framing the bubbling hole with yellow tape. Hopefully it would be enough to keep the partygoers away. Not that they were sticklers for municipal rules. They were more about social rules—the rules that mattered to them. But as the police, Leo and Pappas were obligated to try.

Lottie and I were left standing by the hell pit. Good thing the wind was blowing the other way.

"If you defeat the demon and stuff him back in his vessel, will the bubbling hole from hell go away?"

"Perhaps. There is no physical hell," she said. "Only other dimensions. This one is from a world of fire—his home world. He brought it here to this world. There will be others, if there are not already. I do not know how long the vessel has been open."

"The Man in Black mentioned other cases of that dimension bleeding through."

"Then I must act and soon. If the demon's vessel is broken, I must find some other way to contain him."

I called Adonis Diplas. He actually answered. Surprising, because I figured he'd already blocked me.

"What do you want now?" he said, panting. Someone was still running.

"When did George steal the demon vessel?"

"What?"

"You heard me. Are you wheezing?"

"I'm running because somebody announced a sale at my shop."

At least he didn't call me bad names. That was a point in his favor. A tiny one, but a point was still a point.

I repeated the question.

"I don't know. Years ago. *Yia sou*, Kyria Marika," he said, managing to observe social customs while he was running. "Why?"

"And his housekeeper broke it when?"

"I don't know."

"Wait—we're not done here yet. George asked you to ask me to find the other vessel because he needs an exterminator, right?"

"Yes."

"So how did he end up with the first vessel? Why didn't he take both to begin with?"

"Don't know. You want those kinds of answers, you'll have to ask him. I've got to go before they tear my market apart and Stephanie gives everything away."

I ended the call. That would never be as satisfying as hanging up.

"The demon vessel left the island years ago," I told Lottie, "and it's possible it's been open for that long, too."

"The demon will try to turn this world into his own."

"So there's a burning pit here because … he's homesick?"

"I do not know what this means."

"It means he's misses his own dimension."

"No, he does not have feelings of nostalgia and loss. His only goal is to sow chaos and misery."

"And watch daytime TV."

"Daytime TV is misery," Pappas said on the way past. "I know. My mother watches all the shows."

"Why here?" I said. "Why, specifically, is the pit here? He's in Athens so why not put the pit there?"

Lottie sniffed the air. "Perhaps he knows I am here and he is trying to throw me off his path."

My phone rang.

"Please tell me you've got something I can use," I said.

"Sam Washington the magic man has come through again. I don't know if it's something, but it's not nothing. Your boy Diplas, the dates all match the murders."

"So it's kind of nothing?"

"Was I done yet? No. No, I was not. Let me finish."

"Yessir."

"Atta girl," Sam said in my ear. "Like I told you, the dates match, but that's not the whole picture. The times, they're what doesn't align. Tracking George Diplas's cellphone data, I'm seeing that he was *wher*e the murders took place, but not precisely when. There's a delay with some of them."

"What kind of delay?"

"Minutes. Hours in a couple of cases. I'd be surprised if he killed all of his victims."

"Can you extrapolate?"

"You want the big brain's opinion? All right. If it were me, I'd be looking for someone that's got it in for your boy. Someone keeping tabs on his movements and trying to make it look like he's the bad guy."

"Framing him?"

"Wouldn't be a stretch to consider that Diplas has a stalker. He's on most televisions in the country five days a week. That kind of visibility attracts the weirdoes. I almost sent him a fan letter myself. Then I looked at my man Luther on the wall and changed my mind. This heart could never be untrue."

"You old romantic, you."

"Who are you calling old?"

"Thanks, Sam. Looks like I need to talk to George again."

"Just be careful, okay? This one smells like kimchi after a week in the sun. Stalkers have a tendency to go bad fast. Wait—one more thing. The Baboulas angle? Used to be she was a big fan of the weatherman. Then he—or whoever is after him—killed someone connected to the family. So she figured she'd repay him by replacing his real legal team with the one stooge."

"Who did he kill?"

"A young man whose grandmother lives in the nearby village. Baboulas is a good friend to have."

Now that I had some answers, I kissed Leo goodbye, waved at Pappas, and Lottie, Cerberus and I set off in the direction of my place. I needed a jolt of something strong to get the old brain moving. This level of thinking required Merope's Best.

The next ride to the mainland wasn't happening until tomorrow morning. That was hours lost at a time when we didn't have hours to lose. Lottie needed to stuff her foe back into his vessel and rocket the pair of them back to the island, and then I had to figure out the George Diplas situation.

She was thinking the same thing. "We must go."

"It's winter. The next ferry isn't until tomorrow."

I waved to a few people who were peeping out at us from behind their sheers and shutters. Although they were trying to hide, not acknowledging them would have consequences.

"I will open a portal."

"You can do that?"

Her face fell. "Yes, although I do not know how."

"So, theoretically you can open a portal?"

A shadow pulled away from the wall. "What portal?"

Tomas Bakas and his enormous ears. "Tomas, what are you doing here?"

"I was on my way to the burning hole that used to be the spa."

"Is the hole tomorrow's headline?"

He snorted. "No. Best place to get news is at a party. People yelling secrets at other people over the music, all I have to do is sit and listen, and the news falls right into my lap."

"You're a cockroach, Bakas."

"Thank you." He looked Lottie up and down. "You are new. Are you married? Do you want to be?"

"Ugh, look somewhere else for your chins, Bakas."

He touched the place where a chin was supposed to be. "What do you mean?"

Lottie glared down at him. "I am older than the rock you are standing upon."

"He means new to the island," I told her. "This is Tomas Bakas. He's the local media. Like a town cryer. Sometimes he reports the news and sometimes he makes it up."

"A gossip," she said.

"A *professional* gossip," Bakas said. "The paycheck makes me respectable."

No amount of money could make the Bakas family respectable, but Tomas maybe had something I needed so I kept my mouth shut.

"Have you found out anything useful and actually true yet?"

"You haven't, I know that much," he said. "If you had, I would know."

That was disconcerting and probably not true. All the same, I made a mental note to check my home and devices for bugs. Sam would hook me up.

"I've been busy with other things," I said.

"Like this woman?"

Lottie flicked him between the eyes. "I am not a woman. I am a guardian, a protector of mankind."

Tomas's eyes lit up. "Are you from Greece?"

"I am from everywhere, and nowhere."

I stepped between them. "Enough. She's not a story, and right now we have somewhere to be."

"But first I must make a portal," Lottie announced.

Tomas's eyes lit up.

"That's what she calls walking through a door. She's foreign."

He didn't look convinced. "I know you know something about Stephanie Dolas and the others. I am not done with that story."

"There's no story."

"I will keep following you anyway."

My eyes cut to Lottie. "Coffee?"

"Yes, take me to your coffee."

The reporter and senior editor hung back until we reached Merope's Best. Across the road, the fisherman was still fishing in the fountain. Sitting next to him were a series of plates and bowls with snacks that had gone untouched.

Interesting.

I called Diplas yet again. When he answered he sounded harried and slightly dazed. "What now?"

"Is she eating?"

"Who?"

"Stephanie?"

There was a pause. In the background a skirmish had broken out. Several someones were fighting over cans of NOY NOY evaporated milk. Sounds of rage wafted through the speaker.

"Not right now," he said.

"I mean in general. Is she eating at all?"

"Now that you mention it, I don't think so. Why?"

"Simple curiosity."

He barked a laugh. "We both know that isn't true. Why don't you tell me what's on your mind, Allie?"

"Ha! That will be the day."

If the zombies weren't eating, what was fueling them? That's what was on my mind. But he'd never know that.

I ended the call and looked around. Lottie had vanished.

Wait. No. She was at the counter inside Merope's Best.

This crowd was more caffeinated, so they didn't freak out and run. One look at the guardian and they naturally assumed she was as desperate for coffee as them. I traipsed in after her.

Different barista on duty. This one looked as bored as the last. I held up three fingers. "Three frappes—sweet with milk."

The barista oozed disdain. She was judging me—hard. "It is cold outside."

"Okay, so make it three hot frappes."

She rolled her eyes and verbally tossed our order at her coworker. "Three cappuccinos."

The other barista worked fast. The coffees were ready before I could check my email for work-related messages.

I took two coffees and gave the third to Lottie. "Wow. You're efficient today."

"Thank the new drugs I am taking," the barista said. "I am capable of anything at high speed now."

"What drugs?"

"Sugar," his coworker said. "He eats sugar straight from the bucket under the counter."

"Using a spoon, right?" I said.

They stared at me.

"Using a spoon ... right?"

No answer. Holding a polyethylene cup in each hand, I backed slowly toward the door.

Lottie pulled off her cup's lid and drank from the cup like it was a trough. When she came up for air she was sporting a milk mustache. She eyed the other coffee in my hand. "Why do you have two coffees and I have one?"

"Only one is for me." I pushed through the door with my back and held it open for her to exit. She ducked under the frame and we stepped out into the cold. Outside, Tomas Bakas was shivering in his coat. I handed him the second cup.

He stared the coffee in his gloved hand. "Why are you being nice to me?"

"Because you're a human being and also because I can use you."

He thought about it a moment. "Okay. I am good with that."

Lottie and I went back to my place, where it was just the two of us, Yiayia, the fisherman's ghost, Dead Cat, and Cerberus, who was beside himself with joy to see the couch. He leaped onto the cushions and sank into the softness. As gratitude for me owning a couch, he hit me with the puppy dog eyes.

Lottie watched him roll on the cushions to give his whole body some comfort. "That one loves you."

"All he's ever known is love, and his new family will adore him."

She stared at me. She was still staring at me as I rinsed and refilled Cerberus's water fountain bowl.

"What?"

"You know."

"What I know is that you mentioned a portal. Let's revisit that now that we haven't got the *Merope Fores'* one and only reporter eavesdropping on our conversation.

Hands over face, she plopped down onto my office chair.

"What's wrong?"

"The problem is me. I do not know what to do."

"I don't follow."

"As I told you, I can make a portal to our destination, but I do not know how to do it. I require instructions. Nobody gave me instructions when they created me and magicked me in to the vessel."

"That is a problem. Just out of curiosity though, if you can make portals but don't know how, why didn't we have this conversation earlier? You could have opened a portal to your island, right? I mean, if you knew how to do it."

She shook her head. "No portals to or from the island. It is a security measure, so that my nemesis could not leave the island by portal. To leave he required someone to come to the island and physically transport his vessel. I am bound by the same law, in the interest of balance."

"Okay, fine, so how do we get instructions so that you can make a portal?"

"I do not know."

"Yiayia?"

"I can go through walls," my grandmother said, "but I do not know a thing about portals."

While my eyelid twitched, I paced. Cerberus followed me with his eyeballs. "Why didn't they leave you an instruction manual?" My feet slammed to a stop. My brain found the answer all on its own. I grabbed my backpack and located the salt jar with its spectral passengers.

Yiayia gave it the stink-eye. "I am not getting in the jar."

"There's no room at the inn right now." With that, I wiggled the cork out. "Do you two want to stretch your ghost legs?"

There were bumping noises from inside the jar. Then: "It is very cozy in here. We are quite comfortable."

"Now I am more interested in going in there," Yiayia said.

"Keep your underwear on," I told her. "Do either of you know how to make a portal? A certain someone needs to know."

"Me," Lottie said.

Things like humor and subtlety hadn't been invented in her time.

There was murmuring in the jar. "Did we not teach her how to do the portal?" Gnec said.

"I did not do it. Did you do it?"

"Ach, it has been so long that I cannot remember. Maybe I did, maybe I forgot."

"We had a lot to do during the ritual," Tut said in a louder voice. "There was very little time before the guardian was created and bound to the vessel."

"Changed my mind," Yiayia said. "I do not want to get into the jar with those two old women who cannot find a single *kolos* between them."

I went into the kitchen for a glass of water. Coffee wasn't fixing the headache brewing in my temples. This was a job for non-caffeinated liquids. I guzzled the water and went back to the living room. "Doesn't matter who forgot to tell her, and we don't have time for debate. Give her the portal-making instruction manual so that we can get from here to Athens before we die of old age."

"She will never die of old age," Gnec said. "You, on the other hand ..."

"We mortals are dying from the day we are born," Tut said, his voice morose.

"Thanks, Socrates," I said. "Let's save the philosophy for later. Portal?"

"All she has to do is think about the portal," Tut said.

"And she has to want it," Gnec added.

"It's that easy?" I said.

He sounded amazed that I would question him. "But of course. How else would you make a portal?"

"Magic words?"

The pink jar shook with laughter. I stuffed the cork back in and shoved it deep down in my backpack so I wouldn't have to listen to their cackles.

"Okay," I said to Lottie. "You heard the ghosts. All you have to do is think about the portal and want it to appear."

She handed me her vessel. I carefully placed the glue scarred clay in my backpack. "I am thinking about it, and I do want it. How else will I catch the demon? That is my whole purpose. Is the portal here yet?"

"Not yet."

"I will think harder."

She thought harder for a good twenty minutes. Finally, the air shimmered. A hole opened right there in my apartment. Big enough to accommodate Lottie's towering height. I'd say it was custom made to fit.

She grabbed me by the arm and stepped through to the other side. The portal closed with a *whoosh*, and we were standing in a field in someplace that definitely wasn't Greece.

CHAPTER EIGHTEEN

"Athens has changed," she said, glancing around.

Because this was her first time, I gave her a supportive and encouraging smile so her confidence wouldn't be ruined. She was an all-powerful and ancient being, but I felt responsible for her. "That was a good first try, but maybe a bit closer to Greece next time?"

The portal reappeared. This time when we popped out the other side we were standing on a hilltop.

Good news: We were in Athens.

Bad news: We were in Athens when the Parthenon was brand-spanking-new.

I tried to stay cool about the fact that we'd just time-traveled. I tried to take a picture but my phone was dead.

"So that's what the Acropolis looked like before Elgin robbed Greece. Okay. Let's try the same location, but today."

The portal reappeared.

We emerged in Athens in what appeared to be the right time. My phone was working now, so that was something.

Did I say we?

There was no *we*.

I was the only one to exit the portal, into a claustrophobia-inducing alley, with strings of laundry crisscrossing the air above me, the scent of barf and urine swirling through the gloom.

Virgin Mary. Just my luck.

"This is ridiculous," I said to no one in particular, seeing as how I was in the alley alone—unless the half dozen ghosts of dead hobos picking through the dumpster counted.

There was nothing here besides he grimy backs of shops whose prettier windows were facing in the other direction.

Was I stranded? Should I stay here so that Lottie could find me?

Crap.

This wasn't good. I couldn't even slump on the wall because it was covered in unidentifiable stains—and worse, identifiable stains.

I texted Leo to tell him the bad news, that Lottie and had caught a portal to Athens and we'd been separated.

No answer. He must be struggling with the whole portal thing. Poor Leo. The things he endured.

Then my phone pinged. My message was undeliverable.

Dang it.

Further down the alley, a door opened. A figure stepped out. Short. Round. Head covered in corkscrew curls. A wide, welcoming smile.

"There you are!" Betty Honeychurch said. "I knew I could hear you. We were just about to send you a cake, weren't we, Jack?"

Jack Honeychurch's voice drifted out behind me. "That we were."

I was saved. Yippee. I threw my arms around Betty and we took several moments to squeeze each other. Then I stepped back.

"Another cake? Not that I'm complaining, but you sent me one a couple of days ago."

"That wasn't us, luv."

"It was in a Cake Emporium box. Gingerbread cake, with Christmas scenes."

"Don't quote me, but I think that's the cake Jack was planning to make for you."

She looped her arm through mine and we entered the kitchen, where her brother Jack was whipping cream in a stand mixer the size of an oven. As we passed, he dipped a spoon in the cream and handed it to me. "Honey-whipped," he said.

The delicate sweetness made my eyes roll back in my head.

"Allie just told me that we sent her a gingerbread cake a couple of days ago," Betty told her brother.

He looked surprised. "That's the flavor we were going to send."

"That's what I told her, didn't I?"

We moved out of the kitchen and into the confection shop —the exact same shop that I'd frequented in Merope. The Cake Emporium existed everywhere there were people and everywhen, except present day Merope. A glitch that I hoped wasn't permanent. Only people with a touch of the woo-woo could see the shop. With my ability to see the dead, I definitely counted.

In the fireplace a fire crackled, filling the bakery with a warm glow. Half the shop contained genuine curios and objects fascinating to those with the ability to find the Cake Emporium. The other half was almost identical, but every item was spun from sugar and spice and everything nice.

One shop. Myriad locations. My mind rolled over and gave up struggling. There was a limit to how much weirdness my brain could consume before it decided it was easier to let everything pass through unregulated.

Betty plucked a tray off the counter. Sitting atop the silver tray, coils of steam rising up from the mugs, were two hot beverages. They were accompanied by an assortment of Christmas themed cookies—or biscuits, seeing as how Betty and Jack Honeychurch were British. Or British-presenting. Their faces were youthful, but their eyes said their origin story began long before Great Britain's.

"That must be why I made these hot chocolates," Betty said with a touch of wonder. "Some part of me knew you were coming." She set the tray on the table and gestured at me to take a seat. We were back to our usual routine, like the shop hadn't vanished from Merope to protect itself. "I can hear your thoughts clear as day, luv. Let me ask you something. What day is it?"

"Wednesday."

"It's Monday, luv."

My mind shrugged and muttered something about how this was more weirdness and it was better to give up the tum-tum than struggle against the tide. Still, it was two days ago?

Go with it, my brain said. Resistance is futile.

Anyway, I already suspected what went wonky.

"The portal," I said, groaning. "Lottie's portal brought us to Athens, but not on Wednesday."

Betty's button nose scrunched. "This sounds like one of those long stories I do so love. Have some bickies and tell me all about it."

The cookies were iced with nostalgic Christmas scenes. It seemed impossible that they'd been hand painted, but the Honeychurches worked a kind of magic when it came to baked goods and other confections. As I ate and sipped creamy chocolate, my stress levels dipped into the tolerable zone. Sugar wrapped the ragged edges of my thoughts in soft cotton candy. My eyelid quit twitching.

Betty listened attentively and made all the right noises as

she listened to my tale of murder, adventure, and woe. She asked thoughtful questions and pushed the plate of emotional support cookies closer.

"I'm so full of questions," I said. "And I don't really have any answers. How did George Diplas know about the vessel that's in his possession? Did the demon inside the vessel kill all those men and pin it on George? Where is Lottie? *When* is she? What about the zombie people on Merope? Who—or what—is the Man in Black?"

Betty leaned forward and gathered my hands up in hers. I was still gripping a cookie. She didn't seem to notice or mind.

"Your Man in Black was made by man for the protection of mankind. More than that I can't tell you, luv."

"Because it's a secret?"

Her curls bounced as she shook her head. "I don't know everything."

"Finally, she admits it," Jack called out from the kitchen.

"Don't listen to him," Betty said, suppressing a laugh. "Even if I did know, the man himself seems to be circumspect. He's playing this close to his chest for some reason, and it's up to him to tell you his story if he chooses."

"So he's a good guy, right?"

"*Protective* is not a synonym for *good*. That's our storytelling way of explaining things; the one who saves us from the evil is always painted as evil's counterpart. In reality it's never that simple, is it?" She patted my hands and let me have them back. I stuck the cookie in my mouth. "What I know is that your mysterious Man in Black has stepped in to protect you from harm more than once, which means he has an interest in keeping you safe. That doesn't make him a good man, but it means he's good enough for me. Maybe in time he'll tell you where he came from and what he's doing on your island. But all the same, don't be surprised if he doesn't. Now, as for your zombie people, I don't believe they're your classic zombies, which you already know."

"Are they dead?"

"Oh, yes. Mostly dead, by the sounds of things. But not completely dead. This is a necromancer's doing. They brought the dead back but botched the job and didn't complete a full resurrection. Sounds to me like the souls aren't completely severed from their mortal bodies. They're clinging by a thread. Which is why you've got flesh and blood being tailed by their ghosts."

"How do I fix them, and how do I find this necromancer?"

"I'm not sure you can fix them, luv. This necromancer of yours doesn't strike me as someone skilled at the job. The tie needs to be severed so their spirits can move on and their bodies can rest in peace."

"Is putting them back in their bodies an option?"

"Maybe. If they were resurrected in the first few moments after death, when that spark was still there. But I'm no expert."

"Because it's dark magic?"

Her laugh was like wind chimes. "You've been watching Buffy again, haven't you? I can hear the intro music from here. No, luv. There's no dark and light magic, just magic. It's what you do with it that matters. This doesn't feel like malice to me. Just someone who means well or doesn't even know what they're doing."

A novice. Or someone who didn't know their own power.

I was already making a list of suspects and questions as I stood.

"I need to go," I said. "I have to find Lottie and return to Wednesday."

Betty slid back in her chair and patted her lap before standing. "I hate to see you go so soon, but at least let me give you something for the road. Jack?" she called out. "What have you got that Allie can take with her?"

He emerged, wiping his hands on his white apron. "How do you feet about some eclairs?"

"Christmas eclairs?"

He chuckled. "Regular eclairs with pastry cream filling, chocolate ganache icing, and a touch of confidence."

Warmth unfolded inside me. "Sounds perfect."

He delivered a grin that was as warm and comforting as his baked goods. "I'll box them up for you."

"And we'll make sure we send you that gingerbread cake so that the timeline stays intact," Betty said.

While she prepared a plastic bag so I could carry the box, I leaned on the counter. "Are you ever coming back to Merope?"

"The shop is trying, luv, but something is blocking it."

"Any idea what?"

"No idea. But it'll be back just as soon as it can."

"Where can I find you until then?"

"Apparently we've got a lovely spot on Mykonos, but I'm not entirely sure where. We had a lovely wereweasel from Mykonos come in the other day. Sweet girl. She was on the run after someone caught her eating a chicken."

A wereweasel? Nope. Not even a blip on my weirdometer. The world—my world—was made solely of weird things now. Nothing normal was left except maybe my parents, and they were busy living on a ship in the middle of nowhere. If I was honest, even that wasn't remotely normal. Parents didn't do that. Not Greek parents, anyway.

"Huh," I said. "Looks like I'm catching the ferry to Mykonos next time I need a snack."

Jack popped out of the kitchen with a Cake Emporium box and slid it into the waiting bag. He winked and vanished back into his sanctum.

Betty hugged me hard and escorted me to the door—the front door this time. "Be seeing you soon, luv."

Out in the street, I tried to get my bearings. The Cake Emporium's storefront was a scene from the Nutcracker and the perfect distraction while I tried to ignore the fact that I was lost and it was two days ago. What would happen if I went to George Diplas's place now? Would I bump into the me that went to his place today? Was this like when the Man in Black took me to the past and we peered through a window even though we walked through a door?

My mind was flexible, to a degree, but time travel expected me to be a gymnast.

Where was the DeLorean when I needed it?

Should I stay put or move on? I had things to do and two days worth of time to do them, now. This backwards time jump could be a blessing.

I ran through my to-do list. The club where George's alleged first victim was murdered was close by, in the Gazi area. Sam said the times were off even though the dates were right, but I wanted to scope out the situation myself. This was my chance to start at the beginning.

GPS told me where to go. Fifteen minutes later, I arrived on foot at the Big Rooster. The big neon boy chicken out front was switched off right now, and the door said business hours were 8 PM to 3 AM, but I tried the door anyway, just in case.

My ability to think inside the box paid off. The door opened and I slipped inside.

The club was full of dancing bears, otters, twinks, and foxes, all shaking their groove thang to the sound of no music. Sitting at the bar was Marilyn Monroe with a five o'clock shadow and a laptop. She, he, or they was/were poring over a spreadsheet.

"Club does not open until eight," Marilyn said without

looking up. Someone had no idea that their club was jam packed with dancing ghosts.

I introduced myself and offered my hand. Marilyn gave it a firm shake and went back to the spreadsheet. "Now that we are best friends, I can tell you to get out. Unless you are from the AADE."

The AADE. Those letters made all Greeks raise their middle fingers.

"What happens if I *am* from the AADE?"

The ghosts all quit dancing. A collective gasp happened.

"Then I put my foot up your *kolos* and punch you in the *archidia*."

"Watch out," a ghost called out. "He did that once!"

"Twice," said another.

I did my best not to react. "Virgin Mary, am I glad I'm not here about your taxes, and not just because I don't have any *archidia* for you to punch."

Satisfied that there wouldn't be an ass-kicking, the ghosts went back to dancing to music only they could hear.

I leaned against the bar and tried to look non-threatening yet authoritative.

"What do you want?" Marilyn said without looking up.

"One of your customers was murdered a while back."

"Hazard of being a gay man in the world," he murmured.

"This man was maybe one of George Diplas's victims, and the murder happened here."

Marilyn's head slowly swiveled on its stalk until he was staring down his significant nose at me.

"I know George likes men, even though most of Greece doesn't," I went on. "And that knowledge won't go anywhere else." He continued staring at me. More specifically, the twitch in my eye. "George's cousin hired me to prove to the authorities that George Diplas didn't murder anyone, including your customer."

Marilyn looked away and closed the laptop's lid. On break-neck high heels, he tottered around the bar and slapped two shot glasses on the counter.

"I need a Big Rooster special for this conversation," he said.

He set a bunch of bottles on the bar and painstakingly layered liqueurs in the tiny glasses one at a time, creating an out of order rainbow. When it was done, he gestured for me to take one. He raised his glass. "*Yia mas*."

"Too bad nobody drank to my health," a ghost said beside me. He sniffed once and returned to the dance floor.

Marilyn knocked back the shot and smacked his lips. "That will be thirty euros," he said to me. "You want information about George Diplas, you can pay for the dry cleaning my Aliki Viougouklaki dress needed after I cleaned up the mess George made—although of course I did not know it was him at the time. The police and the coroner took the body but they left everything else."

The math wasn't math-ing.

"My understanding is that George—or whoever—strangled his victims. Where did the blood come from?"

"Not blood. The otter and George went into the bathroom for some fun. He was naked when he died. *Kaka* and *ouro* everywhere."

"And George?"

"He was gone by then." He drummed his nails on the bar and peered down his artfully highlighted nose at me. "Do you think George Diplas really killed him?"

"You tell me."

He swiped away my shot glass and stashed both our glasses in the deep sink on his side of the bar. "George Diplas has been coming here for a long time. We are not friends, but we are friendly, understand" I indicated that I understood. "Lately he has been different. Not himself."

"Different how?"

"Aggressive. Mean." From under the bar, he produced a cloth and wiped down the spot where our glasses had sat. "He used to be charming, but now ... he is someone else."

"When did he change?"

"About a year or so ago, maybe. At first I thought he was sick, but now ..." He jerked his chin up then lowered. "I do not know what to think. If George Diplas did not kill that man in my club, then who did?"

"That's what I plan to find out," I said, and it was true. Part of clearing George, if I could clear him, meant pointing the finger at someone—or something—else. "Thanks for your help." I placed thirty euros on the counter and said my goodbyes.

I almost made it out the door without a ghost incident. At the last second a burly lumberjack of a dead man barged right through me and planted himself in front of the door. Because I wasn't expecting him, I slammed to a stop. That gave him enough time to wag his finger at me.

"You can see me!" he crowed.

I bent down to tie my bootlace. Classic avoidance tactic.

The ghost didn't buy it. He was onto me. "I know you can see me, so what is with these *malakies*?"

"If I stand here and talk to you, what will Marilyn back there think?"

"You are a woman, and a badly dressed one. He has already forgotten you."

"Badly dressed!" I looked down. My clothes were functional for my job, and clean. How was that badly dressed?

He folded his arms. "Sweatpants? In public? Really?"

Bold criticism for a man with glitter tangled in his chest hair. With that pelt, I guessed he was killed by a fur trader.

"They were clean," I said.

He waved my words away with his hand. "Our favorite

weatherman didn't kill anyone in this club. He was already gone when the murder happened."

"How do you know?"

"I saw it with my own eyes." He pointed to his eyes in case I wasn't familiar with rudimentary physiology.

"You witnessed the murder?"

"Yes, and I wish I never saw it. What was in that bathroom was not a man."

"Was it ... a demon?"

With a theatrical gasp, he slapped his hand over his mouth. "You know about them, too?"

"Let's say I have some experience."

"Yes, it was a *daimonos.* It looked like something vomited into a cake mould. It did not even have a proper face."

That sounded like a certain something that loved daytime television and satin sheets.

"And it strangled the man?"

He held up his big paws. "With its vomit hands. If you can call them hands. They were more like shovels."

"Did it see you?"

He jerked his chin up once for "no."

"Then what happened?"

"It left the bathroom and went to dance."

"Why are you still here?" Marilyn Monroe called out.

"Just tying my laces! Thanks for the help," I told the ghost.

He nodded. "Now you owe me one."

Of course I did. Typical ghosts. They rarely did anything for nothing. "What do you want?"

He told me.

CHAPTER NINETEEN

An hour later, for the second time on Monday—if memory served—I was on the run. This time from the cemetery's caretaker. He had a shovel and I had a robust cardiovascular system from all the bicycling. This was one of those moments when I really didn't regret not owning a car.

What did I do?

What the ghost asked. He'd been helpful, after all, and he'd earned his request.

I just wished his request hadn't been to paint "Her cooking was *skata*" on his mother's tombstone—the worst insult he could think of for the woman who had never accepted him. I could think of at least ten worse things, but he didn't ask. I let him have his moment of glory.

I should have waited until night to do the deed. Now I was running for my life.

No. Wait. The caretaker was giving up. The thundering footfalls had stopped. The chase had devolved into screaming insults at me.

Virgin Mary, he really hated my ancestors. Yiayia would be fine with some of his serving suggestions—probably she'd invented those sexual shenanigans herself—but the rest of my forebears would be mortified.

Gasping for air, I stopped and turned around. The caretaker was leaning on his shovel, sweating like a hog. With his free hand, he chopped at his groin.

As much as I enjoyed the activity he was recommending, he wasn't exactly my preferred partner.

"Sorry!" I called out. "I had to do it!"

Then I took off again at a fast clip.

As an object out of time, my phone was messed up but my GPS was still functioning. It took an hour at a fast pace, but eventually I made it to George Diplas's fancy neighborhood.

This time I knew how to break in and made my way around the back before anyone spotted me. A quick glance at my phone told me I didn't have a lot of time before I showed up in the rental car.

"What are you doing?"

I froze. It was the ghost I'd met on Monday—today. Now that I was here, I recalled our strange interaction last time. This was the first time we'd met, even though we'd met previously.

My head hurt.

"My name is Allie, and I'm breaking in to George's house. You're going to see me here in a while, too, but this time I'll be in a car and I'll have a huge dog with me. When we see each other you're going to tell me about this window, and in return I'm going to do a favor for you."

"What favor?"

"Your name is Mitsa and you think your former neighbor over there" —I pointed down the street— "is a mounoskeela."

"My name *is* Mitsa," she said, "and she is a *mounoskeela*."

She looked from me to the window. "This is a time travel thing, yes? I will play the *vlakas* when I see you again, okay?"

"Great idea. Thanks!"

I boosted myself through the window and performed the same handstand, forward roll maneuver as last time, this time smashing my shoulder into the tub.

This go around, I didn't waste time searching the house. I headed straight for the master bedroom.

The demon was sitting up in bed, snacking on a sack of live chickens. The TV was blaring, rapid fire Greek spitting from the speakers. I waved my hands in front of the screen.

The demon's face bunched up harder. "Have we done this before? I feel like we have done this before. What do you think?"

I played dumb. I was good at it. "Done what?"

"You, me, this bedroom. But something about it is different now, and I think that it is you."

"Different how?"

It lifted its nose into the air. Took a deep breath. "You reek like a person out of time."

I sniffed my pits. Fresh and fruity. Splurging on good antiperspirant was really paying off. "I am out of time in a way."

He sat up and fluffed the pillows before falling back on them again. "Explain yourself before I get out of this bed and tear off your limbs. I am experiencing an urge to beat you with the soggy ends of your arms."

With confidence I didn't feel after that death threat, I gestured at the television, where a youthful woman was dressed up as an elderly Greek widow. I knew how that storyline was going to play out. Living in the future had its perks. "In about two days, you'll find out that she's not dead." I jabbed my finger at the screen. "She's been in disguise as her own grandmother for the past year."

He smacked the bedcovers and hurled chickens at me. I opened the window and shooed them out before he could round them up again and eat them. "What! You spoiled it for me! I hate spoilers!" His mind moved to the next conclusion. "Wait—how did you know?"

"I'll tell you, but it will cost you. I want some answers."

"I will tell you nothing."

"Then I won't tell you how I know that that guy" —I poked George Diplas's television screen— "is in love with her brother and has a secret baby with her sister."

"Noooo!" He flew up out of the bed in a tangle of ... could I really call them limbs? They were limb-ish. "Why would you do this to me?"

I folded my arms. "Have you been a bad, bad demon?"

"Of course! That is what demons do. It is right there in the name. We do demonic things! Who ever heard of a good demon? Nobody!"

He leaped back into the bed and rolled around in the covers until he was a demon burrito.

"Okay, so I guess I need to be more specific."

"Can we do this when my show is over?"

One of us was buying time and I hoped it was me. The longer I waited, the higher the chance that Lottie would find me. Of course the longer I waited, the sooner I was going to squeeze through the bathroom window and run into myself. And now that he was out of chicken snacks, the demon would be looking for its next dose of junk food. I didn't want to be junk food. I wasn't gourmet but I figured I was at least a nice pot roast.

"I guess we can finish watching it."

"Sit," he barked. "You are a distraction."

I hauled over a chair from the corner of the fancy bedroom, where there was a standalone bookcase set up and a small table. Despite all the books, George Diplas didn't seem like a reader, but then he hadn't struck me as a serial killer either ... until he had. Then he tried to kill *me*, which was another nail in the coffin his reputation was destined to be buried in if I didn't get to the bottom of this mystery.

The demon waved a pustule crusted hand at me. "You. Human. Go fetch snacks."

"Do I look like a servant?"

"All mortals look like servants."

For crying out loud, the ego on demons was staggering. But a snack did sound good.

"Wait," he said. "What is in the bag?"

I looked at the Cake Emporium bag dangling from my hand. "A box?"

"And inside the box?"

I said nothing. I didn't want to share my cake.

"What is in the box?" he asked. "What's in the box?"

"Fine, it's eclairs."

He stared at me. "I like eclairs."

"Fine. I'll share my eclairs, and these are the best eclairs ever, but you have to do something for me."

"Rip off your head and suck out your brains?"

"Answer questions."

He sighed and flopped back on the pillows. "Ask your questions."

Come on, Lottie. Before I have to share my goodies. "Did you murder a bunch of young men and make it look like George did it?"

He blanked. "Who is George?"

"The man whose bed you're sleeping in."

"Oh. Him. I forgot about him. He was fun for a while, but now he is trapped in a mortal prison. I will not go to a prison. Never again. I cannot be contained in that itty bitty living space. Now I have a whole world to myself." He sniffed. "I am redecorating, you know. This world does not have nearly enough fire and despair. The volcanos are nice, but they need more ... pizazz. A good wake up call would fix them."

"Are you, by any chance, creating hell pits?"

"Maybe," he said slyly. "Why do you ask? Have you seen one?"

"Just one."

"Did you like it?"

"It was ... hot. Kinda stinky, too."

He sighed. "That smell, it reminds me of home sweet home."

Great. The boiling pit was part of his remodeling project. Somebody needed to call this guy a real interior decorator, because fire and brimstone weren't about to become this year's shiplap.

"When you say George was fun for a while, do you mean you killed those men and framed George?"

"Of course not." He looked as offended as something with very little face could manage. "I killed those men and George took credit for it because sometimes I did it in his weak human body."

"I don't think he actually took credit for the murders."

"Murders! You call it murder, I call it—" He made a sound like an elephant coughing up a bucket of peanuts.

"Bless you."

He shrieked. "Do not do that! No blessing!"

"What was that noise then?"

"That is what we demons call the first day of our week."

For crying out loud, he'd just called a whole lot of homicide basically another day on the demon job. And now not only were a bunch of young men dead, but George Diplas was sitting in a jail cell, waiting to get started on a lifetime prison sentence.

Where was Lottie? I had the guy right here. What I needed now was her. Then I could decant the ghosts and they could work their magic mojo to get everyone back in their respective vessels, safe and sound.

Question number two: Where was George hiding the demon's broken vessel?

I excused myself to go to the bathroom. Not the master bathroom because I'd be climbing through it any time now. I went in search of the backup bathroom.

"Leave the eclairs," the demon said.

"The eclairs comes with me."

"Fine, but if you eat them without sharing I will rip off your skin and wear it as underpants."

Good enough incentive not to eat eclairs alone, if you asked me.

I scurried off to black bathroom with my bag of eclairs First thing I did after I locked the door was locate the pink jar buried in my backpack. I wiggled the cork out.

"Is it time to come out?" Tut or Gnec asked.

"Not yet," I said. "I need help. I found the demon, but I'm missing the guardian. We got separated after she sent me back in time."

"How far back in time?"

"Two days, but that's a good thing. The demon doesn't exactly remember us meeting previously. He's suspicious, though."

"When did you meet the demon before?"

"Two days ago."

There was rustling and some "oofing," then: "What happens if she meets herself?"

"Who can say? Catastrophe, perhaps."

"An apocalypse?"

"Maybe a small one, maybe a big one."

"Nobody prepared us for this."

Virgin Mary, why me? "Okay, so I won't run into myself. Apocalypse averted. But if the guardian doesn't show up, how do I defeat the demon and shove him back in his bottle, where he'll hopefully languish until another Aladdin shows up to give him another rub?"

There was bewildered silence.

I gave them a nudge. "Anyone?"

"We cannot beat the demon," Tut spluttered. "That is why we created a guardian in the first place, so that someone else would do the fighting and the magic. Unless you can do it."

"I can't fight! I find things. I can ride a bike, sure, but that's the extent of my physical fitness. Demons are way out of my skillset."

"Tell us about your weapons and we will decide."

"Weapons? What weapons? I've got salt, holy water, pepper spray, a hand-held fan, and a plucky attitude. On a good day my comebacks are solid, but most of the time I only win arguments in the shower."

"She is no good. We will have to find some other way," Tut said.

Gnec went *tst*. "The only other way is to locate the guardian and bring her here."

I paced in front of the jar and nibbled a hangnail. "Do I need the vessel? The demon's vessel, I mean,"

"Of course! What else would you use to imprison the demon? Where is it?"

"Broken, and I don't know where the vessel is or where George keeps his glue."

"We are doomed!" There was a bump inside the jar, which I suspected was Tut throwing his hands in the air.

"Can't we use something else?"

"No!" he yelped.

"Why did you use pottery? Is the clay magic?"

"What else would you use to make a vessel?" Gnec sounded bewildered.

"Something less fragile. George Diplas seems like the kind of person who knows about Gladware. It's plastic, so even if someone drops it the demon won't escape."

"Why did we not think of this plastic?" Gnec asked his pal in a low voice.

"Probably because it had not been invented in our time."

"Greeks invented everything."

Now wasn't the time to tell them about Alexander Parkes and Leo Hendrik Baekeland, neither of whom was Greek.

I crouched down by the jar. "So can we imprison the demon in a plastic container or not?"

"Perhaps, if the ritual can be completed."

"And we need the guardian for that?"

"It is imperative."

I glanced around the bathroom. It was heavy on black with black accents, but light on supernatural communication devices.

"Can you call the guardian somehow? Let her know when and where we are?"

"If we were alive, maybe. But not in our present condition."

I dropped the toilet lid and sat. "First thing's first. We need a vessel. I'm going to the kitchen to find a plastic container with a matching lid, if there is such a thing in George's kitchen. Then we're going to brainstorm and figure out how to get Lottie here so she can drag Blobby in there away from the soap operas and stuff him back in a box."

Inside the jar, the ghosts huddled together in a little whisper-fest.

Then:

"Good idea," Tut said in a louder voice. "You should do that."

Feeling less than enthused about the positive outcome of

this plan, I snatched up the jar and hoofed it to the kitchen to find a plastic container.

Same as last time, which was actually this time when I thought about it, George Diplas's kitchen was a post-apocalyptic wasteland. Cabinet doors hung off their hinges. Boxes were torn. Rice and pasta formed a painful rug on the floor. Good thing I wasn't barefoot or I'd be making sad noises. Last time I'd assumed it was the work of the police. This time I knew better. The demon wasn't big on housework and he'd been rummaging through the kitchen for live animals and charcoal briquettes to munch on.

Plastic containers were right where I expected, in one of the few lower cabinets that hadn't been mauled. Miracle of miracles, they were neatly stacked, with their matching lids present and accounted for. Not knowing what size would best contain a demon, I chose one closest in size to Lottie's vessel. One that would fit a whole pineapple.

I headed for the kitchen door.

A hand grabbed me by the back of the coat and hauled me backwards. It dragged me down behind the kitchen island, out of view of the doorway.

I twisted away from the hand and came face to face with the Man in Black.

CHAPTER TWENTY

"You!" I hissed. "What are you doing?"

"You are here," he muttered.

"Thanks, Captain Obvious."

He nodded to the doorway. "No, *you* are *here*."

Rattling could be heard from the bathroom, and then the telltale sound of someone opening a window. A moment later I heard a woman spitting out a handful of curse words as she landed on the toilet.

It was me.

"Do I really sound like that?" I said, outraged.

A small ditch appeared between his brows. "Like what?"

"Like that!"

"I do not understand."

Someone had never heard a recording of his own face or voice. "What are you going here?"

"Preventing you from meeting yourself. That cannot be allowed to happen."

"Apocalypse. I get it. I went over this already with the dead wimps from the island."

The ditch between his brows dug in deeper, until you

could almost float a barge along the gap. "I still do not understand."

"There's a lot of that going around. Let's long-story-short this. I know you're a guardian of humanity of sorts, and there are others like you. Stephanie Dolas broke an object I was hired to find, a very tall woman popped out, accidentally killed Stephanie, and then she came back to life-ish. Apparently that's a necromancer's fault, and I'll deal with that later. But for right now, Lottie—the other guardian—and I got separated when she portaled us to Athens, and I've time traveled to two days ago. This me is from Wednesday. The one bumbling around the bathroom is Monday's Allie Callas. I'm in the kitchen holding this plastic container because the demon's vessel is broken and we have to put him in something before we send him back to the island. The ghosts responsible for watching over the demon and guardian vessels are in Yiayia's pink jar." I held up the jar as proof that I had a jar.

He stared at me, nonplussed. "I remember when your life was less eventful, Allie Callas."

"You and me both. I'd really like to be searching for a stolen doily right about now, but here we are." Deeper in the house, I heard the grating sounds of me talking to what I now knew was the demon. There were soft footsteps and chuffing, then Cerberus appeared around the side of the island. He glanced at me and the Man in Black, then back at the doorway, and then dragged his tongue from my chin up to my forehead. I scratched behind his ears, then he trotted back to find the other me, tail wagging.

Time travel was weird.

Without Lottie here, I'd assumed that I'd have to wrangle the demon alone, while Gnec and Tut shouted orders and fed me my lines. But this was good, this felt like it could work. The Man in Black was a Lottie or something like her.

I gave him a hopeful sort of look. "Do you know how to shove that demon into this container?"

His face said he was happy about none of this. "How did you learn what I am?"

"The other guardian, Lottie, told me."

The muscle in his temple tightened. "She lacks circumspection."

"I think she wanted someone to talk to after an eternity trapped inside a rock, and I was the closest set of ears. So it's true?"

He looked uncomfortable, like something pointy was being shoved up his posterior. "Yes."

"Were you in a clay pineapple, too?"

"All guardians rest in their vessels until they are needed."

"Were you? Needed, I mean."

His face said that stick was burrowing deeper. "Yes."

"Did you vanquish your foe and shove them back into a handy container that probably won't ever degrade and is appallingly bad for the environment?"

"I ... did not."

"You didn't put them in plastic container or you didn't vanquish them at all?"

His gaze slipped down to my mouth before rising up and settling somewhere beyond my ear. Probably on a box of shattered pasta. "I was created with one purpose and I failed. I do not like to speak of it. For now we must work together to contain the demon. Do you have the guardian's vessel?"

I patted my backpack. "She doesn't have a handbag yet, so it's right here."

He stared at me. Hard. "Yet."

"If Lottie wants a handbag someday, who am I to stand in her way?"

Giving off serious Mr. Darcy vibes, he stared at me down the length of his patrician nose at me. "Once the demon is contained, the guardian must be returned to her vessel to wait once again in case she is needed. There will be no time for shopping."

"What do we do?"

"Give me the vessel and I will try to reach out to the guardian."

All this time we had been whispering and moving so we stayed out of sight. We went quiet again as Other Me returned to the bathroom and scrambled out the window. I knew from experience that I wouldn't be back and it was safe for us to come out.

I withdrew the vessel from my backpack. Discarded the makeshift wrapping. Sat it on the island's marble counter. In case we needed their assistance, I placed the pink jar next to the vessel.

"Should I decant them?"

The man whose face normally gave so little away winced a little. "Their expertise could be useful, as much as it pains me to admit it."

I eased out the cork and set it beside the jar. "Come on out—but do it quietly."

With a gust of wind, Gnec and Tut poured out of the jar and materialized in the kitchen. There was a chorus of oohs and ahhs as they took in the scenery.

"This temple is still standing!" Gnec clapped his hands together. "Where is this marvel?"

"Keep your animal skins on," I said. "You're in a kitchen."

"This is not how I remember kitchens," Tut said. "In my day we had a fire pit, and there was always an animal carcass close by."

"We keep those in the refrigerator now, but I think the owner of the house is a vegan."

Tut blinked at me. "A what?"

"He doesn't eat meat. Only plant-based food."

More blinking. "Is he a goat?"

The Man in Black was waiting impatiently with his arms folded. It took the a moment, but the ghosts suddenly realized he was there. They collectively gasped.

Gnec clutched his chest. "Can it be?"

"You!" Tut said, his voice slathered with a combo of awe and disgust.

"This sounds juicy," I said.

The pair of them fell to their knees. Tut looked up with an expression of shock.

"Why are you here, Disgraced One? Do you seek to redeem yourself?"

"Impossible!" Gnec swore. "No redemption for you!" He spat to the side a couple of times.

The Man in Black—AKA: Disgraced One—kept his gaze level. "I only wish to contain the demon."

Gnec got to his feet. "Now you want to save the world? Ha!"

"What makes you think I care about the world? This is the one I have promised to protect." The Man in Black nodded toward me.

That got my attention. "You promised?"

"Indeed."

"Promised who?"

He said nothing.

I held up my index finger. Pointed it to him. Pointed it to me, "You and me, we need to have a conversation."

"After we have contained the demon. But first I must try to locate the missing guardian. Do nothing without me."

A portal opened directly behind him. He took one step back and he and Lottie's vessel vanished. Wow. He was good. I bet he'd arrived precisely when and where he meant to. Probably he'd had way more practice than Lottie, so comparing them wasn't fair.

I turned to the ghosts. "What can we do while he's doing that?"

"We can do nothing. We have useless hands that go right through things." To prove his point, Gnec performed another round of jazz hands and spirit fingers.

"All those centuries and millennia as ghosts and you didn't learn how to manipulate the real world? No even a chain rattle? A door slam? A twitching curtain?"

"We did not have curtains in our time. They are a frivolous modern invention."

Frivolous? Ha. Greece relied on sheer curtains, shutters, and other forms of window coverings that allowed them to spy. "Work with me here. I have hands. What can I do?"

They exchanged glances. "I suppose you could make ready the intended vessel."

"Great. I can do that—I think. What do I do?"

"You are already doing it. You have the new vessel."

There was movement from the bedroom. "Yoohoo?" the demon said. "Are you still here? You know what I think? I think I remember where we have met each other before. A funny thing just happened. Would you like to hear about it?"

"No, thanks," I called out. "I'm good." I lowered my voice. "Thinking about this time travel thing, what about the pit on Merope? If it opened up after today, so does that mean we didn't defeat the demon and catapult him back to the island in his new sleeping bag?"

They splayed their hands at me. "We do not know."

For a pair of ghosts who were in charge of all of this, they didn't know much.

"So how do we get him" —I gestured in the direction of the bedroom— "into this container? What's the process? Do we set a trap? Maybe a nice piece of cheese or chocolate? Then slam the lid on him when he hops in to get the snack?"

They looked bewildered. "No, you must fight," Tut said.

"Well, not you," Gnec added. "The guardian."

"Yes, the guardian must fight until he is subdued," Tut agreed. "Then there is a ritual to seal the demon inside the ... what did you call it?"

"Plastic."

"Once the ritual is completed, the demon will be sealed inside, and then it must be returned to the island for the rest of eternity."

I rubbed my hands together. "What do we need for the ritual?"

He snorted, which annoyed me because I was really trying here. "You will not find the required items in this kitchen."

"Try me."

"Leaves of the laurel. Do you see a tree?" With his hand shading his eyes, Tut made a big production of looking around the kitchen. "I do not see a tree."

"I do not see a tree either," Gnec said, so he wouldn't be left out.

Laurel leaves.

Ha. They'd have to try harder than that if they wanted to confound me.

"Lucky for you, we don't need a tree." Somewhere in this kitchen was a spice rack. I started opening and closing cabinet doors and drawers until I located George's herbs and spices. He owned a full complement, including bay leaves. I held up the glass container and shook it at them. "How many do we need?"

"Four. Place them around a bowl, if you can find such a thing in here."

Bowls. I'd spotted them earlier. They were sorted by material and nested in nooks on the sides of the island.

"We've got glass, metal, plastic, and ceramic."

"No clay?"

"Ceramic it is," I said, withdrawing the stack of ceramic bowls. "Size?"

Gnec seemed overwhelmed by the range of bowls. "Uh, that one will suffice."

Medium-sized. Good choice. I returned the others to their space in the island and raised my eyebrows at the dead men. "What's next?"

"Salt."

"What kind?"

Tut replied in a lofty, superior voice. "There is only one kind of salt, and that comes from the sea."

"Au contraire, there are myriad salts now. But George does have sea salt." I pulled the kosher sea salt out of the spice cabinet and slapped it next to the bowl. "What else?"

"A guardian," Tut told me.

"We don't have one of those," I admitted, "at least not at the moment. We might have to wing it."

"Can you keep the demon distracted while we wait for the guardian—any guardian—to return?" Gnec said.

"As previously mentioned, I have pepper spray, a stun gun, and withering sarcasm. I can also do dad jokes."

They stared at me.

I performed a game show model's flourish toward the knife block. "And I know how to use a knife. You should see me slice bread."

"A knife is good," Gnec admitted.

"A knife is terrible. Do you know how quickly a demon can heal?" Tut clicked his fingers. "Like that."

"Those voices, I know those voices," the demon said from George's bedroom. "But from where? It will come to me. Are you from the magic box?"

"It's a television," I called out. "And there are no people actually inside it."

"I do not believe you!"

"Open it and find out."

"And leave this bed? Wait! Come here. I need to tell you about the thing that just happened."

"After I use the bathroom," I said.

"Again? You were just in there."

I appealed to the ghosts. "What do I do?"

"Weaken him if you can."

I blew out a long sigh and hoped I wasn't signing my death warrant. I wasn't ready to die yet. Clients were waiting on me to find their things. Toula still needed babysitting services. Leo and I hadn't consummated our alliance, so to speak. And then there was Cerberus. He'd lost one family. Another one would have a negative effect on his psyche. I couldn't do that to him.

Oh my God. Everyone was right. Cerberus was *my* dog.

I had to get home to my dog.

In the master bedroom, Plastic and electronics shattered as the demon followed my advice.

"The demon!" Tut hissed. "Go! Go! There is no time to wait for the guardians to return."

The Man in Black wouldn't be happy if I charged into a fight with a demon. But he should know me by now. Charging in was kind of my thing, even when it was accidental. "What happens if I don't?"

Tut mimed a big, melodramatic explosion with his hands. "Big bad-a boom!"

"Quick question. If I'm back in the past, didn't what happened already happen? Did we win? Did we lose?"

"Why is she asking us these questions?" Gnec said to his pal.

"Never mind," I said.

My Greek Orthodox programming moved my hand in the form of the cross: forehead to chest, right shoulder to left. It might not help but it wouldn't hurt. With that out of the way, I yanked a serrated bread knife out of the knife block. Maybe the jagged teeth would buy me a few seconds. With the knife in one hand, pepper spray in the other, and everything else within grabbing distance, I crept toward George Diplas's bedroom.

The demon had finally risen and shone. He was wearing the covers as a cape, stomping on the television's battered remains with a foot in dire need of a podiatrist's services. There were claws on that thing that could gut me, curly things that corkscrewed upward and ended in a vicious tip.

Thank you, but no thank you.

And yet, there was no other option. Forging onward was the only way. Surely one of my groovy tools would work. If not the knife then the stun gun, the pepper spray, or salt from the shaker I'd tucked into my pocket. Holy water? Maybe. Hopefully one of those would take him down or hold him off long enough for the Man in Black to return with Lottie. In my imagination they kicked demon butt together.

Here and now in reality, however ...

The demon's foot crashed down on the bones of George Diplas's television one more time. His head rolled around to face me. "You. You are up to something."

I played dumb to buy time. "Who, me? I don't know what you mean."

He raised what I think was a hand. "You were here, then you left, and then you were here again. But you were wearing a different skin and you were accompanied by a familiar. And now you are back again in this skin, and without your familiar. You know what I think?"

"No. Please enlighten me."

"I think perhaps you have a twin—maybe an evil one. Or is it you who is the evil twin?"

Was he high?

Yes. Yes, he was. High on a diet of soap operas.

"You've got me," I said. "I have a twin. But she's the evil one. I'm the nice one."

"Did she reproduce with your mate when you were sick in a physician's bed?"

"She did." I shook my fist in mock anger. "The dirty, rotten she-dog."

"I understand. I, too, was deceived once."

"You were? How?"

The demon let out a big chest-shuddering sigh and plopped down on the edge of the bed, all bundled up in the covers. "I was running around the universe, doing regular demon things—murder, destruction, mayhem, wedgies, you know—and then some men performed a silly ritual and trapped me in a clay pot. A clay pot! I was trapped in pottery, and now I am the laughing stock of my kind."

"Rude."

"I was just trying to live my authentic life, you know? Who am I if I am not allowed to be myself? Woe is me."

"That is truly woeful." Were the guardians back yet? My ears said no. I hoped my ears were wrong and that the guardians would charge in at any moment. "Then what happened."

"I lay in wait for thousands of years, with only my nemesis and some ghosts to keep me company. But I could not talk to any of them. I could only feel their contempt for me. Then one day, a man came to the island and carried my vessel to the mainland."

"What man?"

"Who cares?" He threw up his hands. "Your mortals are all the same."

"I could say the same about demons."

"Why is she taunting him?" the ghost whispered in the hallway. "Taunting a demon never goes well."

"Wrong!" he bellowed. "We are all different! How many demons have you seen, eh?"

He had me there. "Three, including you."

"There are trillions of us. Three is nothing. Maybe the other two were my cousins, though The family resemblance is strong between us."

"They're succubi."

He hissed. "They are no cousins of mine."

"But they look like you. At least when they're not dressed as people."

"I could look like people, too, if I wanted."

My muscles unclenched a fraction. Here I was trying to buy time, and he was practically giving it away.

"Really?" I poured oodles of doubt into the question.

"You do not believe me?"

"Now you're putting words in my mouth, but ... seeing is believing."

He swung his legs off the bed. "I will prove it!"

"You don't have to. I believe you. Really, I do." My tone said no—no I did not.

"I am going to prove it and there is nothing you can do to stop me!"

Shucking off the covers, he stood, resplendent in all his gory glory. Goopy bits of viscera everywhere. Limbs where limbs didn't go. An excess of holes. Strange hair. This time both my eyes twitched. They couldn't believe I was forcing them to look at the demon.

Then he went up in cloud of glitter. When the bits landed, there was a puppy in their place. A roly poly chocolate Labrador.

I bit back the cooing noises.

The dumbass ghosts rushed in to the bedroom, tittering like a pair of old ladies. "Look at it!" Gnec cooed. "A dog! I have not seen one of those in thousands of years!"

I rolled my eyes. No wonder they needed a guardian to kick butt. They couldn't be trusted to exist on their own, without a supernatural babysitter.

"It's not a puppy," I said. "That's the demon."

"A puppy?" the demon-puppy said. "What kind of person is that?"

"It's not a person at all, although the best people I've ever met were dogs."

"What about this?"

The puppy vanished in more glitter. This time he was a dolphin.

"Even less of a person than before."

"I am out of practice, okay? You try shapeshifting after thousands of years in a clay vessel."

More glitter.

Poof. He was a horse.

"Not even close."

Poof. A guinea pig.

"Nope."

Poof. Potato.

"That's a vegetable."

"Humans, potatoes, who can tell the difference?"

Poof. A toddler.

"Right species, wrong size."

"Have you seen the damage a small child can do?" Gnec asked me. As someone with a niece and nephew, the answer was yes.

At the sound of Gnec's voice, the toddler froze. "You."

The ghost glanced around in sudden panic. "Me?"

"I know you and I know your voice. It just now suddenly came to me."

"Well, I do not know you, therefore it is impossible that you know me!"

"Or me!" Tut said.

"Now that I think about it, that whining voice is familiar to me, too." The human toddler assumed the thinking position.

"Do something," Gnec hissed at me.

The demon snapped his fingers. "You are the two that imprisoned me in that clap pot!"

Gnec huffed. "I most certainly am not!"

"Yes, you were. You and that other one with the bad hair."

Because his ghost-skin was thinner than cling wrap, Tut wafted into the bedroom. "What is wrong with my hair?" His feelings sounded hurt.

"Did you look in a still body of water recently?" the demon said.

"Of course not! I live on an island! All our water moves."

"I knew it!" The demon poked a hole in the air with his pointer finger. "It is you! Both of you!" He glanced around, suddenly terror stricken. "Where is she?"

"Don't tell—" I started, but the dead man cut me off.

"Missing!" Tut wrung his hands. "We cannot find her. The other guardian went to find her but he is still not back."

Wow. Someone had actually put these clowns in charge of managing a demon. No wonder they were dead—they had no survival skills whatsoever.

"Are you kidding me?" I said. "You two are the worst."

Terror melted off the demon's toddler face, revealing a wicked grin. If he told me to close my eyes and open my mouth, there's no way I'd fall for it. Nothing good happens when a toddler tells you to open your mouth and close your eyes.

Nothing.

The demon swayed. "So there is no guardian here, is that what you are saying?"

The dead men looked at me. I swallowed. There were no good answers here, only correct ones. And the correct ones were a one-way street to certain death. Mentally, I catalogued my weapons. Surely something would work. At the very least, work-ish.

Holy water, pepper spray, personal sized fan, salt …

This was a job for eenie, meanie, miney, and mo. Mo chose pepper spray.

I did it, I pepper-sprayed the toddler.

The toddler fell back, kicking its arms and legs. Anyone watching would think I hadn't let him have ice cream before dinner. His screams shook the house on its earthquake-proof foundations.

"What did you do?" the ghosts cried.

"What did I do? Are you kidding me? You started it! Did you have to tell him there was no guardian around?"

The demon was up on his feet again, hopping around, clawing at his eyes with his baby fingers. Against my better judgment, I experienced a pang of empathy for the injured kid. I hated to see a child in peril, even when they were a demon in baby form.

That didn't stop me from tipping holy water on his head and experiencing relief as steam poured off his tiny body.

And then he went up in a cloud of glitter—black this time—and the demon was back.

This time he was furious.

CHAPTER TWENTY-ONE

When I was a teenager I hated horror movies. Not because so many of them were poorly produced, with limited storylines, but because I knew the things in them had the potential to be real. When you have tea parties with ghosts, it's not a leap to assume the other monsters are real, too. Maybe zombies didn't always crave brains. Maybe some werewolves were content to be vegans. Maybe a vampire could develop the smarts to stay away from Buffy. None of that changed my mind. I preferred movies that provided genuine escapism; no one wants to sit and watch films about their life.

And now here I was, living my horror movie of a life, for however long I had left. Seconds, if the boiling fury in the demon's eyes was any indication. All five thousand or so of them. I'd never noticed it before, because he was wearing one of those sleep hats like Wee Willie Winkie or Ebenezer Scrooge when the ghosts rocked up to give him the Come to Jesus spiel, but his whole head was covered in tiny, blinking eyes.

Good thing I wasn't ommetaphobic, or I'd be freaking out like these two buffoons who had accompanied me. They were waving their transparent arms, scrambling down the hall. Why didn't they just dematerialize?

If we made it out of here, Yiayia needed to give them a crash course in being dead.

If.

The odds, the way I was calculating them, were not in my favor.

"Scream, mortal," the demon said with its gaping gash of a mouth. Saliva pooled on the floor.

"No."

He recoiled. "Why not?"

"Because if I scream, people might run to my aid. I'm not going to put them in harm's way."

He rolled his thousands of eyes. "By all the stupid deities, not another one."

"Another one?"

"A goodie goodie. A defender of humanity. A decent ... *person*." He pressed down on the last word like a boot squishing down in dog poop. "Your kind are all so gross. The smell alone makes me want to vomit. Anyway! Now I am going to kill you, because I can. And then when I am done pulling your eyes out of their sockets and absorbing them, I will deal with those dead *malakes*."

"I think that's you," I called out to the dead men, who, by the sounds of things, were scrambling to climb back into the salt jar. "By the way, do you have issues with salt?" My weapons were still on my mind. A fan wouldn't do diddly to a demon, so I was down to sodium as my final weapon of choice. At the very least I could give the demon high blood pressure. Monday me had made a salt circle around the room. The line was still unbroken. Maybe it would slow him down.

"Salt? What is salt?"

"Why do you think he was on an island surrounded by sea water?" the Man in Black said, stepping out of nowhere.

He had returned alone. There was no time to grill him about Lottie's whereabouts. I reached into my pocket and flung a handful of salt into the demon's eyes.

The demon roared. He must have had an endless supply of oxygen in his lungs—if he had lungs—because the scream kept on coming. The air vibrated, thumping against my eardrums. My inner ear filed a complaint and sent me tilting sideways, waves of vertigo crashing over me. The demons myriad eyes steamed. As I struggled to stand upright, they began to pop out of their sockets, landing on the floor with dull thumps and rolling under the furniture.

Dead Cat's dream come true.

The demon lunged at me. Monday me's salt circle bounced him back to the center of the room.

The Man in Black rushed to my side. "Where is the vessel?"

"Kitchen."

"Get it," he ordered.

"Can't you get it? I'm the one with the salt." I threw more salt at the demon for fun. It was easier to be mean to him now that he was no longer a toddler.

The Man in Black glowered at me. "I am a guardian."

"Was," Gnec called out. "Now you are the Disgraced One."

The vibrations ratcheted up another notch as the demon continued throwing his tantrum.

"It matters not that I am no longer an official guardian, bound to my vessel. What matters is that I am the only one here who can commit this demon back to his."

That's when the demon whipped out his leg knives.

Technically, if you wanted to be nit-picky, they weren't actual knives. The sharp, pointy things protruding from his lower limbs were made of something like bone and they were conical, ending in a sharp point. Leg lances. That was more accurate. And from the way he was kicking them around, I gathered he wanted to joust.

"Do you have a plan?" I asked him.

The Man in Black flicked his eyes to me for a millisecond. "I was created with all the knowledge and power required to defeat a demon."

"And that includes a plan for his leg lances?"

His hands flexed. "The vessel, Allie Callas."

He didn't have to tell me a third time. With my stress levels pegged out at the max, I raced down the hall, slid into the kitchen, and snatched the plastic container and its lid off the island. The ghosts were tussling, struggling to be the first one back into the jar. So I grabbed that, too. If they wanted inside this jar, they would have to follow me back to the bedroom.

I skidded down the hall again. Things were heating up. The Man in Black had a big sword that he hadn't been carrying before. I didn't want to ask where he'd been hiding it. Some things, such as butt swords, were better left as mysteries. The demon's lances were on fire now, and he was waving his arms like he was trying to board a bus in any village, town, or city in Greece.

There was no fighting that. The Man in Black couldn't possibly be prepared to battle a creature mimicking a Greek widow boarding public transportation.

As I stood there juggling the GladWare and the jar, the Man in Black stepped over the salt line and swung his sword. The blade sliced clean through one of the demon's arms.

Victory.

Wait. Not victory.

Before the limb hit the ground, another one sprouted in its place. Small at first—a teeny tiny baby hand and arm—but within seconds it was full size.

The demon sprang at the Man in Black.

The guardian was ready. He angled out of the demon's reach before the demon collided with the salt's protective wall.

I flung more salt at the demon. His skin bubbled, oozing foul smelling liquid. He howled again and the whole house rattled. Somewhere, a window shattered.

The Man in Black darted behind the demon and thrust his sword in its back, burying the blade up to the hilt.

The house heaved. Monday me's salt line was no match for physics. Grains scattered, breaking the protective magic.

The Demon's foot shot out, slamming a wall. The force sent the wall crashing from one end of the house to the other.

"I hope that was not a load bearing wall," Tut said.

Gritting his teeth, the Man in Black pushed out instructions. "Shut up and make ready the ritual."

Gnec wafted to my side. "Do you have the items?"

I presented the ghosts with the goods.

They did jazz hands and spirit fingers at me. "You will have to prepare the items for the Disgraced One."

"The Disgraced One is the only thing saving your bacon right now."

They made faces. Neither was happy about that situation. Too bad.

"What is bacon?" Tut asked.

There was no time to explain bacon. While the demon and the Man in Black whirled around the room, body parts and weapons flying, I crouched down and followed the dead men's instructions. Plastic vessel in the bowl with the lid sealed. A moat of salt. Bay leaves placed at the four cardinal directions.

"Now what?"

"We wait for the guardian to say the words," Gnec told me.

"They're just waiting on the words," I called out to the Man in Black.

After that, things unfolded in slow motion.

Twisting his whole body, the Man in Black swung at the demon's head, pouring every ounce of energy into what was intended to be a deathblow.

The demon ducked.

With no neck to stop the sword, the weapon kept on going, and the guardian along with it.

With the flick of his foot, the demon kicked the Man in Black through the exterior wall. That had to hurt. Like all Greek walls, the wall's bones were a combination of concrete and rebar and steel beams.

Gnec and Tut huddled together and tutted like a pair of old hens. "This guardian cannot win. He was created to fight another. We need the other guardian. Only she can find the demon's weakness and wield it against him."

"You're saying Lottie doesn't intrinsically know the demon's weakness?" I said.

"No. She must discover that for herself during the battle. But she has an instinct for such things. She was created that way."

It was useless. The Man in Black couldn't defeat the demon, and his female counterpart was missing in time and space.

We were going to lose. I should have known this. The earthquake. It happened here, at George's house. It wasn't a regular earthquake. It was the result of us losing and the demon winning.

I tried Googling the precise time, but my phone's browser freaked out and refused to open. The earthquake hadn't happened yet.

Text messages. On Monday—the other Monday—Leo had texted me while I was on my way back to Merope. From there I was able to extrapolate approximately when the earthquake occurred.

The clock said we only had minutes before the big bang.

But for some reason I couldn't focus on the time. Something else was niggling me, something I'd missed. Tut or Gnec had said something important and in the heat of the battle my brain had slipped right over it.

I rolled back the reel in my head and hit replay.

They said Lottie had to *find* the demon's weakness.

Find it.

Seeing ghosts was something I did. It wasn't a talent as such—at least I didn't see it that way. You try attempting to pee in your elementary school bathroom with the ghosts of long dead teachers and lunch ladies trying to get your attention. My actual talent was finding things. My whole career hinged on my ability to locate items, people, information, anything that eluded others.

What if I could find the demon's weakness?

Was that arrogant? Was I a fool?

Toula would probably say yes to both. Good thing my sister wasn't here.

Armed with one bad idea and not a lot of hope, I charged into the fray. The Man in Black had dropped his butt sword on the way out. I slid across the floor and snatched it up.

Well, tried to snatch it up. That thing was heavy. But I managed to get it up off the ground and into the air. Now I had to find a good place to put it. Somewhere in the demon, preferably.

"What are you doing?" the demon said with utter amazement. "You are not one of those loser guardians. You are some type of loser, but I have not decided what kind yet."

"I'm not, am I?"

"Who are you?" He inspected me with what was left of his eyes. "What are you?"

I waggled the sword a bit for dramatic effect.

("That is good," Gnec said. "I like the drama.")

"As Buffy Anne Summers said, I'm just a girl. But older. Look, I'm a woman, okay?"

The demon held up two of his hands. "Okay. Should we fight now?"

"I don't really want to, but I feel like I have to. Are you good with that?"

"Fighting and destruction is kind of my thing."

"Cool. Finding things is mine."

"I do not see how that is relevant."

The sword felt unnatural in my hands. Clumsy. Clearly made for someone else.

The Man in Black.

Who was limping through the place where the exterior wall used to be, gripping his arm, his black overcoat tattered, tall leather boots scuffed. His mouth was murmuring words I couldn't make out. He sought out my gaze with his and held it steady. Then, he nodded once. Granting me permission to proceed or permission to die.

I nodded back.

Closed my eyes.

Listened to my heartbeat.

And swung.

The demon never made another sound after that. But he didn't go quietly. The ground began to heave beneath me. The Man in Black threw himself across the room, pushing me to safety just as a schism appeared in the floor, ripping George Diplas's fancy bedroom in two. The air was filled with terrible noise that reverberated in my chest and clogged my ears. Furniture toppled as, with our arms around each others waists, we navigated the hallway.

When we reached the front door, the Man in Black went to shove me out ahead of him.

There was an almighty groaning, and then everything went black.

CHAPTER TWENTY-TWO

I woke to the sound of ghost chatter. Tut and Gnec were arguing over whether or not fish was better cooked over coals or boiled in sea water.

So. I wasn't dead. That was nice.

I opened one eye to see George Diplas's well-heeled neighbors, sweeping in their yards, pretending they'd held brooms before. One of them was sweeping the dust back toward her front door.

"I'm okay," I called out, even though no one had asked. I rolled onto my stomach and flailed like a seal. Finally, I made it to my feet.

The earthquake hadn't stuck around long. Greece's never did. And this one was as specific as a tornado, targeting one home and leaving the rest untouched. George's house was a pile of shattered building materials and furniture. Not a single wall stood upright.

"Man in Black?" I called out.

Nothing.

For crying out loud. "What's his name?" I asked the ghosts.

They had the audacity to look surprised. "Who?" Gnec said.

"The Man in Black. The other guardian."

They shrugged. "Guardians do not have names," Gnec said. "He is just a guardian."

"You can call him the Disgraced One. We do," Tut added.

I spotted something sitting neatly on a pile of rubble. The plastic container with its lid sealed. Previously clear, the plastic was now the color of oil smoke. I picked through the mess to scoop it up. Sitting nearby were the original clay vessel I'd pilfered from the unnamed island for Adonis Diplas and Yiayia's pink jar. I placed them beside the new and hopefully improved demon vessel.

"Surely you mean the guardian who saved my life and managed to get the demon back into its prison."

"Pfft! You were the one who felled the demon," Gnec said, shaking his hands at the sky. "We saw it with our own eyes."

"That was a lucky swing. He did all the set up." I glanced around. "Where is he, anyway?"

"We saw nothing. We heard nothing. We know nothing."

The pair of them were about as useful as boobs on a boar hog. But I didn't miss the way they both went shifty eyed.

"Where?"

"Would you look at the time?" They lunged at the pink jar. Too slow. I was there with the handheld fan. I blasted them away from the jar and put a cork in it. They dead men wailed but they didn't talk.

They would. Eventually.

In the distance, emergency vehicles were clanging their sirens. They were headed this way and I didn't want to stick around to give them answers. Not when I didn't have anything useful to tell them. They wouldn't believe me and I didn't feel like lying. I just wanted to go home.

Crap. That was the one thing I couldn't do. I was still in

the past, and other me was already on her—my—way back to Merope. The only thing to do was hole up in a hotel here in Athens for a couple of days and figure out how to reintegrate myself back into the proper timeline. Now that I knew where the Cake Emporium was located here in Athens, maybe Betty and Jack Honeychurch could help.

Speaking of Betty and Jack ...

The only other thing to survive the demon-quake were the eclairs from the Cake Emporium. The plastic was torn but the box was intact. I flipped open the lid and scooped a handful of cake into my mouth. The sugar rushed through my body and got to work lifting my mood. The crash wouldn't be pretty, but right now I didn't care.

With the container under one arm and the clay vessel in the crook of my other arm, I set off down the street. I didn't look back.

There was a noise behind me.

I looked back, making a liar out of myself.

Lottie was standing by a portal, gripping a familiar woman by the neck. Kyria Ekonomou's feet were kicking the air. Her dress and shoes were still smeared with pumpkin pie. "This one was trying to attack you."

"Let her go," I said.

She dropped the woman, who sprinted back to her yard.

"I have crossed oceans of time to find you, and at least three lakes."

I offered Lottie the box. "Chocolate eclair?"

"I will try your chocolate eclair."

We sat on the sidewalk and ate choux pastries while emergency vehicles trundled up the street. They stopped outside the remains of George Diplas's house. I really hoped he had better insurance than the average Greek. God, Jesus, and the Virgin Mary weren't known for writing timely checks.

"I like this eclair," Lottie said as we ate with our hands

right out of the box. "I like your coffee, too. And cheese. What else does this time have?"

"One less demon, I know that much. What happens now? Do you go back to the island?"

Gnec's indignation was palpable. He threw in hand waving for effect. "She cannot go back to the island! She failed to do the one job she was created for! She is as much a disgrace as that other!"

Lottie burning gaze bored into me. "He was here then?"

I indicated yes, the Man in Black had been here. She slumped and reached for more pastries. "I have failed."

"You are a failure!" Tut said with entirely too much glee. I wasn't about to sit back and let them make Lottie feel bad.

"Let me point out that the two of you failed, too."

That squeezed a pair of grumbles out of them. At least they had some self-awareness. "We did not think about it like that," Tut said.

Lottie was morose as she stuffed more eclair in her mouth. "I have nowhere to go," she said, spraying crumbs. "No purpose. What am I for if not guarding the demon vessel?"

"You could come back to Merope. Wait—can you get us a portal back to my time?"

Her big shoulders rose and fell. "Of course. After thousands of jumps I have fine tuned my ability to use the portals."

Small mercies.

The ghosts spluttered. "She cannot just go and live on Merope!" Gnec said.

"Why not?"

"Because she cannot!"

"One good reason," I said.

"Give us one moment to think."

They huddled together in the middle of the road. Then: "We cannot think of one."

"That settles it," I said. "Come back to Merope with me. I have a couch. You can stay there for now."

"I have no need of sleep, but it would be my honor to protect you from harm."

It seemed my life was full of protectors now, and yet I still felt battered and bruised.

I stood and brushed myself off, then I placed the clay vessel in my backpack and tucked the plastic container under my arm. I offered the guardian my other hand and tried to pull her off the sidewalk. That didn't work, with our size and weight difference, so she had to do most of the work. Once we were up, I opened the jar and herded a grumbling Gnec and Tut inside using the handheld fan.

Lottie opened a portal and moments later we stepped into the courtyard at my apartment building, where the fisherman was still fishing for fish that weren't there. His ghost was at my window, the tip of his nose visible on this side of the glass..

Lottie raised her face to the thin winter sun and inhaled. "The pits have returned to their own dimensions, and balance has been restored. All traces of the demon's stench in this world have gone."

Another small mercy. Or maybe a big one. Right now I felt weirdly unlucky. Something had changed but I couldn't put my finger on what.

"That's good news."

We trudged upstairs. In the stairwell, she stopped me

"What was he like?" she asked, almost shy.

"Who? The demon?"

She nodded.

"He had a lot of eyes and a serious addiction to daytime television. You never met him?"

"No."

There was a knock in the jar. I wiggled out the cork and

Tut squeezed out. He cleared his throat. He held up an authoritative finger. "Guardians are never allowed to meet their foes until they are needed. It prevents fraternization. You cannot kill your friend."

Julius Caesar and countless others probably begged to differ.

We went home. I set the demon vessel and the guardian vessel in my closet until tomorrow. I cuddled my dog and gave him the good news about his forever home. He grinned at me like he always knew.

Then I settled in for a call I didn't want to make but had to.

"Allie Callas! It is me, Pavlos Makris!"

Given that I'd called him, his identity was never in doubt.

"I need to speak to George. Can you arrange that, please?"

"Maybe, I am not sure." His voice moved away from the phone. "Laki, can I arrange calls to my clients?"

There was a pained sigh somewhere in the background, then, "Yes."

"Yes!" George announced in my ear.

"Want me to take care of it?" Laki, I presumed, asked him.

"Good idea! This is exactly the kind of thing I do not pay you for."

Somebody had obviously acquired an unpaid intern to do all the work.

The phone swapped hands and Laki took over. "I can arrange that for you, but it will take some time. Can I call you back on this number?"

I assured him that was fine and I'd be waiting for the call.

Next up: the other thing I didn't want to do. When we left, I locked the door. Then Lottie, Cerberus, and I set out for the More Super Market. Adonis had hired me to do a job, and now I was finished. All that was left was delivering the truth.

At least he believed. That was half the problem solved.

There was no sign of Stephanie cleaning roofs or roads this time. When I went inside, Adonis Diplas was tearing open boxes of baby formula. Stephanie was polishing each one before she placed it perfectly on the shelf. Her ghost was flat on her back on the counter, sighing.

Adonis smiled at me. I hated to see it. Bringing him joy made me rankle—and boy was I about to bring him joy.

"You look like you've got good news," he said to me.

"Really? Because my face doesn't feel like it's doing the good news thing. I've got this set-in frown that might be sticking around for a while."

"You don't like me, do you?"

"I don't trust you any further than I could kick you, and physics says I couldn't kick you far at all. Unless we were on the moon."

"This is interesting," Ghost Stephanie said. "Too bad I am not alive to tell anyone."

"You can trust me," he said. "Nobody can keep a secret like me."

Ghost Stephanie sat up. "I know his secrets. I have seen them on his phone when he does not know I am looking."

My eye twitched. Sooner or later Ghost Stephanie and I needed to talk. She had information, and in my business it was important to know things. But for now, my business was family business.

"You were right, George didn't kill those men."

He broke down the empty box. "Go on."

"The pest he was trying to get rid of was a demon, who was responsible for the murders. He won't be a problem again."

Fingers crossed.

"So George is off the hook?"

"Theoretically, yes. In practice, probably not." He shot me

a questioning look. "There were times the demon did the dirty work on his own, after George left the scene. But there were other times he took George's body for a spin and committed murder. There's no way to explain that to the police or a judge. They deal with facts and evidence and packets of money they can see and touch. A demon using George's body is still George's body doing the crime. That's if you could even get them to believe in demons."

His lips flattened into a thin, tight line. He tore into another box. "I paid you to get him out."

"No—you paid me to prove he didn't do it. And I did. To you. But only because you believe."

"*Gamo tin panayia mou.*"

The Virgin Mary wasn't about to help him—not with that mouth.

"I'm sorry," I said.

"Can you get him out?"

"I already—"

"Not legally."

"What? No."

"Please."

I plucked a bag of chips off the shelf. Oregano and feta. "Leave the money on the counter?"

"Sure," he said. He didn't look happy. Adonis Diplas wasn't done with me. I could almost hear the hounds in the distance. But I couldn't stick around. There was other business to put to bed. Seeing Stephanie made me remember that we still had a growing zombie problem. And as luck would have it, my phone rang, giving me another reason to bail.

"Samaras said you had been asking questions about my job," Panos Grekos said from his desk in the coroner's office.

I pushed through the door and reeled slightly as the cold air slapped me. "No, I asked him to ask you if any other dead people suddenly became undead."

"That's the same thing."

"It's really not."

The chair creaked as he leaned back and settled in for a tall tale. "Explain how."

"Stephanie Dolas was dead when you examined her and made the call. You got it right."

"I knew it."

"But then, for whatever reason, she suddenly got up and continued about her day."

"Someone is messing with me."

"Do you believe in zombies?"

His silence suggested that I'd lost my marbles. Which wasn't out of the question, except that everyone else could also see that Stephanie wasn't her old, do-nothing self.

But then he surprised me. "I believe in most things. That way I am never surprised. I do not like surprises."

Me either. Even good surprises needed to arrive after ample warning, and preferably on the heels of a written invitation.

"How many have come back after you pronounced them dead?"

"Five. The Dolas girl and four others."

"Walk me through it."

"What is there to tell? The calls came through for me to take them away, and after I confirmed they were dead, they came back to life. Except for Kyria Stamati. She jumped up just as I was arriving."

"Maybe she wasn't dead."

"She was decapitated."

"Then she was definitely dead."

"That is what I would have said if the paramedics had not claimed otherwise. They think we are playing a game, competing to see which of us can get more wins."

"You turned it into a game?"

"In this business you have to take your fun where you can find it, otherwise things get dark. But now they are winning, and now I will have to kill some people myself to catch up." He laughed at his own joke, which made one of us. Then his laughter died and his voice registered concern. "Do you think Ketty and that Dimi Pantazis boy are turning my dead people into zombies to win?"

"I think life is strange and so is death."

"Maybe you are not so bad," he said. "Even if you are weird."

"Coming from you, that's a series of words that I don't know how to react to."

I disconnected and considered my next move. During the call, the penny had finally dropped. The common denominator. It was obvious when I thought about it. I should have realized on day one, but I was swept away with playing Indiana Jones and then my life devolving into a comedic retelling of *The Exorcist*. My life wasn't itself lately. Or worse, maybe it was.

I threw my leg over my bicycle and turned the front wheel toward the hospital. Lottie tailed me, invisible to the rest of the world. Once she scared a couple of chickens and almost hit a power pole, but otherwise she did just fine. Cerberus kept an eye on her.

There were two ambulances in the emergency bay, but only one paramedic in sight. Dimi Pantazis was crouched down, polishing the ambulance's wheels with a soft cloth.

"We meet again," he said, throwing me a warm smile.

"How are you finding Merope?"

"I like it here. Of course my *mama* and *baba* keep calling to say they are dying now. Between them they have had half the cancers and some fatal diseases the internet has never heard of. But they always recover."

I kicked the stand on my bicycle and sat on the curb close

to where he was polishing. Lottie landed nearby and kept her eye on our surroundings. Cerberus seemed to know hospitals were a no-pee zone, so he sat by my bike, ever vigilant. "How long have you been a necromancer?"

He took his sweet time answering, and when he did, it was without tearing attention away from his task. "Since I died last year."

"But you're not dead." If he was, I would know.

"Not now. But I was for about five minutes. When they brought me back, I came back different."

"What happened?"

"Electrocuted. You know how wiring is in some of the old villages. Ground is something you stand on. I went to plug in a hairdryer and ... *bzzt*. Next thing I knew I woke up in the hospital with my *mama* crying over me."

"She must love you very much."

"She was practicing for my funeral."

Made sense. Nobody did performance grief like Greeks. "When you did you first realize what you could bring the dead back?"

"Not for months. I just thought I was good at my job. Then I realized I'm not good at my job, I'm raising the dead without even trying."

The accidental necromancer. "There's a tiny problem."

He bobbed his head. "They come back different, yes?"

That was one way of putting it. "Whatever you're doing, it's bringing their bodies back but not their souls. They're coming back in two pieces."

He looked horrified. "Two pieces?"

I winced. There was no way to soften the blow. "A zombie and a ghost."

He sat back, cloth in one hand, face buried in the other. "I have to ... I can't ... what do I do?"

"Unfortunately I have no idea. Yet. But for now maybe stop bringing people back. Can you do that?"

"But they will die."

"They will, but sometimes that's supposed to happen."

"Is it? Was *he* supposed to die?"

"Who?"

"The man from the waiting room. He said he knew you. He said he left you too soon."

My heart didn't stop, but it felt that way. Icy wind sliced across my cheeks. The whole island was suddenly wreathed in low-hanging cloud. But when I focused, the sun was hitched to the pale blue sky, not a stratus in sight. "The man? What did he look like?"

He shrugged. "Tall. Dark hair."

My phone rang. The screen said Pavlos Makris but I knew it was the intern, Laki. "I have to take this."

"I am afraid there is a problem with Kyrios Diplas. He is—"

"Gone!" Pavlos shrieked in the background. "He is gone! Who will pay me now? I was going to move out of this shed and into a bigger shed!"

"Gone," Laki confirmed.

"I don't understand. Did they let him go?"

"No. He vanished earlier today."

I thanked him for his time and blew out a long sigh as I tried to compile my thoughts. George Diplas had vanished. That was a problem for later. For now, my head was trying to wrap itself around Dimi Pantazis, unintentional necromancer.

Squeezing details about a man's looks from another man was futile, and Dimi was new to Merope. He wouldn't know Andreas, the man I'd loved. The man who had left me before we'd had a chance to really live.

Frantic, I thumbed through the pictures on my phone until I located one of Andreas. I showed Dimi the screen.

"Is this him?"

He nodded once. "I think so. Who is he?"

"Was. He was my fiancé, Andreas. What else did he say?"

Dimi twisted the cloth in his hands. His face was suddenly pale. "He wants to come back for you, and he wants me to help him."

ALSO BY ALEX A. KING

Kat Makris: Greek Mafia Series

Disorganized Crime (Kat Makris #1)
Trueish Crime (Kat Makris #2)
Doing Crime (Kat Makris #3)
In Crime (Kat Makris #4)
Outta Crime (Kat Makris #5)
Night Crime (Kat Makris #6)
Good Crime (Kat Makris #7)
White Crime (Kat Makris #8)
Christmas Crime (Kat Makris #9)
Winter Crime (Kat Makris #10)
Party Crime (Kat Makris #11)
Safari Crime (Kat Makris #12)
Family Crime (Kat Makris #13)
Big Crime (Kat Makris #14)

Penny Post: Myth Agent Series

So Much Bull (Penny Post Myth Agent #1)
Pain in the Asp (Penny Post Myth Agent #2)
Sirentology (Penny Post Myth Agent #3)

Greek Ghouls Series

Family Ghouls (Greek Ghouls #1)
Royal Ghouls (Greek Ghouls #2)
Stolen Ghouls (Greek Ghouls #3)
Golden Ghouls (Greek Ghouls #4)
Holy Ghouls (Greek Ghouls #5)
Mean Ghouls (Greek Ghouls #6)

Revenge Services Inc.

Kick the Bucket (Revenge Services Inc. #1)
Belly Up (Revenge Services Inc. #2)

Women of Greece Series

Seven Days of Friday (Women of Greece #1)
One and Only Sunday (Women of Greece #2)
Freedom the Impossible (Women of Greece #3)
Light is the Shadow (Women of Greece #4)
No Peace in Crazy (Women of Greece #5)
Summer of the Red Hotel (Women of Greece #6)
Rotten Little Apple (Women of Greece #7)
The Last of June (Women of Greece #8)
Forever and Never (Women of Greece #9)

Stand-alone Titles

Pride and All This Prejudice
The Summer War

As Alex King:

Lambs

Tall (The Morganites #1)

Small (The Morganites #2)

As Hannah Green:

Wood (The Protectorate Series #1)

Reliquary (The Reliquary Series #1)

GREEK GLOSSARY

Ade (ah-thay): An expression of pleasure or anger. A bit like "c'mon" or "go on".

Ade gamisou (*a-they ga-mee-soo*): Go make sweet monkey love to yourself.

Ai sto dialo (*eye-sto-thya-lo*): Go to the devil.

A-pah-pah! (a-pa-pa): A sound Greeks make when they disapprove of something.

Archidia (ar-hee-thee-ah): Testicles.

Booboona (boo-boo-nah): A moron.

Despinida (des-pe-nee-tha): Miss. As in "Miss Jackson, if you're nasty."

Faka: (fah-kah): Mousetrap.

Ftero: (Fff-teh-ro): Feather.

Gamo (*ga-mo*): Fuck.

Gamos (ga-moss): A wedding.

Gamo tin putana (ga-mo teen pu-tah-nah): Make sweet monkey love to a woman of purchasable affections.

Gamo ton kerato (ga-mo ton ke-rah-toh): Make sweet monkey love to a horn. Why? I don't know.

Hezo (he-zo): The act of pooping on something.

Hondros (hon-dross): Fat.
   Kaka (ka-ka): Poop

Kalamari (kal-a-ma-ree): Calamari. Squid.

Kalo ste (kah-lo-stay): Welcome! Good to see you!

Katsika (Ka-tsee-kah): A nanny goat.

Kavla (ka-vla): An erection of the non-architectural kind.

Klasimo (Kla-see-mo): A fart.

Klania (klah-n-yah): Also a fart.

Klanies (klah-n-yez): Multiple farts.

Kolos (ko-loss): Butt

Kolotripa (ko-lo-tree-pah): The hole in a butt. You know the one. (Hopefully it's just one, otherwise please consult a physician.)

Kota (ko-tah): Hen.

Kotsoboles (kot-so-bo-lez): Gossip

Koulouraki (koo-loo-ra-kee): a Greek cookie. Harder and slightly less sweet than its American and British counterparts.

Koumbara/koumbaros (koom-bah-rah/koom-bah-ross):

Kyria (kee-ree-ah): Mrs. A married woman.

Kyrios (kee-ree-oss): A man, married or not.

Lambada (lam-ba-tha): A long, skinny, decorative candle used at midnight service on Easter Saturday.

Loukaniko (loo-kah-nee-koh): Sausage.

Loukoumada (loo-koo-mah-tha): Fried balls of dough, drowning in syrup.

Maimou: (my-moo): Monkey.

Malakas (mah-lah-kas): A person who touches themselves so much that their brain turns to mush. Can be an insult or a term of endearment.

Malakies (mah-lah-kee-ez): Nonsense or bullshit.

Malakismeni (mah-lah-kiz-men-ee): Crazy from an excess of masturbation.

Mana mou (mah-nah moo): My mother. Or rather, mother my.

Mati (Ma-tee): An eye. Could be the evil eye, could be a regular eye.

Mezedes (meh-zeh-thes): Appetizers.

Mouni (moo-knee): Vagina, pussy, twat.

Mounoskeela - (moo-knee-skee-lah): Vagina bitch. It really loses something in translation.

Moutsa (moot-sa): An obscene hand gesture. Open palm, facing someone. Can mean that they're a *malakas*, or that you're rubbing poop in their face.

Nanos (Nah-nos): A derogatory term for little person/dwarf.

Ouro (ou-row): Pee.

Panayia mou (pah-nah-yee-ah moo): My Virgin Mary. Or rather, Virgin Mary my.

Panteloni (pan-te-lo-nee): pants, trousers, slacks.

Papou (pah-poo): Grandfather

Parakalo (pa-ra-ka-low): Doubles as "please" and "you're welcome".

Paralia (pa-ra-lee-ah): The beach or waterfront.

Parta (par-tah): Take it.

Periptero (pe-rip-te-ro): A small, boxy newsstand.

Philotimo (fee-lo-tee-mo): A combination of love and generosity towards other. Does not apply if you disagree with their politics or sports.

Po-po (po-po): An exclamation of sorts. A cross between "For crying out loud" and "I can't believe this person is so boneheaded".

Poutsa (put-sa): Penis, wiener, ding-dong, dick.

Propapou (pro-pah-pooh): Great-grandfather.

Proyiayia (pro-ya-ya): Great-grandmother.

Putana (puh-tah-nah): Person who dispenses nookie for a negotiable fee.

Revithia (re-vee-thee-ah): Chickpea soup/stew.

Schethio (ske-the-o): Scheme.

Servietta (ser-vee-eh-tah): Feminine hygiene product.

Skata (ska-tah): Shit.

Skata na fas (ska-tah nah faass): Consume a meal of shit.

Skatoula (ska-too-lah): Little shit.

Skeela (skee-lah): Female dog.

Skouliki (Skoo-lee-kee): Worms. The intestinal and dirt kind.

Taverna (ta-ver-nah): A small restaurant that sells Greek food.

Thea (thee-ah): Aunt.

Theo (thee-oh): Uncle.

Theos (the-os) God.

Tiropita (tee-ro-pee-tah): Cheese pie - typically feta. Can include feta with softer cheese like cottage cheese or ricotta.

Toaleta (too-ah-let-ah): Toilet

Trela/Trelos (tre-lah/tre-loss: Crazy.

Tzatziki (za-zee-kee): A sauce made with yogurt, cucumbers, dill, and all the garlic.

Vaskania (vas-kah-nee-ah): A prayer to remove the evil eye.

Vlakas (vlah-kas): A stupid person

Vre/re: Kind of like "hey, you idiot", but not quite. Informal and can be mildly negative but also indicative of familiarity.

Vromoskeelos (vro-mo-slee-los): Dirty dog.

Vromoskeela (vro-mo-skee-lah): Dirty female dog.

Xematiase (kse-mat-ya-say): Removing the evil eye.

Xenes (kse-nez): Foreigners. People to whom you have to say, "Y'all ain't from around here, are ya?"

Yiayia (yah-yah): Grandmother.

Yia mas (yamas): Cheers! An abbreviation of "To our health."

Yia sas (Ya-sas): Howdy, y'all

Yiftes (yiff-tez): A common derogatory term for the Roma people.

Yitses (Yeet-sez): Healths. What Greeks say instead of "bless you" after someone sneezes out a nose-full of cooties.

Made in United States
Troutdale, OR
02/04/2025

28672340R10162